Meadow of Stones

A story of a man's faith and love - promised and presented.

ROYCE RYDER

Published by Writers4Truth, LLC.

Printed in the United States of America

Scripture quotations are from the KJV Bible.

ISBN-13 979-8-9950978-0-8 (Hardback)

ISBN-13 979-8-9950978-1-5 (Paperback)

ISBN-13 979-8-9950978-2-2 (eBook)

Dedicated to the Nameless...

Acknowledgements

First and foremost, thanks to the Father Above for placing this story in my heart and my head so I could place it in your hands. He is so good.

Thank you to my wife of forty years for her steady love, prayers, and support.

Thank you to all the men and women who know God and have poured into my life through their teaching, examples, and friendship.

'Now may the Lord bless y'all and keep y'all, may His face shine upon y'all and give y'all peace', (Numbers 6:24-25), as you read this book.

Amen.

Prologue

Panther Creek, North Georgia - Early Autumn, 1970's

"Travis! Mama said not to go past the bridge!" Tommy yelled as dread began to overcome him.

By the time the sky over the hills turned from blue to bruised purple, Travis and his little brother Tommy had already ridden their bikes farther than they had meant to. They had passed Turnerville, the little country store, and even passed the old one-lane bridge where Mama always said, "Don't go beyond..." Now the first porch lights behind them were no more than smudges in the drizzle.

"We're too far," Tommy puffed, his breath smoky in the cooling air. "We gotta turn around."

"If we cut across this way, we'll beat the dark," Travis said, trying to sound sure. He pointed his front tire toward a narrow gravel drive that climbed a hill, disappearing between a fenced pasture and some pines. A rusty mailbox leaned at the ditch, its painted name half-flaked away, unreadable in the low light.

"You don't even know who lives up there," Tommy whispered.

"Don't matter who," Travis answered. "Road goes up, and then the road comes down again. It's faster than backtracking."

He didn't say out loud what both boys knew: they had stayed out too long and gone too far from Turnerville, and Mama would already be worrying.

Thunder grumbled somewhere beyond the ridgeline. A fine mist turned to a steadier drizzle, beading on the boys' handlebars and speckling their jeans. Gravel popped under their tires as they pushed up the hill, their legs already burning.

Halfway up, they heard it.

Clang.

A hollow sound, sharp and lonely, rode the damp air. Steel against rock. Again.

Clang.

Travis squeezed his brakes. The bike skidded sideways. Tommy nearly ran into him.

"What was that?" Tommy's voice came out thin.

"Probably somebody fixin' a fence," Travis said, though the hair on his arms lifted.

There were no house lights ahead, no bark of a dog, no radio from an open window. Just pasture, trees, and that sound.

Clang. Drag.

Clang.

“Let’s just go home,” Tommy whispered. “We can take the long way. I don’t like it up here.”

“Road’s right there,” Travis insisted, though his mouth had gone dry. “We’re almost over the hill. We cut across and drop back toward Turnerville. Otherwise, we’re ridin in the dark the whole way.”

The sound came again, closer now, from past the shadowed shape of a barn on their right, somewhere beyond where the land dipped away toward what had to be a creek.

Clang.

The boys left their bikes tipped against the ditch and stepped off the drive into the damp grass. The drizzle soaked through their shirts, causing cool lines to run down their spines. The world seemed to shrink down to a handful of things: the smell of wet earth, the low growl of water somewhere ahead, and the relentless echo of metal on stone.

“Travis, don’t,” Tommy hissed, grabbing his sleeve. “We shouldn’t be here.”

“Just gonna look,” Travis muttered, “don’t be such a baby.”

They crept past a dark barn and an old logging truck, following the lay of the land as it sloped downward. Panther Creek’s roar grew louder, hidden by a group of trees. The sky flickered, and a distant sheet of lightning lit up a cloud from within.

At the top of the rise, Travis dropped to his knees and peered over, pulling Tommy down beside him.

Below them, an open meadow stretched toward the darker line of trees and the unseen creek beyond. The ground looked freshly disturbed in places–patches rawer and more turned than the surrounding grass, scattered with pale stones that glimmered wet in the low light.

Then lightning split the clouds, sudden and white as a camera flash.

For a heartbeat, the world turned to daylight.

In that flash, Travis saw a man in the center of the meadow.

Coat hanging heavy off broad shoulders. Hair plastered to his forehead with rain. One leg was a little strange, as he favored it without thinking. His hands wrapped around the handle of a shovel, his muscles tight as he drove the blade into the earth. They could see a shadow of something lying over from where the man stood, but they could not tell what or who it was.

The man's face was turned upward, toward the low, rolling clouds. In that slice of lightning, his features twisted with something Travis couldn't name–grief maybe, or fury, or both together. His mouth was moving, but thunder rolled over the hill and swallowed the words whole.

The light died. The darkness rushed back in.

"Travis," Tommy whispered, his fingers digging into his brother's arm. "We need to go, Man! We need to go now! He's – he's buryin' somethin'."

Travis's stomach flipped. He didn't know this man. Didn't know this farm. Didn't know what was lying there, only that every part of him screamed they were seeing something they were never meant to see.

Lightning flared again, farther off this time, just enough to draw a silver line along the shovel as the man pushed earth back into the hole. His shoulders shook once, then again. The clang they had heard became a dull thud as stone met soil.

"Run," Travis said, the word barely more than air.

They slid back from the ridge, gravel and damp roots scraping their palms. They didn't look again. Didn't call out. They just ran—scrambling up to the drive, snatching up their bikes with trembling hands, tires spitting stones as they tore back down the hill the way they had come.

Neither boy spoke all the way to Turnerville.

Later, lying in his bed with the storm stomping across the hills and Mama's voice a low murmur down the hall, Travis stared at the ceiling and saw it over and over again: that flash of white, a shovel in a stranger's hands, and something disappearing under the earth and stones.

He didn't know the farm's name. Didn't know the man's story. Didn't know that, one day, folks would speak in whispers about a meadow on the far side of the ridge.

All he knew was that they had gone farther than they were supposed to, and the mountains had shown them something they could never quite forget.

Some nights, the hills kept their secrets.

And some nights, they let two lost boys from Turnerville see just enough to hold a memory forever.

Chapter 1 - Summer in the Falls

The summer of 1968 hung over Rabun County, Georgia, like a heavy quilt stitched with pine sap, sun-warmed earth, and the distant hum of chainsaws carving through the old-growth timber. Gary Holcomb, pastor of Grace Fellowship - a modest clap-board church perched on a hillside overlooking the winding gravel roads that snaked through the hollows - watched his son Buddy swinging an axe with the steady rhythm of a man twice his age. Each swing bit deep into the oak, sending chips flying like golden confetti, the blade whistling through the humid air before thudding home.

Buddy, whose real name was Gary Jr. but had been called Buddy since the day he could toddle after his dad on unsteady legs, was now fourteen and already built like an old-growth oak himself - broad shoulders, calloused hands, and a quiet strength that came from years under the mountain sun. He was a miracle child, born to parents well into their forties after a couple of decades of an empty nest, many doctors' visits, and fervent prayers lifted up in that very church during many long winter nights.

"The Lord doesn't always answer on our timetable or always give us what we want," Gary said, "but when He does, it's a testament to His faithfulness." He wiped sweat from his brow with a faded bandana. "But He gives us what we need - like the wind, the rain, and the sunshine - that makes us grow strong enough, like the trees we bring in."

Buddy nodded, his muscles burning as he heaved another log onto the stack, the scent of the freshly-cut wood mingling with the constant rhythm of the creek nearby.

He had been around sawdust since he could walk. As a little boy, he would play for hours with his toy cars, pushing them through piles of golden shavings, building pretend roads between the stumps while Gary dropped the timbers nearby.

"Stay close now, Little Man," his daddy would call out over the roar of the saw, but Buddy's world was the sawdust kingdom - tiny fists carving highways through fragrant mountains of wood that smelled like Christmas and eternity.

By the time he was able to carry a stick of firewood, he was shadowing his father. And as soon as he was able to pick up a saw, he spared no sapling. One sweltering summer, they tackled the five-acre tract down by Panther Creek - a tangle of briars, rocks, and stubborn roots where the creek's roar drowned out everything but God's own voice. The noise crashed constantly, loud enough to shake your bones, while thick, black, leafy matter cushioned the ground like a forest quilt. It was so warm by ten o'clock that morning, they had stripped down and jumped into the deep pools. Buddy hollered as he scared the trout darting in the dark shadows.

Later, he began to drag stones - one by one- from the undergrowth and the creek side, stacking them neatly at the field's edge while Gary sent the swing blade singing through the saw briars and wild rhododendrons. Sweat stung his eyes, but each rock placed felt like it was claiming the ground for something holy - the creek preaching its approval with its thunderous hymn.

"Look at that, Son," Gary said one dusk evening, stepping back from their work, "a well-cleared meadow. Room for grass, wildflowers, maybe even a garden someday, or a place to build dreams on a solid foundation."

The boy grinned, hands raw but proud, not knowing those stones would one day mark something far more sacred than any garden.

Mama's calls for supper were the day's sweetest signal, cutting through the valley like a bell from Heaven.

"Buddy! Gary! Food is getting cold!" Eliza's voice rolled sharp and warm, pulling them home from the chainsaw buzz.

He would drop his cars or rocks and run, bare feet sinking into the leafy earth, then burst into the kitchen through the screen door as it slammed behind him with the delicious smell of cornbread coming from the oven and her apron no longer spotless from her labor of love.

"Hands first, Wild Man," she would say, pointing to the basin with a knowing smile.

The water splashed as he began to scrub. Then grace - Gary's deep voice thanking the good Lord Above for His provision and family, followed by plates heaped with garden bounty: pole beans, fried okra, hot cornbread, and sometimes a generous portion of beef.

Evenings ended with her snapping beans on the porch, singing old hymns like "Amazing Grace", while Gary studied or made a connection over his open Bible with one of his members as the lamplight cast shadows that danced like angels. Up at the Holcomb house, life flowed as a steady stream of work and worship.

Patty Hall lived just over the ridge - Buddy's closest neighbor and lifelong friend - same age, with her freckles and a laugh that filled the hollows. They had worn many paths from mountain to mountain, racing through laurel thickets, building forts from fallen limbs, and their childhood laughter echoed like the call of mourning doves. And even now as teenagers, their bond was still strong.

Gary preached forgiveness and the fierce value of family from his pulpit every Sunday, drawing a flock of farmers, loggers, and mill hands alike, who nodded in agreement to his calls for decency in a world gone wild with Vietnam protests, moon landings, and rock ' n ' roll blasting from transistor radios.

Eliza kept the hearth burning–canning tomatoes from the garden until the jars glowed like stained glass on the pantry shelves and mending overalls with the quick flick of her needle, weaving faith into every fiber—always humming a hymn as she worked. They were older parents, wise and patient beyond their years, with a work ethic that turned chores into character-building altars.

Buddy did not always fall in line with that straight and narrow. One night, a few years back, moonlight had not yet burned off the heat of the July day, and the old rail yard at Tallulah Falls felt like a secret place where boys could turn invisible.

The tracks - two rusted lines running along the edge of town - had not seen a full train in years, not since the tourists had thinned and the freight moved to faster routes. But a little inspection trolley still sat there some nights, a squat little cart with a bench and a hand brake, used now and then by the lone caretaker and maintenance man, Harold Jones, but to a young Buddy Holcomb, it looked like adventure on wheels.

"Come on," shouted Danny as he glanced over his shoulder, "just down to the bend and back. Nobody's even gonna know."

Mark stood one foot on the gravel, one on the tie, chewing his lip.

"What if Mr. Harold comes back? Or the sheriff?"

Buddy's heart thudded in his chest, and mixed excitement and fear tangled within him. He had been raised on sermons about honesty, but he had also been raised on stories of boys his daddy's age hopping slow-rolling boxcars, "just to see what it felt like". It did not help that the pump trolley sat there as if waiting for them, moonlight glinting off the handle.

"It's not like we are going to Clayton," Danny reasoned. "Just a little ride. We'll push it back right where it was."

The right answer sat clear as day in Buddy's gut, but the night felt big and daring, and he was tired of always being the "good one".

"Once," he heard himself say, "down to the trestle and back. Then we put it back, and we don't touch it again."

Danny grinned, "I knew you weren't skeered."

Inside, Buddy was trembling, but he climbed in anyway. The trolley rocked under their weight as Danny and Mark scrambled in beside him. Buddy's fingers closed around the cool metal rim of the hand brake - the smell of old grease and rust sharp in his nose.

"Push," Danny whispered.

They shoved off with their sneakers, and the cart began rolling with a squeak that sounded deafening in the quiet yard. For a heartbeat, Buddy thought the whole town would sit up in bed and look out their windows. But the only reply was the chorus of crickets and the soft rush of the river beyond the trees. The trolley picked up speed, its wheels clicking over the joints in the rail - thunk-thunk, thunk-thunk - like a heartbeat under theirs. Wind began to cool them from the stale heat of the July night as Buddy's shirt began to flap. The old depot slid past on their left, its peeling paint and boarded windows turning into a blur along with a billow of white from the Moss House.

"This is great!" Danny exclaimed as he tried to keep his voice just low enough that it would not carry.

Buddy could not help the grin that stretched on his face. Down the line, the trestle bridge loomed back against the sky, the gorge yawning beneath it like a giant mouth.

"Don't go to the bridge," Mark said quietly, his voice thin, "Daddy said if you wreck out there, ain't nobody ever gonna find ya!"

"Relax," said Buddy, but his hands tightened anyway, "we'll stop before."

The trestle crept closer. Buddy leaned into the wind, part of him wide open - part of him whispering, *This ain't yours. You did not ask. Turn it around.*

"I'll pull the brake," he said, reaching for the handle.

His fingers had just closed around it when a harsh beam of light cut across the rails from the side, slicing the darkness. The trolley rolled right through it. Buddy's stomach dropped.

"BUDDY HOLCOMB!"

His daddy's voice cracked through the night, sharper than the flashlight. The trolley clattered to a stop as Buddy yanked the brake hard. The wheels squealed, causing the metal to complain. The cart lurched, throwing Danny forward and off into a patch of kud-zu.

Buddy barely heard him. His heart had climbed into his throat. He could see his father now standing near the crossing with his boots planted wide in the gravel. He had a flashlight in one hand and the other fisted at his side. Gary Holcomb's face was shadowed, but there was no mistaking the set of his shoulders.

"We're dead," Mark whispered.

"Y'all get off that trolley," Gary called. Not loud enough to wake the whole town - but plenty loud enough for the three boys. "Now."

They scrambled out, shoes slipping onto the gravel. Buddy's legs felt like rubber, and his hands tingled from clutching the brake. The walk back to his father felt longer than any highway.

"Evening, Pastor Gary," Danny tried to sound sure of himself as his voice wobbled - pulling leaves out of his hair.

Gary's eyes flicked to Danny, then Mark, then landed and held there on his son. "You two head on home," he said evenly. "We'll talk to your folks tomorrow."

Danny opened his mouth like he might argue, then wisely shut it, and nodded, "Yessir."

He and Mark hurried off into the shadows, leaving Buddy alone in the flashlight's pale circle. Up close, Buddy could see the disappointment in his father's eyes, and somehow that hurt worse than if he had been full-on furious with him.

"Daddy, I..."

Gary raised a hand slightly.

“Don’t talk yet,” he said, “just listen.”

He walked over to the trolley, set his shoulder against it, and started pushing it back up the slight grade toward its spot by the shed. Buddy fell in beside him automatically, the metal groaning in protest. They worked in silence; the only sounds were their breathing, the squeak of the wheels, and the distant rush of the falls. When they had settled the cart back where it belonged, Gary braced a foot against the rail and made sure the brake was set good and tight. Then he turned to his son.

“Buddy,” he said quietly, “what you just did was not a prank. It was theft.”

The word landed heavily. Buddy flinched.

“We were gonna bring it back,” he mumbled.

Gary held his gaze, then stated,” If somebody took your bicycle without asking and brought it back before you woke up, would they still have taken what wasn’t theirs?”

His shoulders sagged, “Yessir.”

“Why?”

“Cause...” Buddy swallowed, his throat dry, “'cause it ain’t theirs.”

“Exactly.” Gary’s voice stayed calm, but there was steel under it. “This trolley belongs to the railroad. Folks use it to keep the tracks safe. You do not get to decide that your fun is worth riskin’ somebody else’s job. Or neck.”

He glanced toward the trestle, its shadow stretching like a warning.

"We weren't gonna go on the bridge," he said as a means to justify himself.

"You weren't thinkin' far enough ahead to know what you were gonna do," Gary replied. "That's the problem." He hooked his thumbs in his belt loops and waited until Buddy met his eyes again. "Son, I need you to hear me on somethin' more important than an old trolley.

His chest felt tight as he nodded.

"One day," Gary began, "God's gonna give you things that are yours to take care of. A home. Maybe a wife, maybe children. People under your roof who count on you to always do the thinkin' ahead so they are always good, happy, and safe," his voice softened, but his eyes did not. "You do not get to be the boy who hops on whatever looks fun in the moment and hopes it all works out. Not if you are gonna be the man I'm prayin' you will become."

Buddy's eyes burned. He blinked fast.

"What kind of man?" he whispered.

Gary stepped a little closer, the moonlight catching the silver just starting at his temples.

"A provider in your home," he said first, "that means you work when it is hard. You tell the truth about money. You do not take what is not yours - not a trolley, not a dollar, not a shortcut. You make sure the people God gives you are fed and safe."

Buddy's mind flickered through memories - his daddy out in the rain cutting a tree off Mrs. Tate's roof, his mama never worrying out loud about whether there would be groceries.

He took a deep breath, "Yessir."

"A protector in your home," Gary went on," you put yourself between danger and your family. You do not *become* the danger with foolish choices. Tonight, you climbed on something that could have killed you if it had jumped the track. You think about your mama wakin' up to Sheriff Palmer, hat in hand, sayin' he found your body in the gorge."

The picture slammed into Buddy's imagination so hard he felt sick.

His stomach lurched, "I didn't think about that."

"That's what I am tellin' you. You've got to start," his tone softened as he drew a breath. "Third thing: a preacher in your home. I may stand in a pulpit on Sundays, but when you are grown, you will be the one preachin' under your own roof. You preach every day by what you do - when you bow your head at the table, when you choose honesty over easy, when you admit you were wrong and ask forgiveness - your family will learn what God looks like by how you live. You want your boy thinkin' it is okay to take what is not his - as long as he puts it back, do you?"

"No," he whispered, with a humbled face and head low.

"Then you start today," Gary said simply. "Last thing: a prophet in your home. Not fortune-telling. A prophet is someone who listens for God's voice and warns his people about where the road they are on is headed. He looks at a choice and says, 'If we keep goin' this way, we're gonna wreck.' He is not scared to be unpopular if it means protectin' the ones he loves."

He tapped the rail with the toe of his boot. He swung the flashlight toward the line and the trestle standing in the distance. The light revealed the missing timbers ahead. Mr. Harold had just advised Gary that afternoon to warn the members of his congregation, especially the younger ones, to keep away from the trestle due to the rotting timbers that had fallen into the gorge.

"Sometimes a father sees and knows what you don't."

Buddy's eyes grew big as he exhaled his breath at the reality of just how differently the evening could have ended.

Gary rested a big, work-scarred hand briefly on his shoulder.

"Tonight, you followed your friends where they wanted to go, even when somethin' inside you knew it was not right. One day, bein' a man is gonna mean sayin', 'I hold to what's right, even if the whole world takes the other side', that is the kind of man I am asking God to make you."

The truth of it lodged under Buddy's ribs. Shame pricked behind his eyes.

"I'm sorry," he said, his voice shaking, "I'm really sorry, Daddy."

Gary's hand squeezed his shoulder once.

"I know you are," he paused, letting the night sounds fill the space between them.

Buddy chewed his bottom lip, a question nudging at him.

"Daddy?"

"Yes, Son."

"Does Mama gotta do all that too?" he asked. "Do girls have to be all those things?"

Gary huffed out a quiet breath, something like a tired chuckle.

"Not by design," he said, "most of the time, it is when a man will not step up that a woman ends up tryin' to carry it all. She will be provider if she has to, protect if she has to, preach and prophesy if there is no one else standin' in the gap," his face holding a gentle grin, "but that's a heavy load God never meant her to shoulder alone."

He thought about his mama standing at the sink, humming her hymns, about the way she set the plates on the table for supper, and how she would lay a hand on his daddy's back when he came in late from a hospital visit.

"So, what's she supposed to be?" he asked.

"Your mama's called to be a helpmate, a nurturer, a woman of faith," he responded, "and she is strong in her own right.

But, Buddy, I don't ever want her havin' to be the man of this house because I laid down on the job. And I sure don't want your wife someday havin' to do your part and hers both!" A wry smile tugged at his mouth. "Truth is, I don't want to have to do your mama's part either. I couldn't be stuck in the house all day with laundry, bread dough, sewing bees, and all that hot canning! But Mama seems happy as a lark doing those things and takin' care of us."

Buddy let out a small, startled laugh.

And then his daddy added, "And she does not want to have to do mine. That is how God set it up - we each carry what He hands us, so nobody is crushed tryin' to carry it all."

Buddy nodded slowly, the pieces fitting together in his mind in a way that they had not before.

"I'm sorry," he said again, quieter.

Gary's hand squeezed his shoulder once more.

"I know you are. Tomorrow, you are gonna march yourself back down here and tell Mr. Harold what you did. You are gonna apologize and ask if there is a way you can make it right. Haul scrap, maybe sweep the floors, whatever he says."

He nodded, the humiliation already burning.

"Yessir."

"And when we get home," Gary added, "we're gonna talk about consequences. But hear me, Buddy." He waited until his son looked up. "You are not doin' this alone. I am not givin' you these four things and walkin' off. I will be here. I will be here asking God to shape you into that man. I will be prayin' over you as long as the good Lord gives me breath."

Buddy's throat closed.

"What if I mess up again?" he whispered.

His father's expression softened, the sternness easing.

"And you will," he said simply, "and so will I. And you will learn about grace. But each time, we get back up, we tell the truth, and we let the Lord keep sandin' the rough edges off. Understand?"

Buddy nodded hard, a tear slipping free and cutting a track through the dust on his cheek. Gary reached up and thumbed it away, quick and gentle, like he had done when his boy was little and had scraped his knee.

"Let's go home," he said.

They walked side by side along the tracks with the depot behind them; the only sound between them was Buddy's sneakers crunching on the gravel. In his chest, the thrill of the stolen ride had gone sour and was replaced by something heavier - but more meaningful.

The seasons would turn over them like pages, boyhood scrapes, and hard lessons stacking up as steady as the woodpile by the Holcomb house. And before long, the dares got bigger than trolleys.

Chapter 2 -

High Dive

By the time the next summer rolled around, Buddy and Patty were taller, stronger, and just bold enough to mistake daring for wisdom. Down at Tallulah Lake, Patty Hall talked Buddy Holcomb into the wildest dare of their childhood.

Tallulah Lake spread out below them like a sheet of polished green glass with the afternoon sun turning the ripples into little coins of light. Just off the rocky bank, Big Rock shouldered up out of the water - a hefty thirty feet of jagged granite rising from the depths, its top worn smooth by the bare feet of generations of brave, or foolish, lake kids and grown men who swore they "weren't skeered" of anything.

"Come on, Holcomb," Patty said, hands on her hips, freckles bright against her summer-browned face, "you ain't telling me all those muscles are just for haulin' firewood."

Buddy snorted, but his gaze stayed fixed on the rock. Even from where they stood across the water from the massive granite face, he could see the dark water pooled deep at its base, a shadowed emerald that seemed to go straight down to the bottom of the world.

"I haul firewood cause Daddy says," he answered, "he ain't never once said, 'Son, go jump off a cliff for fun."

Patty rolled her eyes, her braids swishing between her shoulder blades.

"It ain't a cliff, it's a rock. Folks do it all the time. I've seen Henry Irvin's brothers, and they didn't die."

"They're half crazy," Buddy muttered, "and older."

"Buddy, we ain't little kids anymore," she said, glancing back at him with a grin. "You know you swim like a trout. You could go from here to that rock and back before most boys finish thinking about it."

He made a face, but his chest puffed out a little in spite of himself. He knew these coves and inlets like the back of his hand, knew where the bottom fell away and where the rocks lurked just beneath the surface. He also knew how fast cold water could steal a breath and a heartbeat. He did swim strongly - years of creek plunges with Gary and long lake afternoons had carved good muscle into his arms and shoulders. But Big Rock was different. It loomed.

"Daddy will tan my hide if he knew I was out here," he said, "and yours too. That jump is higher than it looks," he continued, "if you hit the water wrong..."

"That's why we ain't gonna tell him," Patty shot back with mischief flashing in her eyes. "Besides, what is he always sayin' in those sermons, 'God don't give us a spirit of fear...'" she wiggled her fingers at him like she was conjuring the verse. "You do sound like your daddy," she teased, "next you'll be preaching about consequences and self-control."

"The four P's," he shot back before he could stop himself.

"The Four what?"

"Never mind," he muttered, ears burning as he remembered Gary's talk beside the tracks.

"He also says use the sense that God gave you," he replied, though the corner of his mouth twitched upward.

Patty saw the crack and pressed in.

"You scared?" she asked, her head tilting, her tone light, but her eyes were sharp. "Big, strong logger's boy like you afraid of a little lake water?"

Buddy squared his shoulders.

"I ain't scared of water. I am cautious about hitting it from thirty feet up, though."

She laughed, the sound bright enough to bounce off the water.

"Oh, come on," she said, "just be... brave."

They picked their way down the bank with their bare feet sliding on pine needles and red clay until they reached the small strip of the pebbled shore. Buddy kicked off his worn sneakers, peeled his shirt off over his head, and tossed it onto a dry rock. Patty didn't look away fast enough.

“When did you get all that?” she blurted and then turned scarlet, not meaning to say her thoughts out loud.

He glanced down, suddenly aware of the hard lines work had carved across his chest and arms. “Choppin’ wood,” he said, flustered, “haulin’ logs, growin’ up.”

She dipped her toe in and murmured something about the water being warm enough and jumped in before he could see her blush again.

She came up and pointed across the glittering expanse.

“I'll race you!”

Before he could answer, she dove back under, slicing the surface clean. For a second, all he saw was bubbles and the flash of little feet. Then her head popped up, her hair slicked back, and her grin still wide.

She called from over her shoulder, “Come on!” as she made her way toward Big Rock.

“Patty!” he hissed and glanced over his shoulder at the tree line, like Gary might step out from the rhododendrons with a Bible in one hand and a belt in the other. But he did not appear.

He cursed under his breath - but only a little - then dived in after her. The water wrapped around him, cool and familiar, and the shock of it took his breath, but only for a moment, before his muscles remembered what to do. He caught up with her within a dozen strokes, his longer frame cutting the distance easily.

"Show off!" she puffed, but there was admiration under the word.

They reached the rock together, fingers scraping the rough stone up close. It loomed taller than it had from shore - the granite face towered above them, wet and slick in places where waves had splashed up, dry and sun-warmed higher up, where boys had climbed for decades. Faded initials and dates were carved into the lower ledges, some so old the lichen had nearly swallowed them.

"There's a path around the back," she said, catching her breath, "Henry showed me."

"Henry showed you?" Buddy repeated with a frown.

"When?"

"Last summer, when you and your daddy were cuttin' over at the Monaghan place, I believe you actually were fishin' more than you were workin', but who am I?" she answered back sarcastically.

"Don't go lookin' at me like that. I didn't jump," she went on. "Tina Irvin hollered from the boat that I was too skinny to splat right. Today I'm proving her wrong."

Buddy ran a hand along the stone, feeling for footholds.

"You sure?" he asked.

Patty's eyes met his, dark with fear and something fiercer behind it.

"We're already here," she said, "might as well see the view."

He nodded and started up, his fingers finding cracks and ledges by instinct. He hooked his fingers into a crack and began hauling himself up. His bare feet gripped the roughness, and his toes searched for holds as well. Patty scrambled after him, hands and feet searching the rocks. They pulled their way around to the backside, where scraggly mountain laurel clung to the slope, and a couple of young pines had twisted their roots into the rock. The climb was steep, dirt crumbling under their toes, laurel leaves slapping at their arms.

"Hands where I put mine," he called down, "Feet two notches lower. Don't rush, take one step at a time."

She followed, trusting his directions more than her own trembling legs. Halfway up, she froze, plastered to the rock as a gust of wind slapped her wet skin, reminding her of just how high they already were.

"Buddy?" her voice wobbled, "I can't... I can't look down."

"Don't," he said calmly, though his own heart was hammering, "look at me."

She swallowed and lifted her eyes. His face, a few feet above hers, was calm and sure in a way that also calmed her spirit.

"You're doin' fine," he stated, trying to encourage her, "just a little further and you're on top. You quit now, and we'll just have to climb all this again another day to prove you ain't scared."

She made a face at him, but the spark was back.

"I hate you," she muttered and pulled herself up another handhold and continued on.

"Liar," he said, grinning.

Then, sooner than she expected, he was reaching down a hand for the last stretch.

She grabbed his hand, her fingers cold, yet his were strong, as he hauled her onto the flat, sun-warmed top of Big Rock.

By the time they reached the top, both of them were breathing hard. The wind felt stronger up there, brushing the sweat from their faces and carrying the clean smell of wild honeysuckle. The water below was intimidating - Big Rock dropping sheer into a bowl of dark green.

They stood there for a moment, the entire lake spread out around them like a promise. The mountains rose in layers of blue-green. A hawk circled high above the ridge, riding invisible currents.

Patty breathed in, "Wow!", all the fear momentarily knocked right out of her by the sheer beauty.

"Yeah," he said softly.

From up there, the cabins looked so tiny, and the canoes appeared as sticks on the water. The world felt both huge and small at the same time.

Patty stepped closer to the edge of the rock, her bare toes curling over the warm stone. She spread her arms wide like a bird.

"Look at it," she whispered, "feels like you could fly."

"You scared?" she then asked, tipping her head to look at him.

"Yes," he said promptly, "and not ashamed to say it."

But he walked to the edge and peered down at the dark water, waiting deep and still. He measured the distance with his eyes, the way he measured yardage on a football field, picturing where they would hit and how long until they resurfaced.

"Remember," he said, turning back to her, "if we are goin' to do this, we are goin' to do it right. Feet first, legs together, arms crossed over your chest, tight. If you hit flat, you'll sting as if you got hit with a board."

"Yessir!" she said, giving a mock salute, but there was respect under the teasing.

"Are you sure you want to do this?" he asked again.

Her eyes twinkled up at him as he could hear her laughter echoing off the rocky edges of the lake.

"Yes, I do, and I want to do it with you. And for the record, I'm scared too, but I want to do it just once to know that I did. I'm more scared of sitting on this bank when I'm old and gray, sayin' remember when we almost jumped off Big Rock, but chickened out?"

Buddy pictured Patty at eighty, still bossing him around with the same spark in her eyes, and he had to grin. It also tugged something deep in him he didn't have words for yet. Loyalty, maybe, or love that had not learned its name.

"Are you sure you wanna do this?" giving her one last chance to change her mind. "Patty, this might not be... smart."

"Since when have you worried about smart?" she retorted.

"Since I saw a boy get pulled out of the river with his neck bent wrong," he answered. "Water doesn't care how brave you are. If you hit it wrong, it will break you regardless."

Something in his tone made her eyes soften. However, she knew he wasn't just being a scaredy-cat. Buddy Holcomb carried caution like other boys carried pocket knives. Always handy, but mostly for someone else's sake.

"I don't feel good about this," he confessed, "my guts twisting. Daddy always said pay attention when your gut and the spirit start hollerin' together."

Patty chewed her lip, gaze flickering between his face and the water, fear and stubbornness warring inside her. She was tired of being the girl who watched the boys climb, jump, and holler, then brag about it all week while she stayed safe on the shore.

“If you're not goin’, at least don't try to talk me out of it,” she said, her voice tight, “I need to know I can be brave, too.”

“Brave don't mean stupid,” he snapped, sharper than he meant to.

Her chin lifted.

“Fine,” she shot back, hurt flashing in her eyes, “cause maybe I'm both.”

Before he could grab her and find better words, she took three quick steps and launched herself off the rock.

For one frozen breath, he saw her in the air - her limbs flung a little wide, not tucked like he had told her to do, her freckles stark against her pale, upturned face. Then she hit the water flat. The slap echoed up like someone had smacked a board on concrete.

“Patty!” Her name tore out of him - raw.

She disappeared in a burst of white froth. A heartbeat. Two. The green closed over her like a lid.

Buddy didn't think. The fear that had gripped his belly broke apart under something older and stronger - the part of him that had stepped between his mama and a coyote once without stopping to calculate. He jumped straight off the edge, his arms tight to his sides, trusting what his body knew about water more than his mind screamed about height.

The jump stole his breath, the wind roaring in his ears, then the lake slammed up to meet him. He knifed through deeper than intended, the cool pressure wrapping his skull. For a second, there was only green and bubbles and the burn in his lungs.

He kicked hard toward the place he had last seen her, his eyes straining in the dim water. A shape drifted a few feet below, her hair streaming and her limbs slack. Panic flared so bright he almost swallowed water. He reached for her, his fingers finding her wrist, then hooked an arm around her middle and yanked them both upward as fast as he could.

They broke the surface in a rush of air and spray. Patty gasped, or at least tried to. The breath had been knocked out of her. Her chest struggled to expand, her eyes round and wild.

"Easy," Buddy panted, drawing her close, keeping her head tipped back.

"You're all right. You're gonna be all right. Just knock the wind out of you. Breathe, Patty. Come on, breathe. Breathe for me."

A shudder tore through her, and then her lungs remembered their job. She sucked in a ragged gulp of air that turned into a cough. Tears spilling hot down her face, mixing with the lake water.

"It... it hurts," she gasped, "my belly, my...my back... everything."

"That's cause you tried to belly flop from the top of the world," he said, trying to be funny as his teeth chattered from the adrenaline rather than the cold. "You're lucky it appears it's just bruises."

Big Rock's shadow loomed above them, but the bank where they started curved nearer on this side, brush hanging low over the shallows. Buddy looked that way, calculating.

"We're going back to shore," he said. "You. Just hang on to me. Don't fight me. Just float."

"I can swim," she protested weakly.

"Not like this, you can't," his tone brooked no argument. "Put your arms around my shoulders. Don't choke me, but don't let go either. I got you."

"It burns," she whimpered, clutching to his shoulders, her voice shaking, "my leg... my side..."

But she did as she was told, slipping her arms around his neck. Her weight dragged him under in the water, and for a second, he wondered if he had misjudged and if he could do it. The years of Panther Creek's current and previous long lake laps answered for him. He turned toward the far bank and started kicking, strong and steady.

He said to her as they started off, "That was a bad hit, but you're breathing, that's what matters. Just keep holding on. And breathe with me - in... out..."

And he continued the long swim back toward the shore with her clinging to him like a cocklebur. He swam in a slow, strong crawl, his legs doing most of the work, his arms adjusting to keep her face above water. Each stroke burned, but he set his jaw and kept going, counting quietly to keep the panic from rising in his own chest. Patty clung tight, her breath hot and uneven against his ear. Twice she whimpered when a wave slapped against the bruised parts of her, and each time he grunted,

"I've got you. You're all right. Don't let go. We're getting there."

By the time they reached the shallows, his muscles shook from the strain. He staggered when his feet touched the bottom, then hoisted her higher on his back and carried her the last few steps onto the pebbled bank. He half-dragged, half-carried her onto the warm rock. They collapsed side by side, with chests heaving. Her skin was pale beneath the freckles, teeth chattering as adrenaline drained away. Angry red contusions were already blossoming along her thigh and ribs where the water had slapped her.

"Do you hurt? Do you hurt anywhere else?" he asked, dropping to his knees beside her.

She tested her fingers and toes and winced as she moved her leg.

"Just feels like somebody took a board to me," she said weakly, "I'm not broken, am I?"

He ran his hands lightly down her arms and then along her shins, carefully and respectfully, the way Gary had taught him when checking a parishioner after a bad fall.

"Don't feel like anything's out of place," he said, "but that bruise is going to be something else, though."

She let out a shaky laugh that turned into a hiccupping sob, "I really messed it up."

"But you jumped off Big Rock," he corrected gently, "plenty of folks never get that far. You just forgot. You can't argue with gravity halfway down."

She sniffed, wiping her nose with the back of her hand, "I thought I was going to drown for a second."

"You almost did," he said bluntly, "but I wasn't going to let that happen. Don't you ever do that again, do you hear me?"

Their eyes met, and for a moment the whole world narrowed to the space between them, the scrape of stone on their knees, the lake whispering behind them, and the knowledge of what he had just done for her.

"I just wanted to prove I could. I didn't mean to scare you," she said. After a pause, she added, "Thank you," and there was more in it than gratitude for being pulled out of the lake.

"You're welcome, but you scared me half to death," he shot back, but there was more relief than anger in it. "Patty, you can't go jumpin' off every high thing just cause some Irvin boy did it first. One of these days I ain't going to be close enough to catch you."

She studied his face, the way his jaw clenched, the crease between his brow, the wet hair plastered to his forehead. It hit her then, clear as the ring of Big Rock's splash, that he hadn't hesitated. Buddy Holcomb, who thought everything through twice, had jumped without a second thought when she went under. For her.

"You didn't have to come," she said, "could have stayed on the shore like an old man," the ghost of her usual sass returning.

He snorted.

"And listen to your daddy holler at your funeral cause I let you drown? No, thank you," then he added, "what kind of protector would I be if I had let you sink?" he tried to make it sound like a joke as the words slipped out before he could stop them.

"Protector," she repeated softly, tasting it.

Heat crawled up his neck. "Forget I said that."

"Maybe I won't," she said, a hint of that spark returning.

He helped her sit up slowly. She winced but managed it, leaning against a rock. Younger kids down shore were staring wide-eyed, whispers already starting about Buddy Holcomb and Patty Hall jumping Big Rock.

"You realize we're gonna be legends by suppertime," she said, managing a crooked grin.

"More like fools," he grunted back. "Daddy hears about this, I will be learning a whole new sermon on wisdom."

"You won't tell him, will you?" she asked quickly, her eyes wide.

“I don't know yet,” he said honestly, then, looking over at the kids at the shore, he stated simply, “We may not have to.”

She sobered at that, chewing her lip. “Maybe we should stop with dares?”

He looked at her, really looked at her then, the wet hair plastered to her cheeks, the bruise continuing to darken on her thigh, and the stubborn line of her jaw.

“That’d be a good start,’ he responded with a small grin.

They sat there a long while, letting the sun do its quiet work on their chilled skin.

“We'd better get home,” he said, “you're going to be sore as sin tomorrow. We'll probably be barred from the lake till we're thirty.”

“So you're not gonna tell?”

“I don't see how that will help. Lesson learned without all that.”

“You sound like a daddy yourself.”

“Somebody's got to think ahead,” he said, “come on, lean on me.”

He helped her up the path, letting her use his solid frame like a walking stick, both of them quieter than usual. The late sun slanted through the trees, turning the lake golden as they left it behind.

That night in her small room, Patty lay on her side with one hand resting lightly over the bruised patch on her leg, moonlight leaking through the curtains, pale and soft. Each breath was a reminder of how close she had come to real trouble, but under the ache, something warm began to glow.

She replayed the moments in her mind. The way Buddy's eyes had gone wide with fear when she had disappeared, the hard slap of his arms around her under the water. His hand pulling her up the rock, his body cutting through the water below, and the clamp of his arms around her when everything had turned upside down. His voice in her ear saying, '*I got you, don't let go.*'

"Protecter," she whispered into the dark, the word warming her more than any blanket. She thought about Gary's deep voice on Sundays, of Eliza's gentle hands, of the way Buddy had always stepped between her and trouble, even when he was little, and trouble was just older boys on the playground.

"Buddy Holcomb," she whispered into the dark, testing the sound of his name on her tongue in a new way. He had always been her best friend, the boy who had raced her through laurel thickets and split biscuits with her at Eliza's table. Tonight, he had been something more - strong and sure, and willing to jump from high places if it meant pulling her from the deep.

Her cheeks heated, though no one else could see.

“One day,” she murmured, “some girl's gonna be awfully blessed to have you.” She paused, her heart thumping, “Maybe... maybe that girl could be me.”

She pressed her hand carefully to her tender ribs, winced, and then smiled anyway. The lake had stolen her breath and given her another kind back - an innocent, stubborn little hope that tucked itself quietly in the corners of her heart, right beside the memory of Buddy's broad shoulders cutting through green water like he was born to carry somebody besides himself.

Down the road, in his own room, Buddy lay awake too, listening to Panther Creek's distant roar through the open window. He thought about the trolley and the talk beside the tracks, of Big Rock and Patty’s small body clinging to his as he kicked desperately for shore.

The lesson came back to his mind. The words did not feel quite as far-fetched as they had the night his daddy first said them. Today, for a few hard, cold seconds under Tallulah Lake, he had gotten a taste of what it meant to be responsible for somebody else.

“Lord,” he murmured into the darkness, “I don't know much about bein’ a man yet, but if you keep putting folks in my care, please don't let me fail them.”

Outside, Tallulah Lake lay still under the stars, and Big Rock rose dark against the sky, awaiting the next daring soul...

Chapter 3 -

Lakeside Sparks

In the hot summer of 1972, seventeen-year-old Buddy Holcomb logs beside his dad before dawn every morning, hauling timbers down slick, dew-kissed slopes, shouldering lumber across rocky acres for many hours as the demanding work shapes his body and his character.

At Rabun County High, he channeled that strength into football, rising as head quarterback whose arm could thread a needle through a defensive line as thick as briars. His grades shone even more brightly with straight A's in every subject - marking him as a boy who would go places if the mountains would loosen their hold on him.

Lake Rabun shimmered like a sapphire cradled in the Appalachians, its cool waters drawing Atlanta's high-society crowd as they built their weekend retreats amid the wild rhododendrons and azaleas that bloomed as orange fire come the spring.

One sticky July afternoon, Gary and Buddy were clearing a tract near the shore for a new cabin site, their chainsaws echoing off the glassy water. Buddy paused to take a swig from his canteen, his t-shirt clinging to his solid frame that was slick with sweat and sawdust, when he heard laughter carry from across the lake - high and free – like a Carolina Wren in the morning.

There was Donna - slicing ripples through the water with strokes that were as graceful as a heron. Her dark hair streamed like ink against the blue of the sky above. Shyness rooted him like a stump, but boldness won out. Wiping the sawdust from his face, he flashed a confident smile - boyish, yet sure. Her head turned toward him in mid-stroke. Their eyes locked as their grins hooked instantly.

The lake witnessed old secrets, and new promises quietly glisten between them.

Two weeks dragged by in what felt like years through the July heat, the kind that turned shirt collars into wet rags and made every breath feel borrowed. But fate - or more likely, the Lord's own perfect timing - hauled Buddy and Donna back together again at Mathis' Diner, that ramshackle joint slung low on the highway where Rabun County's hard lines blurred - loggers in grease-stained caps rubbed elbows with Atlanta lawyers in pressed khakis with the air heavy with onion rings, strong coffee, and country music's top ten twanging from the jukebox.

Buddy was hunched over a platter of ribs slathered in tangy sauce as his three teammates were joking around between bites - Big Jim with his gap-toothed grin, skinny Leroy nursing a Coke, and bull-necked Hank pounding the table with gusto, "Pass the ketchup, Holcomb!" he hooted with ketchup already smeared on his chin. The bell above the door jingled loudly, and time slowed like sap hanging in the winter cold.

Donna swept in like summer lightning, her sundress fluttering pale yellow against tanned legs and her dark hair hanging loosely down her back. Tom and Gail Hargrove, her parents, trailed behind her while her dad was barking about "needing to close that Buckhead deal before sundown". Buddy's gaze locked on her like a quarterback sighting the end zone through a blitz - his heart thumping louder than the diner's grease-popping grill and the music from the box.

The boys noticed instantly and erupted in jeers that rattled the saltshakers.

"Holcomb's mooning over lake money!" Hank bellowed.

"Pastor's boy goin' soft for Atlanta silk!" Leroy grinned slyly as he elbowed Buddy in the side.

Buddy flushed hot from his head to his toes but held his gaze steady on her without blinking. His confidence flickering. He flashed her a smile across the room - easy and sure - the kind that said, "I see you" without saying a word.

She felt the stares like a spotlight - her pulse hammering wildly as her eyes caught his. Her courage overrode the flutter. While her folks were claiming a booth and some menus, Donna slid into his table. She was close enough for him to smell vanilla and a light hint of tanning lotion.

"Hey Quarterback," she said, her voice trembling just a touch, yet her eyes were a little daring at the same time, "my 17th

birthday bash is tomorrow at our lake house. You in? Bring that arm, maybe we will need a game."

Buddy swallowed hard, his heart slamming within his chest.

"I'll be there," he responded, his words hurried but steady as if he were calling a play under pressure.

The boys whistled low as she sauntered back, her hips swaying naturally, leaving a vanilla trail as she went. Buddy was already counting the hours - ribs all but forgotten.

The bash blurred into magic under a bonfire sky as orange flames licked logs Buddy himself had split. The lake house glowed with lanterns strung like stars as Atlanta kids in madras shirts mixed awkwardly with locals in boots. Music was blaring through the speakers - Creedence Clearwater Revival cutting through the night - while kids danced barefoot on the dew-wet grass. Donna found him by the dock, pulling him into the shadows as loons called out lonely songs across the dark water.

Their first real kiss happened there.

Tentatively, then fiercely, with her hands framing his handsome, sun-tanned face and his arms strong around her waist as if he would never let her go.

"You're different," she whispered against his lips, as fireworks began popping distantly over the ridge. "Real," she simply said.

They talked till the fire died down - her spilling about Atlanta life pressures, her parents' lofty expectations for her, and with him sharing about Gary and Eliza and the way of the mountain life.

For the next two months, weekends fused them together when the Hargroves escaped the city heat. Fall practice bled into Friday Night Lights with Buddy slinging passes like bullets. But Saturdays belonged to her. He would slip two miles through the woods and cross two creeks down to the roadside pay phone at the old depot that had shut down a few years back, every evening, where he would drop in as many dimes as he could muster to just hear her voice.

"Mountain Man Calling," he would say with a grin into the receiver in the night air - her voice crackling through the copper wire across the miles.

There, they would bare their souls to one another - her dreams of breaking free from Daddy's deals, his vows of faith and family forged in Grace Fellowship pews - talking until the operator's cold call, "Time's Up!", cut them short and left them each with an ache that would not stop until they could hear the other again.

Gary raised a brow at the mud-caked boots and late returns but held his tongue, wisdom as quiet as a prayer. Donna's parents tolerated the local boy as harmless summer fun, yet they were blind to the fire that kindled deep into a love-starved soul. The coming October chill turned maple and sourwood leaves to flaming torches on the mountainsides, and frost etched the windowpanes, but Buddy knew this was no fleeting spark. She was his, and he would run through Hell's own defensive line to claim her forever.

Chapter 4 - Moonlit Promises

The last Friday night in September crackled alive under Rabun County's stadium lights, the air thick with the season's coming chill, fresh mowed grass, and the electric roar of a packed crowd spilling from the bleachers to the sidelines.

Buddy dropped back off the line, scanning the defense like a hawk flying over misty ridges, his broad frame calm despite the blitz howling in his ears, "Blue 42! Set! Hut!" he barked, voice cutting through the chaos like one of Gary's sermons.

Then the snap - Buddy rolling right, his pass pinpoint perfect to Big Jim, the tight-end, the hometown crowd erupting as he broke free for twenty yards. With the first quarter tied, Buddy was at home on the field as he was in the mountains that surrounded him.

Up in the stands, Donna had begged her parents for an early weekend escape from Atlanta's concrete cage. She had slipped in unannounced amid the peanut shells and wool blankets. Her sweater hugged her figure against the chill as she watched mesmerized as Buddy dropped back again - evading a blindside rush with a spin that drew gasps, then shooting a 60-yard spiral that kissed the receiver's hands right in the end zone.

Touchdown! Wildcats now up 14-7. Her heart pounded in sync with the cheers, her hands clasped tightly, as she whispered his name like a prayer.

Whispers rippled from the bleachers like running water about several major colleges sniffing around the Holcombs - from the Georgia Bulldogs' scout scribbling furiously on his notepad, the Clemson Tigers' rep pacing the sidelines, and even Alabama's Tide had rolled in to scope out this young, amazing talent.

Buddy's senior year stardom was no fluke: his arm was like cannon fire, always hitting his target, his legs churning like logging chains through the mud.

By half-time, with a 28-14 lead, the PA announcer boomed, "Holcomb connects again!"

Donna's eyes never left him as her heart swelled with pride.

Final quarter and Fannin County was clawing their way back - score tied at 28-all with only two minutes remaining. Buddy took the snap a little high, grabbed it up, and rifled to his receiver alone in the end zone.

Victory erupted - 34-28 final - the mountain's natural amphitheater gave way to shouts of,

"Holcomb! Holcomb!" shaking the stands.

As the whistle shrieked its last, Donna pushed her way up from the bleachers, trying not to shiver in the mountain cold and her boots slipping a little on the concrete.

"I'm gonna run down and tell him that was a good game," she said to her parents over her shoulder, already gathering her purse.

"We need to beat the traffic," Tom replied, checking his watch.

Donna was already halfway to the aisle.

"I'll catch a ride to the lake house with Buddy," she called out, hurrying on her way towards the field.

"Meet us at the house then," her dad called behind her.

Gail's mouth tightened, but she did not call her back. By the time Donna reached the bottom of the bleachers, the Hargroves were already headed out of the fence towards their car, hoping to be the first ones out of the parking lot.

She stepped onto the edge of the field, swaddling herself in Buddy's Letterman jacket, as her eyes began searching for number 12. The band played one last brassy flourish and then began to file out, leaving the turf strewn with confetti, paper cups, and trampled grass. Donna stayed rooted near the 50-yard line, waiting.

Buddy caught her wave across the chaos and lifted a hand, his helmet tucked under his arm, his grin wide and boyish. Then the coach clapped his shoulder and jerked a thumb toward the tunnel.

"Locker room, Holcomb! We talk first; you can celebrate later."

Buddy pointed to the grass near the fifty, mouthing, "*wait for me* ", then disappeared with the team under the stands.

The lights hummed overhead, casting the emptying field in a bright, lonely glow. Cheerleaders dragged pom-poms toward the gate, and a couple of little kids chased each other in circles where the players had just battled for every inch. Donna stood on the painted white stripe, hands jammed into her pockets, her heart still racing from the game and from the look he had given her.

The locker room under the stands smelled like sweat, grass, and cheap cologne. Steam curled from the showers, turning the air hazy as the boys laughed and hollered, replaying every hit and pass as if the game were not already settled.

"Holcomb, that last drive," Hank thumped Buddy's shoulder pads with a wet palm, "they're gonna be talkin' about that till we're old men on this same bench."

"Speak for yourself," Big Jim snorted, wrapping tape around his wrists like it might hold his whole future together. "I ain't sittin' on no bench in Rabun when I am old. I will be in Atlanta, big money, big suit. You will be right here, Hank, shouting at referees through dentures."

Laughter broke out, easy and loud.

Buddy grinned, tugging his jersey over his head, the fabric still damp with victory and the autumn chill. His muscles hummed with the good burn of work well done. Outside, the band's drums boomed faintly as the last of the crowd shuffled away under the lights.

In the corner, Leroy fell quiet as he unfolded a thin, blue airmail letter, the paper already soft from being read so many times. The chatter around him dimmed.

"How's Johnny?" Buddy asked, nodding toward the page - Leroy's older brother, two years ahead of him and now in Vietnam.

Leroy swallowed.

"Says it's hot as the devil and wet as the bottom of Tallulah Gorge," he said, forcing a crooked grin. "Says the trees look wrong and the bugs bite meaner. Says he misses Mama's biscuits something fierce."

He did not read the other lines out loud - the ones about boys their age not coming back, about nights broken by the sound of helicopter blades and the crack of distant rifles - but his eyes told the story anyway.

Coach's radio, perched on a shelf by the door, crackled with the commentator's voice, half-drowned by the static and the shower spray:

"...More protests in Atlanta over the war..."

“ Another list of draft lottery numbers to be called tonight...”

“Turn that off,” someone muttered.

“Nah, leave it,” Hank said, tossing his towel in the hamper. “I wanna hear it if they pull my birthday.” He puffed out his chest. “Uncle Sam might look at this prime beef, and say, ‘Son, you're being wasted on small-town ball.’”

“Yeah, right,” Big Jim shot back, “you’d last ten minutes in the jungle before you begged them to send you home to Mathis’ onion rings.”

More laughter, but thinner, a little too high at the edges.

Buddy sank into the wooden bench, laces loose in his hands.

“You think they'll still be draftin’ by the time we're out?” one of the younger guys asked, his voice cracking just enough to show that he had been thinking about it longer than just tonight. “My cousin over in Clarkesville got his number pulled in June. Aunt Jean ain't stopped cryin’ since.”

“War’s gotta end sometime,” Danny said quickly, “it can't go on forever.”

“Folks said that back in ‘67,” Leroy murmured, his eyes on his brother's letter. “Johnny wrote they keep sayin’ it now - and he still ain't home.”

Silence settled for a beat, thick as the steam.

Buddy stared down at his muddy cleats, at the grass mashed into the grooves. On the field, the yard lines were straight and clear, the plays written out and choices neat as chalk on a blackboard.

You read the defense, you trust your line, you throw the ball.

The world outside those lights was not so simple.

He thought of Gary's voice on Sunday mornings, heavy with the names of boys overseas, the church bulletin with a list printed between hymnal page numbers, and potluck announcements.

Pray for: *Johnny Garrison. Billy Fain. Earl McCray.* And many others...

He thought about the flag in front of the school, snapped tightly by the mountain wind.

"You worried, Holcomb?" Hank asked, swinging his legs, trying to sound casual. "Big arm like yours, they might just stick you at the front. Quarterback in a different kind of back field."

Buddy lifted his gaze.

"I'd go if they called me," he said, the words surprising even himself with how steady they came. "Dad says you don't run from your duty. But..." he hesitated, choosing the words with care, "I don't reckon wantin' to live and do somethin' good here is the same as bein' scared. I just... don't want to waste whatever the years the Lord gives me, whether they are here or over there."

Leroy's mouth twitched.

"Johnny wrote somethin' like that," he said, "said it feels like he is fightin' somebody else's mess, but the boys next to him make it worth it. Says he wants to come home and build something that lasts. A garage, maybe. A family."

"Family sounds better than foxholes," Big Jim muttered.

Coach's voice cut through the low murmur from the doorway.

"Alright, Ladies," he called, pretending not to hear the war talk the way grown men pretend not to be afraid for their sons. "Shower quickly and clear out. You can solve the world's problems from your tailgates. Lights go off in ten."

The boys groaned, some snapping towels, others grabbing their gear. The moment passed, dissolved into chatter and plans for after the game. Buddy slung his duffle over his shoulder and headed out of the tunnel, leaving the other fellas and the radio's scratchy war news fading behind him.

Donna was still there when he appeared from the tunnel, the field now mostly empty, the lights buzzing overhead like a held breath. She stood on the 50-yard line, her hands tucked in his coat sleeves and her breath puffing white in the cold.

"I thought you might be gone," he called, his voice echoing a little in the open space.

"And miss this?" she asked as she stepped toward him with a smile bright as the stadium bulbs. "Not a chance."

Up close, he could see the flush on her cheeks and the way her eyes shone like little stars.

"Buddy, that was incredible!" she exclaimed. "You're unstoppable."

"Team did their part," he said casually, "the line held. Coach called it right."

She moved closer, her fingers grazing his sleeve, drawing him toward her. Then she leaned in, lips near his ear, and whispered words that lit him like kindling.

The rest of the team came piling out of the tunnel, hollering for the after-game bonfire roaring in the woods off Route 441 - cold beer soaking in Stekoa Creek waiting under the oaks - but Buddy waved them off with a grin.

"Got something better tonight," he simply stated as he steered her toward his beat-up old Ford pickup that was ready to rumble like a faithful coonhound.

He killed the lights when they reached the Hargrove lake house and grabbed a blanket from the truck. Then, hand-in-hand, they slipped down the trail to the dock. The moon was dancing over the water like a silver promise etched in its black silk. Inside, her parents were oblivious to them - Tom pacing and ranting on the phone while Gail was lost in a dog-eared Gloria Weinstein book beside a glass of chardonnay; playing a Big Band record from the 1940's that echoed through the lake valley.

Under that lunar glow, their guards crumbled slowly. Buddy pulled her close on the weathered planks as they creaked under their weight, the lake lapping softly like whispered vows. Hands first - his callused thumb tracing her jaw as her fingers threaded themselves in his thick, dampened hair.

"Donna," he whispered gently against her skin, his voice rough from shouting plays, "This...us... you and me - it's forever - right?"

She nodded, "Yes. Forever."

Their eyes locked as she pulled him down, as passion overtook them like a summer storm.

The community's golden boy, schooled in Grace Fellowship's sanctity of life and love, let the moment claim them fully - whispers turning fevered; her soft "please", mingling with his tender resolve. The soft waves rocked as their gentle witness.

They lay there together later, tangled in each other's souls, stargazing as Orion wheeled overhead, loons calling their lonely song across the water's symphony.

"Our future," she said as she traced his chest, "is right here with the mountains holding us."

He kissed her forehead, his conviction as steel - this was sacred ground, planted as deeply as his faith.

He pulled in at the first gate off Highway 441 at the farm near dawn, then parked and shut the truck door as quietly as possible so as not to wake his folks. He went straight to the shed and began busting wood like most fall mornings - the rhythmic thunk-thunk echoing with the fireplace smoke already drifting sweet across the cool morning. Eliza watched from the kitchen window, hymn soft on her lips - "It Is Well"-

knowing full well her boy had been missing from the Holcomb home last night. She added some more pancake batter to the sizzling griddle as she wondered.

"Buddy, you did all right out there last night," she said as he stomped in, hands still raw from the axe work, with a knowing look.

Gary chimed in, interrupting the moment between mother and son.

"Two different folks came by after the game. Their cards are on the hearth - several college scouts are looking at you. Looks like my boy might have more than logging in in his future."

He then changed gears and said, "We're cutting the Parkers' place this month. That should get us through spring, most likely. Mighty steep over there on that side of Persimmon Gap - we will need longer ropes, maybe even a chain for the big ones. You ready, Son?"

"Yessir. Good trout runnin' that side of the river - might break up the day with a pole. I'll catch them, you clean them!" he told him with a wide grin.

Gary chuckled.

Buddy shoveled in bites all the while burning to see Donna's face again - to know if she felt as incomplete without him as he did her.

After Thursday's practice, Henry Irvin hollered from the field,

"Bonfire before the game - you goin'?"

Patty Hall waved from the bleachers with her quiet eyes, looking at him knowingly.

Buddy nodded, "Yeah, see you there."

He pulled into the schoolyard late, coming from the Parkers' place, and could see the flames leaping wildly in a huge circle of glowing rocks as girls' laughter cut through the darkness like fireflies. Then he saw Donna in her baby-blue sweater, her blue eyes shining across the firelight.

At first glance, Donna's gaze met his, stating simply, "I'm yours."

The city girl stood out among the mountains, bright as a wildflower in a field of hay. It was like Buddy had reached up and grabbed a distant star, and when he was holding it, he glowed just as bright.

The weeks that followed were full of the kind of love Donna had never known and could have only dreamt of. It was as if she were wrapped in a warm quilt stitched with Eliza's kindness, Gary's steady laughter, and the quiet strength of the mountain community built on faith that had raised Buddy. They showed her a world she had only had a glimpse of from the lake - a world where faith and hard work ran deeply, where supper tables were set with grace as much as with food.

Being with Buddy felt like finding crystal clear water at its source after years of drinking from the murky wells of the Hargrove house and the city. The Holcombs' kitchen smelled like heaven and home - yeast rolls, fried taters crisping in an iron skillet, coffee strong and steaming on the counter while the morning's light landed in through the small window over the sink, turning the flour on Eliza's hands to something almost holy.

Patty stood at the table with a big metal bowl of snap beans - fingers moving on instinct against the green pieces planking softly against the sides of the bowl - as her braids hung over her shoulders, dusted with a little flour from when Eliza had "accidentally" bumped her with her elbow.

"Pattygirl, you're makin' those beans nervous - snappin' them so fast," Eliza said glancing over her shoulder with a smile. "They ain't goin' nowhere."

Patty grinned, "Just tryin' to keep up with you, Mrs. Eliza. You move like there are three of you in this kitchen."

Eliza chuckled and turned back to the dough, pressing her palms in and folding, then pressing and folding again, her rhythm as steady as a hymn.

"Only one of me, far as I know. Lord help the mountains if there were more!"

The back screen door creaked and banged shut as the morning wind caught it. Donna stepped in, cheeks pink from the walk up the drive, hair a little wind-tossed despite her careful styling. She paused just inside like she always did, hands hovering near her purse strap, eyes drinking in the sight of the Holcombs' kitchen as if it were a painting she loved.

"Well, there she is," Eliza said, not turning yet, "Miss Atlanta herself. You hungry, baby?"

Donna smiled, the tension in her shoulders easing a little.

"Always, Mrs. Eliza. It smells amazing in here."

"That's cause Patty's workin' so hard," Eliza said, nodding toward the table as she reached for the rolling pin. "Come on in and sit a spell. City folks need some biscuits, too."

Donna slid into the chair across from Patty, setting her purse down by her feet. Patty nudged the bowl toward her.

"You can snap a few if you want," Patty offered, "Eliza says it's good therapy."

Eliza snorted.

"I said it keeps your hands busy, so your mouth don't get you in trouble! That is what I said."

Donna laughed, reaching for a handful of beans. Her manicured fingers fumbled at first, the ends not breaking clean, and Patty showed her how to bend and pull the beans, so they snapped just right.

"Like that," Patty instructed, "they'll talk to you if you'll listen."

Donna concentrated, her tongue caught between her teeth for a moment, then tried again. The bean gave a neat, satisfying snap! Her face lit up.

"Oh. That is kind of nice!"

“Careful,” Eliza said as she rolled out the dough, “we will have you ruined for high society! And in no time at all, you will be wantin’ front porches, clotheslines, and men who smell like campfires instead of fine cologne.”

Donna's hands stilled on the beans, a soft flush rising on her cheeks.

“There are worse things to smell like,” she said quietly.

Patty's gaze flickered up, meeting hers. For a heartbeat, neither of them looked away. There was no accusation in Patty's eyes, only a knowing softness - like she had read the same chapter of life and had underlined different lines.

Eliza dusted her hands and turned her face fully; one hip braced against the counter.

“Pattygirl,” she said, mischief glinting in her eyes, “you got any fellas as a future husband in mind yet?”

Patty let out a groan.

“Mrs. Eliza...”

Donna smiled, eager for the shift.

“Yes, Patty,” Donna said, leaning forward, “anyone special?”

Patty rolled her eyes, but her lips curved.

“I'm just gettin’ me ready for one, is all,” she said, “cause you never know.” She lifted one shoulder. “Figured if I let the Lord work on me now, maybe I won't scare him off when he finally shows up!”

Eliza laughed outright.

“That's right. Better have your heart in order before you start worryin’ about his.”

She tilted her head and began studying Donna.

“What about you, Sugar? Buckhead boys beatin’ down your door?”

Donna looked down at the bean in her hands, turning it over, thumbs stroking the green skin. Images flashed behind her eyes - silver spoons, club dinners, polite handshakes that never reached the heart.

Then Buddy's face rose up - sweat-damped hair under the stadium lights, the way his hand had felt steady at the small of her back, how his laugh filled up a room and somehow quieted her all at once.

“Most boys I know,” she said slowly, “are in love with themselves or their daddy's money.”

She snapped the bean clean in half. “I’m not sure that counts.”

Eliza’s expression softened.

“Hmm,” she murmured as she moved back to the stove, lifting the lid off so steam billowed warm through the room.

“The world is full of boys like that. Takes the Lord’s own hand to grow a man worth tyin’ your life to.”

Patty kept her eyes on the bowl, but her voice was gentle.

“Have you found anyone that makes you feel... safe?” she asked. “Like you can be yourself and the walls don't have to stay too high?”

Donna's throat tightened at the word safe. She thought of Buddy's jacket around her shoulders at the lake, the way he had listened when she talked about things the Buckhead crowd would call "silly" or "sentimental."

She nodded before she meant to.

"I think... I have," she whispered.

Eliza did not press. She hummed a line of "Great Is Thy Faithfulness" under her breath as she moved, and the kitchen began filling with the quiet music of home: the clink of a spoon, the soft thud of dough being cut into biscuits, the snap of beans between the girls' fingers.

"You know," Eliza said after a moment, her voice almost casual, "Gary has a sayin', 'The Lord don't waste nothin': not a tear, not a mistake, not a broken heart.' He can use every bit of it if we hand it over to him," she glanced back at Donna, her eyes kind but keen, "and that goes for mountain girls and city girls both alike."

Donna swallowed, blinking away the sudden sting in her eyes.

"Mom is trying to teach me to 'take' control - I am not sure I am happy with that or that I want that approach. And she does not seem so happy these days."

Patty snorted softly, and Eliza shot her a look over one shoulder, "Hush, Child!" she said, but there was a twitch of a smile at the corner of her mouth.

"Well," Eliza said, turning back to her, "you just remember there's One whose hands are steadier than hers or mine or yours," as she pointed the biscuit cutter covered in dough gently in Donna's direction, "and He loves you more than any of us ever could."

The words landed softly but surely. Donna did not know what to say, so she said nothing. She just kept snapping beans beside Patty, listening to the hymn, and watching Eliza move around the kitchen like she was born to make ordinary mornings always feel like something special.

For the first time in a long time, Donna felt something inside her loosening - a tiny corner of her heart unclenching. Maybe, just maybe, there was a kind of life where expectations did not crush, where love was steady, and faith was as natural as breathing. Her thoughts were sailing between Patty's quiet companionship and Eliza's unshakable warmth. She could almost believe she belonged right there in the center of this precious family for life.

Patty bumped her shoulders lightly, bringing her out of her daydreams.

"You're gettin' pretty good at those," she teased, nodding at the neat pile of beans piled up in Donna's bowl.

Donna smiled back at her and replied, "Good teacher!"

Eliza slid a tray of biscuits into the oven and closed the door with a soft click.

"All right, you two," she said, "let's see if we can feed this family and whatever strays the Lord sends up the hill today," she gave them a knowing look, "seems like he's already sent a few."

Chapter 5 - Present Faith and Fractured Dreams

The very next Sunday, the air over Panther Creek smelled crisp and fresh, mingled with the smoky scent of the BBQ waiting under the pavilion. Cars lined the rutted track all the way down from Grace Fellowship's little gravel lot, Fords and Chevys nose-to-tail between the pines. The last of the leaves were just catching the copper edge of fall, with the first full week of November already passed by.

All week, the Mathis' Diner talk had been about the revival - three nights of preaching, singing, and today's baptisms down at the Holcombs' favorite bend. Half of Buddy's teammates had sworn they would be there, if only to hear Gary "get to hollerin' about Jesus" and see who would be brave enough to walk into the icy water.

Donna stood near the bank, wrapped in a borrowed, crocheted shawl over her dress, bare legs goose-pimpled in the shade. Her parents stayed farther up the hill where the grass gave way to hard-packed dirt - Tom in his pressed khakis and polished loafers, and Gail in a smart wool coat despite the country setting. Tom kept checking his watch like mountain time ran like city time. Gail's lips were set thin, her fingers worrying over the strap of her purse every time somebody shouted, "Amen", which was a lot.

Only Donna and Buddy knew about the dock, about their whispered vows and crossed lines. The guilt sat under her ribs, though she knew in her heart that she was deeply in love with the quarterback-logger.

Buddy stood shoulder to shoulder with his teammates on the flat rocks, his hands shoved deep in his pockets. The roar of Panther Creek wrapped the whole crowd. Gary stepped up on a boulder that served as his pulpit, Bible in hand, his voice carrying over the water.

"Now I know folks got a heap of ideas 'bout what's wrong with this world," he called. "Some say it is the government. Some say it is money. Some say it is them folks down in Atlanta, or them hippies on TV."

A ripple of chuckles moved through the Rabun County crowd. Up the bank, Tom gave a tight little laugh that did not reach his eyes, straightening his tie like he wished he had left it in the car. Gail shifted her weight, one polished heel sinking into the soft ground, her eyes narrowing just a touch at the mention of Atlanta.

"But God's Word says somethin' different," Gary went on, "our real problem started way back yonder before any of us were around. God made this world good. He made a man, put him in a garden, and gave him one clear command. 'Obey me.' If that man had kept on listenin' and obeyin', there would be life and peace as long as the days rolled."

Tom cleared his throat, glancing sideways as if to see whether anyone was noticing him standing this close to such plain talk.

Gail's fingers tightened on her purse strap. Terms like "obedience" and "command" scraped against every 'Women's Empowerment' article folded in the glovebox.

"But that one man - Adam - chose his own way instead of God's way," Gary said. "Sin slipped in through that one door, and death came right behind it. And ever since, every one of us born after him comes into this world with that same bent heart. We do not just do wrong now and then - we have wrong living inside us. That is why this world's busted up. That is why we hurt each other. That is why even good days have a shadow on them."

A couple of Buddy's teammates shifted their feet, their faces somber. Donna felt the words land sharply. She thought of the dock, the breathless "yes', the way joy had soured into a quiet ache.

"Deep down, we know God is holy and right," Gary said, "that is why even lost folks holler for justice when they have been done wrong. Problem is, if God just gives us pure justice and nothin' else, every last one of us goes under. If He pays us what we have really earned, we all die and we all stand guilty."

Tom frowned, his jaw ticking. He was used to being the man who balanced scales his way in business and in closings. Gail folded her arms tightly, as if to shield herself - and her daughter - from a verdict she did not like the sound of.

"But hear me: God didn't just leave us there," Gary's tone softened.

"In His goodness and His mercy, He sent His Son. Jesus did not come into this world like you and me. He was not born the ordinary way, taking on the same bent nature. He was born of a virgin, just like the Bible says. That matters because it means His record started clean - and He kept it clean. Never sinned once. Every thought, every word, every step lined with His Father's will."

Gail's brows drew together. Virgin birth, sin nature - it all sounded a little too primitive, too absolute, for the woman who had been clipping women's lib editorials about "self-actualization" and "writing your own rules". She shifted again, whispering something to Tom that made him nod, though his eyes stayed on the creek.

"Jesus is fully God and fully man," Gary said, his voice rolling sure as the water. "As a man, He obeyed God's law perfectly in our place - living the life we could not live. And then, as God's spotless Lamb, He went to the cross and took the punishment we had earned - dying the death that belonged to us. The scriptures tell us, 'All we like sheep have gone astray...and the Lord hath laid on Him the iniquity of us all.' And again it says, 'For he hath made Him to be sin for us, who knew no sin; that we might be made the righteousness of God in Him.'"

He pointed gently to the water.

"When Jesus hung on that tree, it was like God took all the filth of our record and wrote it across His name. He carried it. He paid it. He died once for sin, the just for the unjust, to bring us to God. Then on the third day, He got up again - alive - for our justification. That is a big word, but it simply means this: God can look at a sinner who runs to Jesus and say, 'Not guilty. Cleansed. Mine.' And still be fair and holy in doing it, because the bill's already been paid in full."

"Not guilty" made Donna's throat tighten. Her hand drifted protectively to her middle; she knew something was different.

There was a faint, impatient sigh from the bank. The idea that her daughter might stand in the same line as "sinners" in need of cleansing rubbed Gail raw. Tom shifted his weight again, eyes scanning for an exit path through the parked cars.

"There's another trade that happens too," Gary continued on with excitement building in his voice, "our sin goes to Him at the cross, and His goodness - His righteousness - gets counted to us. So God is both just and the one who justifies the man, woman, boy, or girl who puts their trust in Jesus. Anybody who comes to Christ in faith can be saved. Not just scrape by, either - but brought into God's own family."

He nodded towards the cluster of young folks.

"When He saves you, He doesn't just stamp a ticket to Heaven for you and leave you be. He adopts you as His child. He starts making you look like kin - shaping you, little by little, to bear the family resemblance. That is what we call sanctified. And the same good news that saved you keeps on changing you, all the way through this life."

"And one day, when it is all said and done, He ain't just gonna save you from sin's penalty. He ain't just gonna break sin's power over you. He is going to bring you home where there ain't even the presence of sin. No more funerals. No more wars. No more secret shame. Just Jesus and his people, whole and clean."

He spread out his work-scarred hands.

"That's the good news we are preaching out here at this creek. That is the only message big enough for this busted-up world. It is enough for a football star, enough for a rich man, enough for a girl who ain't sure where she stands, and enough for a sinner sittin' on the back rock thinkin' they have done gone too far. And it's enough for this old, logger-preacher, that thanks Him for the mercy in my life every day. It is enough."

"So if you are hearing His voice today, do not argue about whose fault everything is. Start with your own heart. Admit what He already knows. And then run, not to this water first, but to the Savior -the Carpenter who went to the cross - and trust Him with all you are."

Down by the rocks, Buddy felt the words burn straight through him.

Up on the bank, Donna hugged herself tighter against a chill that had nothing to do with the creek's breeze.

Behind her, Tom checked his watch one more time and muttered, "Hope this doesn't run too much longer," while Gail's mouth pressed into a hard line that promised this backwoods' religion had already gone far enough for one day.

But the river kept roaring.

And the Carpenter's call kept cutting through their unease, straight to Donna's heart - and to Buddy's - whether the Hargrove's liked it or not.

Seven games into the season, the Wildcats stood unbeaten. Friday nights were electric under those same stadium lights that had seen Buddy's rise from raw sophomore to legend. His arm was a torpedo now - slinging passes like answered prayers - threading tight windows and dropping bombs that split secondaries wide open.

Even Tom Hargrove started showing up at his games. His slacks crisp and clean while sporting a Rabun County Wildcat hat amid the popcorn carnage and peanut shells as he nodded to the local lake folks while boasting loudly, "Holcomb's the heart of it!"

Buddy soaked it all in quietly with his eyes always searching the stands until they fell on Donna - her cheers his fuel. But beneath the noise and the glory, Donna fidgeted with sweaty palms.

During one of their long walks along the gravel road from the lake house, with white pines whispering overhead like uneasy guardians, her silence proved to be deafening. It was a chilly evening, but he stopped her, gently brushed her knuckle with his thumb, and finally asked her,

"What's eating at you, Darlin'? Talk to me - ain't no play we cannot call."

She looked up at the canopy of pines they were standing under as if to offer up a little prayer, as tears began to pour from her eyes, and with her voice breaking, she finally stated in a whisper,

"I think I'm pregnant."

The world tilted like a snapped log rolling downhill, but Buddy pulled her close. He was steady as the mountains cradling them, wrapping her in his strong arms. "Are you sure?"

"I have not gone to the doctor yet, but I am pretty sure. I am late. I keep waking up nauseous."

"It will be okay. I got this," he vowed, his voice firm and strong.

"We will make this right. As soon as I can stand proper-like before your daddy. I will ask him for your hand, clean and true - if you will say yes to this logger's son forever?"

Her sobs melted into "Yes" against his chest as her fears began dissolving into shared resolve.

A wedding.

Scholarships might bridge the class chasm between them; faith would carry the rest.

The gravel crunched as they walked hand in hand, their future sketched in starlight.

The next week was buzzing with excitement: The Wildcats against their archrival Habersham Central - the feud that packed the stands from fence to fence. The air was thick with trash talk.

The rival coaches and students barking out pre-game barbs: "Your golden boy's a leg injury away - watch him limp off!"

Both sides jeered from the bleachers as the marching band's drums pounded out war songs.

Donna and her parents took their places in some prime seats.

Tom slapped Buddy's shoulder before the kickoff and stated enthusiastically, "Show them, Son!"

He channeled every nerve into perfection - with pinpoint spirals carving the air as his legs churned through tackles like a hot knife in butter.

It was the end of the fourth quarter, and the score was tied 14-14.

Coach Smith looked Buddy in the eye and said to him, "Boy, this next play could seal your ticket! The Bulldog's scout is sitting in the end zone, and the rep from Alabama is watching from the fifty-yard line. Go get them!"

The snap came low and bounced wildly like a spooked fawn. Buddy scooped it up on instinct. He juked two defenders with a shoulder dip straight, escaping a linebacker whiffing at air, then rumbled forty-seven yards untouched. His legs high-stepping as the crowd's roar drowned out the world as he entered the end zone.

Touchdown!

Victory erupted... teammates yelling "Dogpile! Dogpile!"

Darkness swallowed him like a blanket under the piling bodies.

Shouts of "Holcomb! Holcomb!" shook the earth.

Snap! He heard it first - deep in his thigh like pines crashing in an ice storm. Then pain exploded white-hot with floating bones grinding against each other.

The coaches swarmed in, and the stretcher ride was nothing more than a blur as the sound of sirens began ringing in his ears, overruling the shouts of his teammates and the glare of the stadium lights.

Rabun Memorial's ER doors swallowed him whole as the x-rays revealed a unique break: bone splintered clean through. His femur shattered like kindling.

Dr. Taylor's words landed heavily on everyone in the room: "Year minimum of rehab. Football? Scholarships? Dicey at best - maybe down the drain."

Tom paced softly in the hallway with his mind drifting to a project waiting on his desk. Gary gripped Eliza's hand while murmuring familiar Psalms.

Buddy lay staring quietly at the ceiling with Donna's hand in his: his pain paling against his burning vow: family first, always.

Dawn found him plotting through a morphine haze - wedding plans, pondering baby names, and thoughts of building a cabin in the meadow by the creek and raising his family there. Naivety was blinding him to the storm that was gathering over Atlanta, but faith was anchored as deep as the Tallulah Gorge in his soul. The field was lost. The real game had just begun...

Chapter 6 –

By the Lake

Donna rolled the window down a crack and let the mountain air rush in, cool and fresh and full of pine. The old Ford rattled a little as Eliza eased it around the curve coming out of town, a brown paper sack of flour and sugar rustling between them on the bench seat.

"Mercy, they've gone and raised prices again," Eliza said, as she shook her head, "if sugar gets any higher, folks will have to start robbing the beehives."

Donna managed to smile, though her fingers stayed tight in her lap.

"You would just water it down and stretch it anyway," she said, "you and your make do's."

"That's right."

Eliza tipped her chin, her eyes on the narrow road. "Women up here have been making do since before there was a sign for Main Street. We know how to feed a crowd with a pot of beans and a pone of cornbread and still send a plate home to somebody worse off."

They passed the last of the storefronts, then the post office, then the faded sign pointing toward the lake and the campgrounds. Trees closed in soft and familiar, the branches meeting high overhead like a green tunnel.

Donna swallowed, looking straight ahead. Her stomach had been in a knot all morning, but it was more than nerves. It was the same rolling, unsettled feeling she had been waking up with every day for several weeks now. Late. She was too late. The calendar squares she had tried not to count kept lighting up in her mind.

She slid a glance at Eliza. The older woman's hands were steady on the wheel, her knuckles browned and strong, her gold band catching the light.

“Mrs. Eliza?” Donna said.

“Hmm?” Eliza did not look away from the road.

“Can I... ask you something?” Donna picked out a loose thread on her jeans. “And you promise not to, I don't know, laugh or think I'm nosy?”

Eliza's mouth twitched a little.

“I can promise not to laugh,” she said, “but whether I think you're nosy or not is between the Lord and me.”

Donna huffed a soft breath that was almost a laugh.

“Okay, that's fair.”

They crested a rise, and the lake flashed blue through the trees. Eliza's hands slowed on the wheel, more from habit than traffic; she always eased up here, as if the view deserved a little reverence.

“It's about you and Pastor Gary,” Donna said, the words tumbling out quicker than she meant for them to do. “About Buddy.”

Eliza's brows lifted the slightest bit, but she kept driving and looking ahead.

“All right,” she said slowly, “what about Buddy and us?”

Donna pushed the thread flat.

“Why did y'all wait so long to have him?” she asked. “I mean, you and Pastor Gary were married a long time before Buddy came along, weren't you?”

Eliza gave a little snort.

“Lord, child,” she said, “come to find out you really are from this county!”

Donna blinked.

“What is that supposed to mean?”

“Means you pay better attention than you let on,” Eliza said, “most folks just assumed we had him right away. Or that we had a passel before him, tucked away somewhere out of sight. Either way, most don’t usually come right out and ask.”

She glanced at Donna then, her eyes sparkling with a smirk.

“Why are you asking?”

Donna looked away quickly.

“No reason,” she said too fast, “just wondering.”

Eliza let the silence sit for a beat.

“You're at that age where just wonderin’ usually means somethin’,” she said, “but I will not pry. Not yet.”

Donna’s throat tightened. She stared at the blur of trees, trying to steady her breathing. She had not told anyone else, besides Buddy. Not friends. Not her mother. Only her reflection in the bathroom mirror.

Her hand drifted, almost without thinking, to rest flat against her middle. She snatched it back and shoved it under her leg.

Ahead, the gravel road turned off toward the lake parking area. Eliza flickered on the blinker and slowed.

“I thought we were going to your house to get Buddy’s things and then back to the hospital,” Donna said in surprise.

“We are,” Eliza said, “but by way of the water. I ain't in no such a hurry that I can't pull over when a girl asks a question with her whole body and not just her mouth.”

Donna flushed, but something in her chest eased. Eliza turned onto the single-laned road that followed the lake and rolled the car to a stop under a big sycamore in a side pull-over. The lake lay out in front of them, calm and wide, with the afternoon sun skipping along its surface.

For a moment, neither of them moved. They just listened to the ticking of the cooling engine and the soft slap of waves against the rocks on the bank side.

Eliza finally shifted, turning so she could see Donna better.

“To answer you plainly,” she said, “we didn't wait on purpose. Not a day. We were married young, and we wanted a house full right off. But wantin’ and gettin’ ain't always the same thing.”

She gave a small, wry smile, the corners of her eyes crinkling.

“So no, honey. It was not from lack of trying.”

Donna's face went hot.

“Oh!” she said, with half a laugh, half a cough.

Eliza chuckled, low and amused.

“Remember you asked!” she said with a little laugh. “Can't stand when folks act like babies just drop out of the sky if you hang your clothes out right. Took us a lot of tryin’ and a lot of tears and a whole lot of prayin’, before the Lord sent Buddy along.”

Donna nervously picked at the seam of the seat.

“Just how long?” she whispered. “Did...did it take?”

“Years,” Eliza said simply. “Long enough, I thought He had said ‘no’ without bothering to write it down for me loud and clear.”

Donna chewed her lip.

"Was that... hard?"

"That's one word for it."

Eliza looked over the water a moment, her jaw softening.

"There were nights I had lain there listening to Gary breathe, and I'd ask the Lord if he was even listening to me at all. Babies were everywhere. Church pews full of them. My cousins were having one right after another. And there we were, just us."

Donna swallowed.

"Did you ever... wish you had not married him? Since it took so long."

Eliza's head snapped back around, and her eyes flashed.

"No! Absolutely never!" she exclaimed, her voice sharp enough to slice the air between them.

Then her tone went gentler.

"No, baby. Not a minute. I might have wished he were a little less hard-headed. Might have wished we had made different choices sooner. But I never wished I had not laid my hand in his at that altar."

Donna watched her, with her heart thudding.

"Mama thinks you all were born in the... as church people," she said carefully, "that you do everything right, or so you think?"

Eliza's mouth did that thing that it did sometimes, where one corner quirked up like she knew a joke nobody else knew.

“Your mama's thinking is as short as her patience,” she said. “We were not always ‘church people’. Not by half.”

Donna blinked.

“You weren't?”

“Goodness, no!”

Eliza leaned back against the seat, her eyes going distant, as if she were looking at a different version of herself across the lake.

“Gary Holcomb was the wildest thing on two feet in this county when I met him. He ran shine up and down these roads in a cut-down Ford, and he thought the law was a game and that he was always winning.”

Donna's eyes widened. “Pastor Gary?”

“That's the one.” Eliza's smile held both mischief and sorrow.

“His daddy had him hauling jars before he could drive. The boy knew every back road from here to the state line. And I...” she shook her head faintly, “I was a good girl who had gotten tired of being good. Fell for that local bad boy just as sure as if the devil had written his name in my diary.”

Donna could not help the small laugh that slipped out.

“Oh, Mrs. Eliza,” she said, “I can't even picture it.”

"Thank the good Lord you can't," Eliza muttered. "We married over both our mamas' objections. Mine cried, his cursed. We thought it was so romantic."

She rolled her eyes at herself.

"Bless our foolish hearts."

"Were y'all..." Donna hesitated, searching for words that did not sound like her mother, "Were you two happy?"

"We were loud," Eliza said after a pause, "we were fun. We were stupid."

Her eyes softened.

"We were in love, best we knew how. But, we were also half-drunk half the time, and Gary was running those roads like they could carry him clean away from his own skin if he went fast enough. I went right along with him, thinking I could hold him steady if I just held on tight enough."

Donna stared at her hands.

"So what changed?" she asked. "You are... You now."

"Don't say it like that, like it's a compliment," she snorted, "but you're right, somethin' had to give."

She looked back out over the lake, her voice dropping.

"I got tired, Donna. Tired of wakin' up, not sure where we had been the night before. Tired of seein' my mama's face at the window wonderin' if we were alive. Tired of the emptiness when the music stopped, the bottles were empty, and it was just me and my own thoughts."

She drew a breath.

"One night, Gary took off with some of the boys, and I could not shake this feeling, like somebody had set a rock on my chest. I walked myself right into a little white church down near the river where they were havin' revival. I did not go forward for the preacher. I went forward cause I was drownin' and they were singin' about Somebody who could pull a body out."

Donna swallowed. "What happened?"

"Jesus. He happened."

Eliza's eyes were misty, but her smile was bright.

"Not all at once, not in a clean, pretty way. But I knelt down that night, and I told Him I could not run my own life one more second without makin' a bigger mess of it. I walked out and knowin' I belonged to Him instead of to my fear. Gary did not take kindly to that at first."

Donna could only imagine. "He was still running shine?"

"And runnin' from the Lord just as hard, maybe harder," Eliza answered with a nod.

"He listened to me talk about Jesus till he couldn't stand it no more, and then he'd slam the door and go peel out just to prove he was still his own man."

She shook her head.

"You know how many times I prayed, 'Lord, catch him or kill him, but don't let him stay like this.' More than I can count."

Donna's breath caught. "Did you mean that?"

"I meant, 'Do whatever it takes,'" Eliza said simply. "Turned out, what it took was a 1940's coupe upside down in a ditch."

Donna stared. "What?"

"Gary was too proud to slow down for a curve he had taken a hundred times." Her voice took on a rhythm, as if she were telling an old, often-told story.

"He hit some loose gravel wrong one rainy night. He spun out and rolled that coupe completely over. He was pinned under it. Broken ribs and broken pride. Folks say they heard the crash halfway to town, but there was nobody close enough to get to him that night. He lay there in the dark, the rain coming down, and the gas smell so strong, it was enough to choke a man."

Donna had a hand over her mouth.

"He told me later," she went on quietly, "that he thought he was going to die right there, with glass jars all around him and his own foolishness sitting on his chest. And right then and there, he remembered every sermon I dragged him to, every late-night 'Jesus talk' I had put him through - though he had pretended not to hear. He said he just started talkin' out loud to the Lord."

"He said, 'If You get me out from under this car, I'll quit runnin', I'll quit haulin', I'll quit all of it. Just don't let me open my eyes in Hell.'"

Donna whispered, "Did anybody hear him?"

"Not that night," Eliza said. "The men found him the next morning, half frozen and barely breathin'. They said it was a miracle he was alive. I said it was an answer."

She let the words hang between them a moment, each deep in their own thoughts.

"He was laid up a long time after that," she continued, "busted up pretty bad. Could not so much as sit up without help those first weeks. Gave me a captive audience, you might say."

A faint smile tugged at her lips.

"It was just me, a Bible, and a man who couldn't climb through a window to get away from the Word for once."

Donna's tight chest loosened on a little shaky laugh.

"He slowed down because he had to at first," she continued, lost in her memories, "then he slowed down cause he found he liked the quiet better than the roar. He started readin' on his own, started prayin' his own prayers and not just noddin' along to mine. And one day he looked at me and said, 'Eliza, I cannot go back to them roads. I cannot outrun what I know now.'"

"So Buddy was..." Donna began.

"Buddy was mercy," Eliza said simply, interrupting her, "plain and pure. The Lord could have left us, just the two of us, and He would still have been good. But He waited till we were more 'His' than we were our own, before He trusted us with that boy. At least that is how I see it."

Donna's hand crept, slow and unsure, back to her stomach.

"Weren't you... mad?" she asked softly. "That it took so long, that He didn't just give you what you wanted right off."

"Oh, I had my words with him," Eliza said, frankly.

"I told Him I didn't see why other folks who didn't care a lick about Him had babies stacked like cord wood, and me and Gary were sitting there with empty arms."

"But looking back..." she shook her head, "we were not fit to raise a dog, much less a soul, those first years. The Lord was more gracious than I understood, making us wait till we had come to the end of ourselves."

Donna blinked hard, her eyes burning.

"I used to think He was punishing me," she added, her voice dropping.

"For the things I had done, for the words I had said. Then I learned all my yesterdays, my today, and all my tomorrow sins - He's already put all those on Jesus. He disciplines, sure, and He may redirect. But He ain't petty. He ain't cruel. Sometimes He just says, 'Not yet', cause He knows the road ahead and we do not."

Donna stared at the shimmering water, Eliza's words thudding against the secret she carried.

“Mrs. Eliza,” she whispered.

“Hmm?”

“What if somebody...did everything wrong?” Donna's voice shook.

“Like... what if they did not wait till they were married, or till they were ready, or till they were pointed in the right way? What if they just...messed up?”

Her hand pressed harder against her middle. “Does that mean...does that mean God's done with them? That He will not help them? Or that the baby's some kind of...” she whispered, her voice trailing off, her throat closing around the word punishment, and before she said too much.

Eliza studied her in the quiet. The only sounds were the soft slap of water against stone and a crow fussing somewhere high in the tree line.

“You seem to be carrying a lot around in that little frame,” Eliza said at last, kindly. “I can see it on you, same as if you have a heavy feed sack slung over your shoulder.”

Donna's fingers twisted together in her lap.

“I'm fine,” she said a little too quickly. “Really. Just thinking too much, I guess.”

“Hmm,” Eliza's gaze lingered a bit longer, then she looked back out over the lake.

"Thinkin' can be a blessing or a curse, dependin' on what you let run loose up there."

Donna pressed her lips together, the words she wanted to say crowding her throat: *Mama is going to kill me. I don't know what to do!*

She bit the words back.

"You ever feel like that? Like you have messed up everything?" she asked instead, her voice small. "Like there's no good road left."

Eliza's brow softened.

"More times than I can count," she said. "I just gave you the short version back there. There were nights I was sure I had run so far sideways that the Lord had washed His hands of me. Nights I stared at the ceiling and thought, 'there is no way back from this.'"

"What did you do?" Donna whispered.

"I told Him that," she answered simply. "I told Him I could not see a way. I told Him if He wanted me, He'd have to come and get me, cause I was plum out of maps."

A faint smile tugged at her mouth.

"Turns out that's His specialty, finding folks who've gone and got themselves lost."

Donna swallowed hard again, her knuckles white where she had gripped her own hands.

“What if you can't...say it?” she asked. “Not to anybody. Not yet.”

“Then you say what you can,” Eliza replied, “even if it is just, ‘help’. He hears that word simply fine.”

She slanted Donna a look.

“And you let at least one person in on the edges, so you do not drown in your own head. Doesn't have to be an old woman in a rattly Ford, either. Just somebody who loves you and loves Him.”

Donna let out a heavy breath.

“I don't know if I'm that brave,” she said.

“You will be when you need to be,” Eliza told her. “Sometimes courage shows up ten seconds before you need it and not a minute sooner.”

Donna huffed a tiny, broken laugh. “You make it sound easy.”

“It ain't easy,” Eliza said. “It's just possible. That's the difference.”

They sat for another long moment, watching light skip across the water. A boat droned faintly somewhere across the lake and then faded.

“You and Buddy...” Eliza began, then stopped, choosing her words.

“Y'all are young. Young folks think every choice they make is the one that's goin’ to seal their whole fate forever. Truth is, the Lord's bigger than that. Doesn't excuse foolishness, but it sure does outsize it.”

Donna's heart lurched at Buddy's name.

“I don't want to hold him back,” she blurted out, then flushed, realizing how it sounded.

Eliza’s eyes narrowed just a fraction, but she let it pass.

“You lovin’ my boy won’t hold him back,” she stated confidently. “What you two choose to do with that love - that's where the road forks. But you ain't at the end of any road yet, Donna. Don't go livin’ like all the doors are locked when you haven't even tried the handles.”

Donna bit the inside of her cheek, holding their secret in place.

“I wish I could just... go back,” she replied honestly, “to before everything felt so...big.”

“I used to say that, too,” Eliza murmured, “then I realized the Lord was already standin’ in all the ‘after’s I was scared of. Don't make them less hard. Just meant I wouldn't get there alone.”

Donna nodded, not trusting herself to speak. She stared at the lake until her eyes blurred, letting the water and the sky run together.

Eliza reached for the keys.

"We best get on back before your Buddy starts countin' minutes and blaming' my old car," she said lightly. "Gonna make everybody eat late."

Donna managed a thin smile.

"Yes, I've got to get back to the lake house before Mama gets upset. She already doesn't like me hanging around y'all so much," she said, "she says it makes me too...mountain."

Eliza snorted.

"Could be worse things to be. The world's full of folks with more polish than sense. A little mountain won't hurt you."

She turned the key. The engine coughed, then settled into its familiar rumble. As they pulled out of the gravel lot and back toward the road, Donna looked once more at the water, small and bright in the side mirror.

The fear in her chest hadn't gone anywhere. She was still late. Still hiding. Still walking around with a secret that changes everything.

But sitting there beside Eliza, listening to stories of wrecks and revivals and a God who came looking for fools, she could almost believe there might be a way through - whatever she chose, whatever happened next.

She folded her hands tight in her lap to keep from touching her stomach, and watched the trees close in around the road, carrying her back toward town, toward Buddy, toward a future she wasn't ready to name.

Chapter 7 –

Hospital Whispers

Morning light filtered softly through the blinds at Rabun Memorial Hospital, casting golden stripes across Buddy's casted leg that was elevated high. The room smelled of antiseptic, sharp as pine rosin, and of Eliza's hidden sweet bread cooling on the windowsill - its warmth a small rebellion against the chill of bleach and metal.

Patty came by early that morning while Gary and Eliza were down at the cafeteria. She slipped in with the sunrise, bearing a gift of peppermint sticks and a dog-eared devotional. Rain traced slow rivers down the hospital window as she sat quietly by his bed. The machines hummed steadily, and Buddy's breathing had fallen into a slow, measured rhythm, as his body seemed to have relaxed somewhat in the midst of his pain.

"Buddy," she began softly, fingers worrying the edge of her sleeve, "you know I love you, right?"

He turned his head, offering a tired, gentle smile.

"Course you do, Patty. You're like my own sister."

The words landed bittersweet. She swallowed, blinking back the sting.

"Yeah," she managed, her voice catching, trying not to feel the flood of disappointment in her spirit. "Your sister," she repeated, flatter this time.

She laid the peppermint sticks on the bedside table, lining them up in a neat row like little red-and-white fence posts.

"Daddy says these will help after surgery," she said, trying to keep it light, "the nurse told him it ain't medicine, but he swears it will keep this patient from fussing so much."

Buddy chuckled a little, winced, and let the smile settle again.

"Tell your daddy I'll take all the help I can get," he replied, "and I hope you know I love you too." Then he quickly added, "Did they give you any news while I was doped up?"

She paused before saying, "Just the same - the break is bad. Long road ahead. No guarantees. But you know doctors."

He nodded once, his jaw tightening.

"The Lord knew before they did," he said quietly. "He ain't surprised."

Patty's eyes went to the thick white cast, then to his face.

“Maybe He figured you needed to slow down a spell,” she responded. “I mean, you usually carry the team with your arm, but you literally tried to carry the whole team!” she then added, a hint of teasing in her tone.

Buddy had to grin at that.

“Maybe so,” he murmured, “just wish my slowdown didn't land Daddy with more work and Donna with...”

He trailed off, the words catching in his throat.

Patty felt something lurch in her chest at the sound of Donna's name, but she kept her features smooth.

“Donna knows you love her,” she said calmly. “She was here half the night, as far as I could tell. I walked past their car twice out in the parking lot. Gail looked like she had swallowed a lemon whole.”

Buddy huffed out a short laugh that turned into a grimace.

“Yeah,” he said, “Tom patted my shoulder like I was one of his investments that had gone sideways. Gail glared at the cast on my leg like it was my moral failure.”

Patty's lips twitched.

“They ain't used to things they can't control,” she said matter-of-factly, “ and you scare them, Buddy, not because you're wild, but because you're different from their world.”

He watched as drops slid down the windowpane.

"I was going to march myself up to the front door," he said, more to the glass than to her, "ask Tom straight out for Donna's hand. Tell him about the baby. Tell him I'd make it right, that I would work twice as hard to take care of her."

Patty's heartbeat stumbled.

"Baby," she repeated softly, "she's ... sure?"

Buddy nodded, his eyes still on the rain.

"She's late, sick in the mornings. She's scared," he answered, "but I told her family first, always. I mean, we can start small, a cabin by the creek. If I can't throw a ball for Georgia or Alabama, the Lord can feed a family out of these hills, same as he did for Daddy and Mama."

Patty swallowed past the ache rising in her throat.

"Not much scares you, does it?" she asked.

He shrugged, then regretted the movement.

"I'm scared plenty," he said. "I am just more scared of standing before the Lord one day and having to say I ran from what He gave me."

Patty looked at her hands.

"Do you think ...?" she began, then stopped, choosing her words carefully, "Do you think He's the one who gave you ... this?"

She nodded toward the cast.

Buddy was quiet for a long moment.

"I know He let it happen," he said finally, "nothing slips through His hands. Whether He sent it or allowed it, I might not know till Heaven, but I know He can surely use it. Maybe it's keeping me out of a foxhole next year. Maybe it's keeping my pride from growing bigger than my britches."

He tried to smile.

"Maybe He figured my head needed knockin' more than a linebacker."

Patty gave a watery laugh.

"Hard to imagine your head any harder than it is already," she said, "but I reckon you're right. He wastes nothing."

Silence settled over them, punctuated only by the soft beeping of the monitor and the soft whisper of the rain.

"Patty," Buddy said quietly, "you ever feel like the Lord's asking more of you than you've got to give?"

"All the time," she replied without hesitation, "except I've learned, He ain't actually asking for more than I got. He's asking me to hand over what I do have and to sit back, watch what He can do with just a little."

She hesitated, then added, "You know you do not have to carry all this by yourself. The leg, Donna, the baby, your daddy's work. You're not the only one in this story."

He closed his eyes briefly, letting her words sink in.

"Yeah," he said, "tell that to my pride."

"I just did," she answered softly with a little grin, "you fuss at me about it later."

The doorknob rattled, and Patty quickly wiped at her eyes. Eliza appeared through the door with her hair pinned up and her cheeks flushed from the walk down the hall. Gary hovered behind her with cups of coffee in his hands.

"We got you some real coffee," Eliza announced, eyeing the hospital mug on the tray. "Not that brown water they serve to you here."

She spotted Patty and smiled.

"Pattygirl, you beat us to it!" she exclaimed. "That's what I like, folks who know where they're needed."

Patty stood, smoothing out her skirt.

"I just wanted to see him before my shift," she said. "Those peppermint sticks are from Daddy, he said to tell you that they are not official medical advice, just a bribe."

Gary chuckled, stepping around her to set the cups down, and then turned to give her a hug.

"Tell Dr. Hall, he is a wise man," he said with a sly hint of sarcasm.

Patty nodded and glanced back at Buddy.

"I'll come by again later," she said quietly, "you holler now if you need anything. A book, a milkshake, a smuggled hamburger."

Buddy grinned faintly.

"Thank you, Sis," he said affectionately, "you always show up."

The word 'Sis' hit her again, but she nodded and forced a smile.

"Somebody's got to keep you humble," she said, "can't leave it all to your daddy."

She slipped past Gary and Eliza, giving them her 'good-byes', and the door clicked softly shut behind her.

Inside, Eliza fussed with the blanket, smoothing it over Buddy's leg, while Gary pulled a chair closer to the bed.

Outside in the corridor, Patty leaned against the cool wall for a moment, pressing the peppermint wrapper between her fingers until it crinkled.

"You're like my own sister," echoed in her ears.

She let the ache come, let it wash over her like the rain against the windows, then drew a slow breath.

"Lord," she whispered under her breath, "if that's all I get to be, then help me be the best 'sister' You could ever have sent him, even if it breaks me a little."

She straightened, slipped the devotional from under her arm, and opened it to a page marked by an old crease. The verse at the top stared back at her:

My grace is sufficient for thee, for my strength is made perfect in weakness.

Patty closed the book gently, tucked it under her arm again, and headed down the hall - a new, quieter resolve in her step.

Later that afternoon, Gary and Eliza sat by the bedside, her hands clasped tightly, and her whispered prayers to the good Lord always settling Buddy's heart. They were the anchors of his world - steady, full of grace, uneducated in the eyes of some, but rich in the only wisdom that mattered. His body ached to confess everything to them: Donna, the baby, the "forever" he had vowed in his heart. But the words were tangled thick in his throat. He had not yet worked it all out inside himself - how to speak of shattered bone and shattered plans in the same breath.

"Boy's tougher than hickory," Gary said with a father's steady grin, squeezing Buddy's shoulder as Donna slipped through the door quite as morning mist rolling off Lake Rabun.

Tears still clung to her lashes. She was drawn by instinct, as if some invisible thread pulled her straight to his side. Her man. Her love. She sank into the chair beside him, her hand reaching under the thin blanket until it found his. His fingers curled around hers like they were a life raft, sure and familiar, in a very uncertain world.

His parents read the room in an instant. Gary met Eliza's eyes. She rose, leaned over, and pressed a soft kiss to Buddy's brow.

“Okay,” she said gently, “we'll step out and let y'all talk.”

They slipped into the hall, the door easing shut behind them with a quiet click.

Donna's tears fell freely now, soaking his hand as her head dropped to the bedrail. Buddy's thumb traced slow circles over her knuckles, rough from years of summers at the lake, now slick with salt. Words felt too small. The silence between them was heavy, thicker than the morphine haze, a kind of vow all its own.

“We'll make it,” he whispered finally, his voice groggy from the pain and the medications. “God doesn't abandon His own.”

She lifted her head just enough to nod, fiercely, squeezing his hand back with promises she could not yet put into sentences.

In the hall, the Holcombs joined the Hargroves - country peace mingling with city anxiety. It was the sort of combination that might make most folks uneasy, but not the Holcombs. They knew who they were in Christ. No airs. No polish. No fakeness - just people who were known to listen before they spoke.

Tom rambled on about occupations and important land deals in Atlanta, his words running ahead of his heart. His little girl was hurting, and he did not know how to slow down enough to see it. Gary's eyes grew misty at the lack of tenderness for a young soul caught in the middle. Eliza, never one to hold back truth wrapped in love, spoke up.

"Well, folks, the doc said maybe a year to recover," she gave a small smile, "but I know the Great Physician. We'll see what He has to say about it."

Tom had already processed the medical facts: the femur bone was splintered. The future in football was likely gone, and so were the scholarships.

"Well," Eliza continued, steady as scripture, "God has a well-established calling for my Buddy, and this is part of it. God's calling is sure."

The Hargroves looked confused at such unshaken hope. Gary stood rock solid beside his wife, murmuring an "Amen" under his breath.

Donna and Patty hung out at the hospital and at the Holcombs' over the next few days. Patty spread the quilt out on the grass with a practiced flick of her wrist. The bright patches fluttering down like a field of stitched wildflowers. Panther Creek murmured a few yards away, slipping over rocks the way it had long before any Hargrove or Holcomb drew breath. Above them, the mountains rose in soft greens and blues, shouldering the sky.

"This is perfect," Donna said, lowering herself onto the edge of the quilt and kicking off her shoes. I almost forgot what real quiet sounds like - that hospital can get a little noisy." Then admitted, "I'm worried about Buddy."

"He's gonna be alright," Patty said. She dropped down beside her, tucking one knee up with the other leg stretched out so her bare toes brushed the clover.

"And you call this quiet?" she teased, "you got birds hollering, water fussing over the rocks, and crickets practicing for tonight. City girl's definition of quiet needs some work!"

Donna smiled, looking out at the trees. "Compared to Buckhead traffic and mama's voice on the phone? This is ... peace."

Donna huffed out a breath that wasn't quite a laugh. "She's added two lunch meetings and a charity committee group talk, all since Monday! I think she believes if she keeps me busy enough, I won't have time to remember who I am!"

Patty glanced at her.

"Do you remember?"

Donna picked at a loose thread on the quilt, the cotton soft and twisting under her fingertips. "Up here I do," she said after a moment. "Down there - it's like I'm another person - smiling at things I don't care about, agreeing with people who don't see me at all." She swallowed. "Sometimes it feels like I'm living somebody else's life, and they'll come back any minute and ask for it back."

Patty lay back on her elbows, eyes tracing the line of the ridge. "I get that," she said, "only for me, it's kinda the opposite. Sometimes I wonder if I should be wantin' what you've got - big city, big plans and high-dollar salads."

Donna laughed, the sound loosening something tight within her chest. "Trust me, you're not missing much with those salads!"

Patty smiled, but her voice stayed thoughtful.

"I mean... I love it here. Eliza's kitchen, my home church, the charm of Clayton, and these hills. But every now and then, I hear folks talking about gettin' out and seein' more, and I wonder if I'm being foolish lettin' my whole life fit between Clarkesville and Clayton," she shrugged. "Then I feel guilty for even thinkin' it."

Donna turned toward her, propping her head in one hand, "You are the least foolish person I know," she said. "You know who you are. You know where you belong."

She hesitated, choosing her words carefully. "I envy that."

Patty's brows lifted, "YOU envy me?"

"Yes, YOU!"

Donna picked up a corner of the quilt and rubbed the fabric between her fingers, as if touching it somehow brought her some comfort. "You have roots. People who don't care if your dress came from the right store or if you said the wrong thing at a dinner party. You have a church that knows your name. A town that would come running if you needed anything," she blinked toward the creek. "I have invitations and expectations and a daddy who checks bank balances more than he checks on hearts."

Patty was quiet for a moment, listening to the creek.

"You have people who would run to you, too," she said softly. "Might take them longer to get there, but they'd come. Buddy would." She glanced sideways at Donna. "You know that."

Donna's throat tightened at the sound of his name. "I know," she whispered. "Sometimes that scares me."

"Why?" Patty asked gently.

"Because when I'm with him," Donna said, "This..." she said as she gestured toward the trees, the creek, the quilt - "Feels like the life I was meant to have. Simple? Yes. Demanding work? Sure. But honest." Her fingers curled into the fabric. "Then I go back to Atlanta and Mama reminds me of every door I'm closing if I choose this kind of life, of every person I would be disappointing, every plan I'd ruin."

Patty lay all the way back now, folding one arm under her head. "Your mama sure is good at counting the wrong kind of losses," she said, "and so does this town sometimes."

Donna looked at her, "What do you mean?"

Patty studied the sky as she spoke.

"Folks down here, they talk about people who leave like they've been unfaithful to the mountains, like leavin' means you've stopped lovin' home. I don't think that's fair. Sometimes the Lord calls people to other places - sometimes He calls them to stay. Folks act like one's better than the other, but it's not. It's simply different." She turned her head to look at Donna directly as she spoke on, "Your Mama thinks Atlanta is the only promised land. Some folks here think these ridges are. The truth is the promised land is wherever you're obeying Him."

Donna let the words sink in. "How did you get so wise?" she asked.

Patty snorted. "You should see me when I get mad! I don't sound nearly as righteous!"

They both laughed, easy and real. A breeze slipped down the hill, bringing the clean scent of pine and damp earth. Donna closed her eyes and let it wash over her.

After a moment, Patty spoke again, a bit softer this time, "Can I ask you something and you not take it wrong?"

Donna opened her eyes. "You can ask me anything."

"Does Buddy feel like home to you?" Patty's gaze didn't flinch, but there was no accusation there, just honest curiosity.

Donna's answer came so fast it surprised even her.

"Yes."

She blinked. "More than any house I've ever lived in."

Patty nodded slowly, as if that matched what she had already seen.

"Then you need to pay attention to that," she said, "Because there's a lot of noise out there tellin' you what you '*should'* do, but not all of it loves you."

Donna stared at her - "And you?" she asked quietly. "Do you...?"

Patty held her eyes for a long moment. Something unspoken passed between them - old crushes, quiet sacrifices, the kind of love that steps back so another can step forward.

"I love him," Patty said simply.

"Always have, far as I can remember, but I love the Lord more. And I love you both more than I love my own way," she gave a small, sheepish smile. "So, if God's building a life for you and Buddy, I'd rather stand off to the side and clap than stand in the middle and get run over."

Donna lowered her eyes.

"Patty," she whispered, "I don't deserve that."

"None of us deserves nothin' good," Patty said. "But that's what makes it grace." She reached out and squeezed Donna's hand. "Just promise me you won't let fear or pride or anybody else's dream steal yours - not your mama's, not this town's, not even mine."

Donna squeezed back, tears slipping free.

"I promise to at least try," she said. "And if I start forgetting?"

"I'll remind you," Patty said with a twinkle in her eyes, "probably with more beans to snap."

They both laughed again, the sound mingling with the creek's song. Below them, the leaves dropped into Panther Creek pools, turning into a collage of yellows and reds. The quilt beneath them, sewn from scraps of old shirts and dresses, cradled their shared weight like memory itself - pieces of two different worlds stitched into one soft place to rest.

For a little while longer, they lay side-by-side, saying nothing, listening to the water and the wind. Donna thought of Atlanta and the mountains, of expectations and quiet kitchens, of a logger's steady hands and a God who might, just might, have a plan bigger than all of them. Wrapped in Patty's friendship and the hush of the hills, she let herself believe that maybe there *was* a way through the tangle.

And Patty, her eyes on the shifting light in the trees, silently handed her own dreams back to the One she trusted, asking only that He take care of their Buddy and the two people lying on that quilt - whatever story He chose to write for them.

In his hospital room, Buddy's thoughts burned, and he purposed in his heart: *As soon as I am standing like a man again,* he vowed, *I'm going straight to Tom, and I'll ask for her hand.* He had no idea how swiftly time would reveal her condition.

Gail Hargrove, on the other hand, had a sharp eye. She came from a world that talked about Women's Awakening with suffrage fire in her veins. During the family's visit two days prior, over cafeteria Jell-o and weak tea, her gaze had narrowed, laser-focused on Donna's waist, seeing the subtle curve and the protective drift of her hand.

Later, cornering her daughter in the bathroom, Gail's voice left no room for evasion.

"Explanation, now! No lies."

Under the pressure, the truth came spilling out in halting words. Gail's face hardened, not from lack of love, but from fear and pride and all the expectations that she had stored up for her only daughter.

Weeks blurred into months of brutal rehab. The hospital became a second home for the Holcombs. The hard crutch still bit cold beneath Buddy's arm, clacking on the linoleum like accusations as he swung forward one-legged, sweat beading at his hairline. Physical therapy had turned into a kind of warrior training.

"Press through it, Mr. Holcomb. One more rep," the therapist barked like a football coach who had traded whistles for clipboards. Gary hauled in fresh firewood for the waiting room stove in between sessions while Eliza delivered pies weekly, stacking apple, still steaming, in the staff lounge - comfort sliced and served to the healers and to her boy.

Eventually, Buddy did make it back to the Holcomb farm and Mama's cooking, way ahead of the doctor's predictions. Gary had whittled him a walking cane from hickory - smooth as river rock along the handle where Buddy's hand would rest. He would take slow walks down to the meadow, to the creek, and back.

"Just to get my gait," he would often tell Eliza over breakfast, making light of the effort it took.

"Panther Creek is calling you back, Boy," she would say each time, smiling as she listened to the water's rolling with that same old rhythm through the trees.

Near the stones he had stacked as a boy - crutches for his soul now - he walked and thought deeply. The meadow felt different with each pass, as if it were waiting with him for something yet unnamed.

He hunted stolen moments to call Donna. Firing up the old Ford, he'd rumbled down to the depot, to that same old phone booth, scarred by initials and weather. But the lake trips had ceased abruptly. Calls went unanswered. The operator's voice turned flat.

"No reply."

Isolation settled in, deep as the ache of the mending bone.

Whispers reached him by way of Patty at Mathis' Diner one Thursday. Over a couple of greasy burgers and a shared brownie with the hum of the jukebox in the background, she leaned in close, her voice low and urgent.

“Donna was able to sneak out a call to me,” she informed him, trying to whisper, “she's holed up in Atlanta. Her mama's fierce as a hornet - no more Rabun weekends allowed. They're planning something. Something permanent,” she stated, looking him straight in the eye until he registered her meaning.

Buddy’s fork froze midair. The diners' sounds slid into the background. His world narrowed to a tunnel around Patty's face. His heart hammered so loudly it seemed to drown out everything else.

A resolve was forming inside Buddy's soul, as hard as the rocks that lay beneath the mountains surrounding him.

Chapter 8 -

Atlanta's Elite

Donna's bare legs stuck to the cracked vinyl booth as the oscillating fan over the jukebox clicked uselessly between hot and hotter. The diner just off Peachtree smelled like fried onions, cigarette smoke, and Coca-Cola syrup - the kind of place Buckhead girls pretended not to know about, yet always ended up there anyway after a Friday night football game.

“Okay,” Cheryl said, snapping her gum as she slid a basket of fries to the middle of the table. “Somebody explain to me why you're suddenly, ‘Miss Country’?”

Donna pulled the paper straw from its sleeve and twisted the wrapper tightly around her finger. “I'm not ‘Miss Country’,” she said. “I just went to visit some friends.”

“Friends,” Laney repeated, arching a penciled eyebrow. “At a church. In a town with one blinking red light and more cows than people? That doesn't sound too groovy.”

“They don't have more cows than people,” Donna muttered, but a smile tugged at the corner of her mouth despite herself.

Across from her, Karen took a sip of her Coke, her eyes narrowing in mock suspicion.

“I saw that boy,” she said, “at the falls. The one who helped you up when you slipped on the rocks. He was far out, Donna.”

“He was... nice,” Donna said carefully. Images flashed unbidden - Buddy’s steady hands, Panther Creek roaring behind them, Eliza's kitchen all warm and welcoming with the smell of biscuits. “His family's been really kind.”

“Kind?” Cheryl scoffed. “That's what my grandma says about the church ladies who bring Jell-o salad.”

“They do bring Jell-o,” Donna admitted, a little laugh escaping. “But they also...pray for each other. They show up. They don't just say they will.”

Karen waved a fry, “We show up. We've been to every game, every slumber party, every time your mother has one of her ‘ladies’ luncheons’ and makes us pass around deviled eggs in pantyhose.”

“That's not what I mean,” Donna said, shaking her head. “Up there, when somebody's in trouble, they don't talk about her behind her back. They sit with her. They read scripture. They cry with her.” Her throat tightened. “They did that for me.”

The girls fell quiet for a moment. The jukebox filled the space with a soft Motown song while outside, a bus hissed as it pulled away from the curb, its headlights cutting across the smudged windows of the diner.

"So, they think you should stay up there?" Laney said, finally. "Marry a nice mountain boy, bake casseroles, pop out babies, and sing hymns?"

Donna stared at the swirling ice in her glass. "They think I should listen to what the Lord says," she stated, "even if it looks different from what my parents planned."

Cheryl rolled her eyes, "Bummer...The *Lord* wants you to throw away law school and your chance at success for some logging town? I don't think so."

"Careful," Karen murmured, but there was doubt in her eyes, too. "Your dad would lose his mind, Donna."

Donna swallowed. "He almost did when he found out about... everything," she said. None of them said a word. They didn't have to. Atlanta had been buzzing with it for weeks - Tom Hargrove's daughter and the trouble up North.

"Soon it will be over," Laney said briskly. "You can put all that...mess... behind you and get back to normal."

Donna flinched. Her mind went back. In Tallulah, Eliza's soft hand on hers had said the very opposite - "*The Lord sees every tear, baby," she'd whispered. "You don't have to pretend it never happened. You just bring it to Him."*

Normal, in Atlanta, meant putting on mascara and a smile, and pretending you were happy with your old circle of friends while, deep down inside, life was hollow and she felt totally alone.

“Up there,” Donna said, her voice low and reflective, “They don't talk like it's nothing. Pastor Holcomb said some things are sin, but there's forgiveness big enough for all of it. He said hiding it just makes the hurt grow.” Her eyes burned. “Down here, Mom acts as if we don't say a word; it will just be erased.”

Cheryl shifted uncomfortably. “Your mama's just trying to protect you,” she said. “People are mean. You know how fast gossip spreads in Buckhead.”

“It spreads just as fast in a town of eight hundred,” Donna said. “The difference is, there, they bring casseroles with the whispers.”

Karen snorted, but she softened, “Look, I'm not against church or anything, but you're talking like those people have all the answers and we're just...shallow.”

“That's not,” Donna stopped. “I'm just saying the advice is different.”

“Okay,” Laney said, leaning in, the numerous bangles on both of her wrists clinging loudly. “What’s their advice?”

“They tell me to slow down,” Donna began, “To pray. To be honest. To be still and know He is God instead of just rushing back to committees and cheer tryouts like nothing's changed. Patty says the Lord might be trying to tell me something, and if I am drowning out His voice with noise, I'll miss it."

"And our advice?" Cheryl asked, raising her chin up just a little.

"You say, if I don't get back on track, I'll ruin my life," Donna answered, surprising herself with the bluntness. "That I'll disappoint my parents. That I'll waste my chances."

Karen sighed. "Well...yeah. I mean, we're not wrong. This is the real world, Donna. You don't get a redo of your Senior year. Colleges look at everything."

"God looks at everything, too," Donna said simply. "That's what they keep saying."

Cheryl shrugged. "Maybe, but he isn't the one reading applications in an office at UGA. Those people are. They're not going to care how many hymns you know–just your GPA and the clubs you're in."

Donna thought about Patty's earnest eyes. *The Lord doesn't care what letters are after your name. Patty had said, sitting on Eliza's porch with the Bible open in her lap. He cares whether your heart is His.*

"Do you hear yourself?" Laney asked. "Those mountain folks want you to be...nice, humble. Girl, your daddy wants you to be somebody! You can't be both."

"That's not true," Donna whispered, but it sounded weak even to her own ears.

Karen reached across the table and squeezed her hand.

“We're not trying to be mean,” she said. “We just don't want you to throw away everything you've worked for because you're feeling guilty, and these church people make you cry in a good way. Atlanta is where your life is, Donna. Your colleges, your future husband, your future children's schools. Not some hollow with an A&P and a bait shop.”

“There's a Piggly Wiggly,” Donna said automatically, then laughed, the sound a half-sob. “You sound like my mother.”

“Maybe because your mother's right,” Cheryl said. “Look, go on up there on weekends if you must. Let them pray over you, bake biscuits, and whatever else they do up there. Then come home and get serious. That's what a grown woman does. She takes the good feelings and still chooses what makes sense.”

What makes sense... she pondered those words in her mind as their voices continued in the background. She thought:

Up in Tallulah Falls, “what made sense” had sounded like: *Trust the Lord, not your own understanding. There's a way that seems right to a man, but the end of it is death.*

Down here, “what made sense” sounded more like: *Forget. Move on. Don't look back. Don't be that girl.*

The fan clicked to a stop and started again. A *Four Tops* song slowed down. A couple in bell-bottoms and fringe vests had slid coins into the jukebox and were dancing by the door - oblivious.

Donna looked at her friends – their hair perfectly flipped, their nails painted immaculately, their true features covered with a heavy layer of makeup and rouge. A thought crossed her heart- *what is really, real here?*

"I wish I could take the best of both," she said. "The way I feel at home up there and the opportunities here. I don't want to choose."

"You don't have to choose 'forever', today," Karen stated confidently. "You just have to not blow it this year!"

"Which means," Laney added, "less mountain revival, more Math homework and finding the right prom dress!"

Donna smiled weakly.

"Patty says the Lord can call people anywhere," she reflected as her thoughts kept going back there. "Even out of Atlanta. Even into the middle of nowhere."

Cheryl rolled her eyes again. "If he wants you in the middle of nowhere, he can send you when you're forty and your kids are grown. Right now, he gave you Buckhead and a brain. Use it."

Donna's chest ached. The words sounded so... reasonable. Sensible. Responsible. And yet, when she pictured going home to silk curtains and granite countertops, something in her rebelled.

In her mind, she saw Eliza's kitchen instead - lamplight on warm wood, Gary's Bible open, Patty humming "Great Is

Thy Faithfulness" under her breath - a different kind of wealth.

"Okay," she said softly because she didn't know how to explain all that without sounding crazy. "Okay."

They relaxed, the crisis averted in their minds. Plans shifted back to football games, outfits, and which boy from Roswell had the best car. Donna nodded in the right places and laughed in the right moments, but her heart was elsewhere.

Somewhere between the booth and that smoky Atlanta diner and the pews at Grace Fellowship, she felt herself being pulled.

And for the first time, she realized that the voices telling her what was "best" for her life might not be the ones that loved her soul the most.

Gail stopped by Tom's office in the Buckhead Plaza. He barely looked up from his briefcase splayed across the mahogany desk, papers rustling like dry leaves under an autumn wind. When the truth about Donna finally settled in his mind, it landed like a blotched land deal that he just wanted off his books. Work ruled him completely - deals closing by razor-thin margins and deadlines ticking like auction gavel walls were the only emergencies he recognized in God's green Earth.

"Handle it, Gail," he muttered without lifting his eyes from the papers, already reaching for the next file, its Manila edges yellowed with coffee rings. To him, his daughter's pregnancy wasn't a life blooming sacred, but a problem to be managed, cleaned away - like clearing a title on a disputed track - final, forgotten.

Gail Hargrove had sharper plans for Donna. Plans that did not include being a logger's wife after a mountain shotgun wedding, scrubbing floors in a house full of squalling babies, chicken-scratched yards, and wood smoke clinging eternally to laundry lines. She saw her daughter as the future face of Atlanta- loudly agreed upon by every framed gold certificate on Tom's office walls, a seat at a gleaming table among Georgia's most powerful women: real estate queens, political rising stars, suffrage heirs - breaking glass ceilings daily. A mountain boy with dirt under his nails and a baby bump did not fit that polished scene. It was like chalk screeching across a blackboard, an ink blot on silk - completely out of place.

For Donna, life in the Atlanta cage seemed it would never bring her true happiness again; the Country Club membership echoed hollowly, Daddy's expectations crushed like granite slabs, and her mother's rants rang falsely against her swelling heart. Until, in Buddy's arms - under mountains, stars, and lake whispers - she finally found what true happiness looked like. It was what Forever should feel like: steady, rooted as deeply as old oaks, warm as fresh bread from Eliza's oven. He made all the stresses of city life - the Country Club whispers, the unrealistic expectations everyone else heaped upon her - fade away as gently as dawn.

After the initial shock of her pregnancy hit like a cold creek plunge, joy mingled with her fear - blooming defiantly. Their child felt like a gift straight from God, her heart flooding with proof of grace she hadn't even asked for. They might not have planned it under that moonlit dock as she whispered to herself: *God doesn't make mistakes.*

Gary's sermons echoed clearly in her memory, now preached from that simple pulpit she had once ignored. She could almost hear his voice again, saying, *"For what shall it profit a man, if he shall gain the whole world..."* the very world the Hargroves chased, *"and lose his own soul?"*

Donna could see it vividly as a photograph: she and Buddy knee-deep in nursery paint, choosing names over dinner at the Holcombs' table - maybe Grace for a girl or maybe Gary the Third for a boy. They dreamed of picking out tiny overalls and quilts patterned with deer and trout, of growing old together on a porch overlooking Panther Creek - hands wrinkled but with love eternal. But her mother was determined to live Donna's life for her. Women's success manifestos were stacked beside Gail's bed like battle plans. Arrangements had been made quickly, efficiently, as if booking any other Atlanta appointment: manicure, power lunch, clinic visit. A crisp letter arrived on heavy stock. The date circled in red: procedure scheduled.

Donna drifted through those days numb as winter fog, feeling her soul slip away piece by piece. Easy closeness with Buddy had already been severed. Now the moral truth that he had tried to plant in her heart twisted like a knife down deep in the gut - his simple sayings backed solid by his father's preaching.

Every child is a sacred gift from its very first breath, she remembered, *knitted by the Lord's own hands.*

The words sat deeply in her, rooted firmly as a mountain laurel. She knew, deep in her bones, that what her mother demanded was wrong. Nights found her curled up in silk sheets, her hand cradling the swell, whispering half-prayers that she hoped Buddy might hear across the miles.

"Hold on, Darling, I'm on my way."

Back at the Falls, Buddy was shaking Heaven and Earth, praying, and reasoning his way from boyhood into manhood.

I was taught what's right and wrong, he told himself, *I know it deep in me. But I let a moment take me. I can't let a life be destroyed because of my own decisions. I still love my creator, even though I'm not perfect. Two wrongs can't make it right. My child has every right to be all God wills him or her to be. Mama and Daddy will love this baby, no matter what happens. They'll understand. They always said God knit me together in my mother's womb. I want the same thing for my child.*

He wanted the same things he had always wanted: a marriage, a baby, a home there in the mountains. *I will trust the sovereign God to work this thing out,* he thought.

He stared up at the cold, clear night, dew already forming on his clothes. Lifting his hands toward the heavens, he whispered, "I submit to Thy will, O God. Whatever it is, use me as a vessel for Your good and Your glory."

Then he rose, climbed back down from Hickory Nut Mountain, cranked up the old Ford, and rode out to the highway, giving the engine all it could muster, and headed out, his dim headlights cutting through the early dawn. He had wrestled with God in the night, and his mind was set.

Chapter 9 - Nameless

Buddy had ridden to Atlanta before, but this was the first time he had ever driven there himself. The closer he got, the more the road signs multiplied, the lanes began splitting and merging from every direction - city traffic swarming like hornets around his old Ford. For a mountain boy, running hot with fear and hope, it was too much noise and too much movement, all at once. His cane rattled against the metal floorboards with every bump, a hollow rhythm that matched the pounding of his heart.

101 Peach Avenue.

He had scribbled the address a dozen times on a piece of scrap paper, traced it with his thumb in the dark, and prayed over it. Now the buildings loomed tall and glassy, each one looking like the next, a forest of steel instead of pine. Patty had helped him find the clinic name in the phone book and had helped him piece together what little he understood about appointments and procedures and the "word" he could barely bring himself to say. But the rest - the talking to Donna, facing Tom Hargrove, and making this right - was all on him. Every phrase he had rehearsed over the past few months ran circles in his mind as he scanned building after building, searching for the right one, searching for any sign of mercy.

He finally spotted it. A small brick building was hunched between much taller ones, its entrance tucked half out of sight. The sign out in front of it was small, almost apologetic, the wording so vague, it felt like they didn't want anyone to know what really happened behind those doors. Broken dreams and dark deeds - that's what it looked like to him.

But he pulled into the parking lot, his hand shaking on the steering wheel. Somewhere inside, Donna was there. And their child.

"Lord, be with us," he whispered, his voice breaking.

He flung the truck door open and started toward the building as fast as his injured leg would let him go - half-limp, half-awkward run, his cane clacking sharply against the asphalt. He was only a few yards from the clinic door when a roaring engine cut through the hum of the traffic. Tires squealed across the pavement as a sedan whipped around the corner of the lot, cutting past him with a burst of exhaust and gravel.

The Hargrove's sedan.

He froze as it flew by. In the back window, Donna's face was pressed to the glass, her eyes were wide and wet. Her hands were splayed flat as if reaching for him through the pane, her fingers desperate. Her mouth moved - no sound reached him over the engine and the city noise, but he read the word all the same:

Help!

The car shot out of the lot, turned right, and gunned it into the flow of city traffic, and they disappeared in seconds.

But he stood there stunned as if his whole life had just driven away in one long, impossible second. The strength drained from his legs. He sank down onto the curb, elbows on his knees, with his head hanging low. Tears spilled hot and fast down his cheeks, burning tracks he couldn't wipe away. He didn't know how long he sat like that - his head in his hands, the world tilting under him, time losing all shape.

A sharp squeak of hinges snapped him back.

He looked up just in time to see a woman in a white uniform push through a side door near the back of the building. Her hair was tucked under a cap, her expression blank as she carried a black garbage bag. Without a glance around, she hefted it into a metal trash bin. The lid banged shut with a hollow echo that sent a chill straight through him.

Something in Buddy refused to look away. A part of him wanted to run for the truck, slam the door, and drive until the skyscrapers shrank to dots in his rearview, leaving this entire day behind him. But another part, the one way down deep inside him, the one that had walked creek banks with his daddy and listened to sermons about life being holy, would not let him move.

He rose slowly. His cane clicked on the asphalt with every step toward the trash can, and with each one he took, it felt as if they were taking years off his life. His hands shook as he gripped the rusted metal rim, and he eased the lid open.

The smell hit him first. Bleach. Something metallic. Something wrong. A smell his body seemed to understand before his mind did.

He peered inside.

There, among bloody gauze and twisted medical waste, lay a small torn bundle of flesh. Tiny limbs, not fully formed yet unmistakably human, slick with blood and thrown aside like refuse.

For a moment, his mind refused to accept what his eyes saw. The world narrowed to a red blur, his breath locking in his chest. Then, like a blow to the gut, the truth forced its way through the fog, brutal and clear.

My baby. My baby.

Six months since that night on the dock. Six months of plans and prayers and waiting. All of it ended here - in this metal bin behind a nameless door.

Before Buddy slowly collapsed to his knees beside the trash bin, he gently shut the lid above him with a terrible, ringing finality. Asphalt bit into his skin.

“My baby,” he choked, his voice raw and shredded, the words ripping out of him like something torn from the bone.

"God, help me."

There was no name he could give, no face he would ever see. Only absence.

The parking lot spun around him. Painted lines and parked cars tilted, as if they might slide right off the edge of the world. In that moment, his father's voice rose in his memory, as clear as if Gary stood right beside him in the Grace Fellowship pulpit.

'You know a society by what it does with its young and with its old.'

Those words cut deeper now than any sermon he had ever heard. They weren't just lines from a Sunday sermon anymore. They were a verdict. A judgment over this place, over this bright, busy city, and over what had just been tossed into a metal bin behind an unmarked door.

How can this be?

Buddy lifted his face toward the sky, with his eyes burning in the harsh afternoon glare.

How can this be?

He searched the blinding light for any sign, any answer, any crack in the heavens that might show God was still watching. Atlanta hummed around him - honking horns on Peachtree, the distant wail of sirens, the muted thump of city life rolling on as if nothing had happened at all. But there was no voice from the clouds, no thunder splitting the sky.

Only the echo of his own grief, and the silent witness of that bin behind the clinic, standing there like a dark metal gravestone no one would ever claim.

His hands trembled as he moved toward the bin again. This time, he reached inside. With the care that belonged in a nursery, not in this alley of shame, he lifted the torn little body out, cradling it as gently and lovingly as a shepherd rescuing a little lost lamb. He unbuttoned his shirt and took it off, then wrapped the bundle inside and knotted the fabric securely, as if tucking a child to sleep beneath a quilt of stars. From the truck, he found an old cloth sack on the floorboard and nestled the wrapped form inside.

Cradling the bag to his chest like the most fragile thing he had ever held, he went back to the truck, and the clicks of his cane echoed off brick and metal. He eased into the front seat as if it were made of glass, one hand resting protectively on the bundle - like a father's palm on a newborn's back, feeling for the rise and fall that would never come.

Then he turned the key. The Ford rumbled to life and rode out of the lot, heading north toward the Falls, toward home, toward the only ground he trusted to receive what he carried.

This day he would never forget.

The drive back felt like weeks stretched eternally, headlights tracing a thin, white ribbon of highway as the mountains began to reclaim the horizon. His mind replayed the last year on a merciless loop: first smile across Lake Rabun, Donna's laughter bright at Mathis' over BBQ, promises whispered on the moonlit dock, the snap of his femur under a dog pile roar, the hollow echo of hospital corridors, unanswered calls, the secretive plaque beside a clinic door, the horror inside a metal bin.

Love and loss tangled inside him until he could not tell where one ended and the other began. How could he reckon this? Life and death, love and hate, faith, and emptiness - all knotted into one small, silent bag on the seat beside him, a sacred witness to a world gone wrong.

He gripped the steering wheel until his knuckles blanched white; his jaw clenched against his sobs that threatened to shatter the cab.

Near midnight, he turned down the familiar gravel drive to the Holcomb farm, tires crunching softly under a canopy of stars. The house stood dark, mama's bedroom lamp long since gone out, her prayers trailing him like a blessing through whatever storm he had driven into.

Buddy parked beneath the ancient oak, its branches reaching toward the sky like pleading hands. He sat there for a long moment listening to the engine tick as it cooled, each soft pop like a heartbeat denied.

Finally, he picked up the bag with both hands, reverently, and slipped into the chilled air that smelled of pine and home.

At the old shed by the first gate, he set the bundle gently on an overturned crate. He found the shovel that had been his companion since boyhood, the handle worn smoothly by his and his daddy's hands. The wood felt warm against his palm despite the cold.

Down at Panther Creek, where stones lay scattered, Buddy dug deep and carefully, the shovel biting into the earth that had fed his family for years. A small grave opened before him - tender as a prayer, final as judgment.

He placed the bundle inside with both hands, his head bowed.

“Tony,” he whispered.

“I'll name you, Tony. Tony Holcomb, you are loved. You are a witness.”

Then he covered the little grave with earth and stone, mounding it gently and padding it firmly. On that night under the stars, Buddy Holcomb made a vow that would reshape the rest of his life.

“I will remember you,” he whispered into the darkness, “every child cast away. Every life discarded. I will remember you all.”

Chapter 10 –

The Calling Begins

Time just seemed to be on hold as Buddy threw himself into his work beside Gary. Spring logging season was just beginning, the kind of busy that used to thrill him, chainsaws buzzing, trucks grinding up the mountain roads, the fresh tang of sap and sawdust hanging in the cool air. Now every climb, every lift, sent a dull ache through his leg. He welcomed it. The pain gave him something to lean into, something that wasn't Donna's face in the moonlight or the picture of a nursery that would never be. It kept him from drowning in the "what might have been" that still haunted him when the workday went quiet.

The last cold snap of winter slipped under the barn doors, with traces of the last snow of the season quickly becoming a memory. He shifted a thick timber of oak onto the sawhorses, his jaw tight as his bad leg protested against the weight. Pain shot up his thigh, white and hot, but he swallowed it down and set the board square.

Gary watched from the shadows near the tool rack; his hands buried in his coat pockets. The single bulb overhead threw long lines across the lumber, catching the stiffness in his son's gait.

"You can outwork most men on one leg, Son," he said finally, his voice low, "but I ain't blind. That bone of yours is going to fuss more every winter."

Buddy wiped sawdust on his jeans, not meeting his father's eyes.

"The Lord will give me strength," he answered, the word shaped by habit more than conviction.

"He will," Gary agreed, "but He also gave us good sense."

He stepped forward, laying his palm flat on the oak. The grain ran straight and true, pale gold under the dust.

"All my life I've cut logs down and sold them rough," he went on, "logs on the truck, boards in a stack. Maybe it's me that's been missin' the trick. These logs could turn into something beautiful - maybe tables, chairs, cabinets - things folks will pass down instead of burn."

He nodded toward the dark mouth of the wood lot behind the hill.

"Shoot, Son, we've got enough logs in that wood lot down there to carve up furniture for the next ten years. Nice oaks, maples, and even good cedars. All we have to do is wait on God to dry them out, and we will use them right. And there's a lot down there that's knotty - trees that nature has beaten and bent. There's still good wood under all that. Sometimes those tight turns and scars are what make the prettiest grain. Lots of character comes out when things face storms. It strengthens them and reshapes them."

Buddy's fingers drifted over the edge of the board, but his eyes were far away, somewhere behind a brick building in Atlanta, where metal lids banged, and tiny limbs bled red against white gauze. The barn smelled of pine and oil; his memory still stank of bleach and death.

"What would you think about a little shop here?" Gary asked. "Nothing fancy. Planer, good blade, maybe a sander. You with that eye for straight lines, me teachin' you what I know - Holcomb & Son Furniture. You'd be workin' wood, not lettin' it break you."

Buddy blinked, dragged back to the barn by the sound of his own name.

"Sure, Daddy," he murmured, "whatever you think is best."

Gary heard the distance in his boy's voice, the way it came from some hollow place that grief had carved. He didn't push. Just patted the oak once, as if it were a shoulder.

"We'll talk more when your mind's not somewhere else," he said gently, "the point is, you don't have to carry logs on that leg forever. There are other ways to feed a family out of these hills. Ways that don't run you into the ground."

Buddy nodded, but his gaze had already slid toward the open barn door, where the meadow dipped away into the darkness. Somewhere out there, by the creek, a tiny stone marked what the world would never see as a grave. Furniture and a future felt a world away.

Gary watched his boy closely, noting the furrow in Buddy's brow, the way his shoulders stayed just a little too tight. There was a shadow on him that Gary couldn't quite name, and it worried him more than the limp.

In the evenings, Patty would drop by the Holcombs' porch as faithfully as the sunset, easing herself into the old rocker beside Buddy. Sometimes they talked, sometimes they didn't. More often than not, they just sat - Buddy staring out toward Panther Creek and Patty shelling peas or snapping beans into Eliza's big blue bowl. The silence between them was its own kind of language, a gentle presence that wrapped around the raw places.

Eliza would lean out of the screen door, wiping her hands on her apron.

“Pattygirl,” she would call in that bold, playful way of hers, “you got any future husbands in mind?”

Patty would laugh with her cheeks pink and her eyes sliding once toward Buddy before she looked back at Eliza. “I'm just getting me ready for one, Mrs. Eliza,” she would say, “cause you never know.”

Eliza would shake her head, smiling, and disappear back into the kitchen. Buddy might not say a word, but something in his chest loosened each time - like God was using Patty's easy loyalty and Eliza's teasing to stitch his heart back together, one tiny seam at a time.

Moonlight sat softly, like silver, over Tallulah Gorge the following evening, its light draping the cliffs in a way that made every edge look gentler than it was. The air was cool enough that Eliza's breath fogged a little as she walked up the hill, her hands wrapped around a chipped thermos of coffee she had insisted on bringing. The old truck's tailgate creaked as she settled beside Gary, the metal familiar against the back of her legs.

"Thought I'd find you up here," she said. She kept her voice low, so it didn't disturb the hush of the place.

Gary didn't look at her right away. His eyes stayed on the dark ribbon of river far below, moonlight catching where the water broke over the rocks. One hand curled loosely around the brim of his ball cap, the other braced on the tailgate, his knuckles pale.

"Truck gave me away?" he asked, a weak, half-smile twitching at the corner of his mouth.

Eliza nudged his shoulder with hers.

"The truck, Buddy not at the house, and your empty spot at the kitchen table," she paused, "and the way you've been carrying your shoulders up around your ears all week."

He sighed, the sound deep and tired, like it came from somewhere under his ribs.

"Didn't mean to worry you, Liza."

"Well, you did."

She took a sip of coffee, the warmth filling her chest.

"So, you might as well tell me what's gnawin' at ya."

For a long moment, the only sounds were the distant rush of the river and a Whip-poor-will calling from the trees. Gary's jaw twitched slowly. Finally, he spoke.

"It's Buddy," he said, "something's off, and I can't put my finger on it."

Eliza glanced at him, brushed the hair from her cheek, and asked, "He say somethin'?"

"That's just it. He ain't sayin' much of nothing," Gary shook his head. "He's showin' up, doin' the work. But his eyes..." he trailed off, searching for the right word. "They look like mine did right after Daddy died. Like he's carryin' somethin' he just don't know how to lay down. "

Eliza let that sit between them. She knew better than to rush him, knew his heart opened slowly like a morning glory-early, but only if the light was gentle.

"He's been quiet at the table," she said, "even Patty noticed."

Gary huffed.

"If Patty's noticed, then I'm late to the party. That girl misses nothing."

They shared a small smile, then fell quiet again. Down below, the falls shone like a trail of spilled stars.

“You think it's Donna?” Eliza asked. “He's been wrapped around that girl's finger ever since he laid his eyes on her. I like her. I believe her heart is soft.”

“Could be.”

Gary tipped his head back, studying the scattering of the stars overhead.

“All I know is, somethin' is weighin’ mighty heavy on him. I see it in the way he picks up his fork, and how he stares past the boys from the team when they pop in and start cuttin’ up. He's in the room, but part of him is somewhere else.”

Eliza's fingers tightened around the thermos.

“Why didn't you say something sooner?”

He smiled without humor.

“What was I gonna say? Son, I see the storm in your eyes, but I don't know the forecast.” He shook his head. “He's a man now. I can't go pryin’ like I did when he was ten and sullen on the porch.”

“You can still knock on the door of his heart,” Eliza said softly, “you're his daddy.”

Gary's throat bobbed, and then he swallowed hard, looking down at his hands.

“Feels like I'm knocking and nobody's answering,” he hesitated, “and I keep wondering if I did somethin’ wrong somewhere along the way. Maybe I pushed him too hard. Or not hard enough.”

Eliza turned on the tailgate, so she faced him fully, her knee bumping his.

"Gary Holcomb, you listen to me!"

Her voice held the steel he had learned years ago, his cue to pay attention. "You have loved that boy straight and steady since the nurse first put him in your arms. You have prayed for him, worked for him, corrected him when he needed it, and bragged on him when he didn't. Whatever he's facing right now, it ain't because you failed him."

He blinked, keeping his eyes still on the gorge, "How can you be so sure?"

"Because I live in the same house as you," she replied. "I've watched you choose that boy's heart over your own pride more times than I can count." Her voice softened. "He knows who to come to. Maybe he's just not ready to say it out loud yet."

Gary drew a long breath and let it out slowly.

"I keep thinkin' about when he was little," he said, "when we used to sit right up here, toss rocks down toward the river, and he had asked a million questions. 'Why's the water move so fast, Daddy?' 'How deep do you think it is?' 'You think God can see us from all the way up there?'" His mouth curved. "Now I'm the one with questions and no answers."

Eliza looked up at the sky with him.

"God can see us from up there," she murmured, "and He can see Buddy, too. Even when we can't."

Silence wrapped around them again, not empty, but full of history, of late-night talks and early morning prayers, of years piled one on top of another like the layers of rock beneath their dangling feet.

"Do you ever worry we're going to lose him?" Gary's voice was barely above a whisper.

Eliza's heart squeezed.

"To what?"

"I don't know."

He shook his head, frustration flickering across his face.

"To Atlanta. To his own mistakes. To carryin' somebody else's burden so hard, it breaks him," he swallowed as he voiced out loud some of his many fears, "to a life he thinks he's got to live alone."

Eliza reached over and laid her hand on his forearm, her touch firm.

"We are not gonna lose our boy," she said, "he might stumble. He might make a royal mess of things. But the Lord's got a hold on him, and so do we. The rope might stretch, but it's not gonna snap."

Gary's shoulders sagged a little, some of the tension leaking out.

"You always did have more faith than sense," he said, but the words held affection, not criticism.

"Good thing," she countered, "since you've spent our whole marriage testin' both."

That drew a real laugh from him, low and warm. He glanced over at her, the lines around his eyes softening. The moonlight traced the familiar curve of her cheek and the silver threads in her hair. He saw the girl who used to climb into his truck with him on summer nights, and the woman who had stayed when money was tight and tempers were short.

"You remember the first time we came up here?" he asked.

Eliza smiled, her eyes turning distant. "You had that old Ford that wheezed worse than your Uncle Earl."

"Hey now," he protested mildly, "that truck got us everywhere we needed to go."

"Eventually," she said playfully. "And then you would spread a blanket on this tailgate and try to impress me with that sad, little radio playin' love songs that kept crackin' like popcorn."

He winced.

"I was hoping you'd forgotten that part."

"I remember every bit of it," her gaze slid back to him, "you were so nervous your hands shook when you poured my Coke."

Gary looked down at his hands now, steadier but scarred, years of work written in calluses and small white marks.

“Wasn't sure I was good enough for you,” he admitted, “still not sure some days.”

Eliza's voice went quiet.

“Gary.”

He met her eyes then, really met them, the weight he had been carrying making him look older than his years.

“You gave me your name,” she said, “your heart, and a home where the Lord’s Name is spoken more than any other. You’ve worked yourself half to death keepin’ us fed and warm. You’ve loved when I was unlovable. There is not one part of me that doubts I married the right man.”

Emotion flickered across his face, raw and unhidden. He looked away for a second, swallowing hard.

“Liza,” he managed, “I don’t know what I’d do without you.”

“You’re not gonna have to find out,” she said simply. “We are in this together. Buddy’s troubles. Patty’s future, the church, these mountains - it’s not yours to shoulder alone,” she squeezed his arm. “You hear me?”

He nodded, the motion small but sure.

“I keep wantin’ to fix it,” he confessed, “whatever it is. March right up to that boy and demand he spill his guts so I can carry half of it for him.”

"You can't fix what you don't know, and sometimes even when you do know," she replied. "What you can do is stay close enough that when he can't hold it in anymore, you're the first one he thinks to run to."

Gary stared out over the dark gorge, "What if he's in somethin' deep, 'Liza? Deeper than we can pull him out of?"

"Then we pray him through," she said confidently, "just like we prayed your brother through that mess with the pills. Just like when we prayed over Patty when she lost her mama and her heart was broken and she was tryin' to hide it. And just like we've prayed over this marriage every time the world tried to pull us apart," she stopped as her eyes shone. "The Lord hasn't dropped us yet. He's not about to start with Buddy."

A breeze swept up from the gorge, cool and damp, rustling the trees around them. Gary inhaled, then let his breath out slowly, as if he were finally putting down a weight he'd been clutching to so tightly.

"You ever get tired..." he asked quietly, "of having to carry everybody else?"

Eliza smiled, a little weary but with a lot of tenderness.

"All the time," she said, "that's why I keep handin' them back to Jesus - sometimes five, ten times a day."

She tipped her head toward him. "And yourself most of all."

He chuckled ruefully.

"I'm not very good at letting go."

"I've noticed," she murmured.

He reached for her hand then, lacing his fingers through hers on the tailgate and squeezed three times to say, I LOVE YOU. The gesture was as old as their marriage and yet still new, every time.

"You are my best friend, you know that?" he said.

"I do," she answered honestly, "and you're mine. Even when you run off to sulk on tailgates instead of talkin' to me in the kitchen like a civilized man."

He grinned.

"You like me better under the stars anyhow."

She bumped his shoulder.

"Don't push it, Holcomb."

They sat there a while longer, side by side, with their hands joined, watching the way the moonlight reflected back the different colors in the layers of the gorge.

Gary's thoughts still circled Buddy, still brushed against a fear he couldn't name, but the edge of it had dulled. Eliza's presence pressed up warm against his side, a quiet reminder that he was not alone in this.

"Will you pray?" he asked at last, his voice rough. "For him. For me. For whatever's comin'."

Eliza bowed her head, their joint hands resting between them.

“Been prayin’,” she said softly, “but I'll gladly do it again.”

Her words rose into the cool night - simple, steady, full of the kind of faith that had been forged over many years of shared times - both good and bad. She asked for protection for their boy, for wisdom they didn't yet have, and for courage to face what they couldn't see. She thanked God for the man beside her, and for all the ways his heart bore the weight of others.

When she finished, they didn't move right away. The world felt still for a moment, the river, rocks, trees, and two aging bodies on an old tailgate under a watchful sky.

Finally, Gary squeezed her hand.

“Whatever it is,” he said, more to himself than to her, “we’ll face it head-on. Together.”

“That's the only way we know how,” Eliza replied.

The Holcombs didn't know exactly what had happened in Buddy's life. They knew it was more than a lost football season and more than a leg that didn't move like it used to. They only knew their boy had come back from the city carrying a weight that wasn't just physical. Gary watched him sit in that shadow and did the only thing he knew how to do: he kept pointing Buddy toward the One who could hold what they could not.

More than once, Gary would stop him on his way out the door, big hands resting heavily on Buddy's broad shoulders. He would turn him, so they were face-to-face, his eyes steady.

"Boy, you know who made you," he would say in a clear, confident voice, "and when He made you, He gave you meaning. Now live your life for Him. We all gotta go back to Him."

Buddy would nod, swallowing hard, not trusting his own voice. The words lodged deeply anyway, joining the old Bible verses and creek bank prayers Gary had been planting in him since he was a boy.

One foggy morning on a new logging road, the air felt heavier than usual, the clouds sitting low on the ridgeline. Gary drove the loaded truck through the tight curve at Persimmon Gap, the tires making deep trenches in the muddy road softened by days of rain. Buddy walked a little way behind him, saw in hand, listening to the engine's strain under the weight of the timber. He was just lifting his head to holler something about taking it slow when the ground gave way.

There was a sickening tilt, a screech of metal, and then the world turned upside down. The truck flipped, its load of logs rolling free, huge trunks tumbling like loose cannonballs down the slope. The squawk of birds exploded from the trees. The air was filled with dust and the splintering crack of wood.

Buddy dropped the saw where he stood and ran. His boots pounded across the timbers that had rolled and locked against one another, his breath tearing at his throat. He leaped from log to log, ignoring the exploding pain in his legs, until he hit the gravel road and slid down the embankment on his knees, his hands already reaching out. One massive log lay across his daddy's chest; the cab had crushed Gary's waist into the earth.

“Daddy! Daddy - I'm gonna go for help!” Buddy gasped, his muscles straining as he shoved the log back enough to see his daddy’s face.

“Oh, Buddy... stay with me a moment,” Gary whispered, each word riding on a shallow breath. “Listen. Listen.” His hand fumbled until it found Buddy's arm and gripped it tightly. “Take care of your mama, you hear? And don't forsake the people who helped raise you here. You've learned well, my son. God is kind. And always know I am so proud of you.”

Tears burned in Buddy's eyes.

“Daddy, don't talk like that. I can get you out...”

Gary shook his head, the movement small, but resolute.

“My ministry is now finished, and yours has just begun. He has planned this very day for me. The good Lord has so many ways to take us home, you know? I have been here before,” as he took a breath, “but this time, I’m ready.”

A faint smile began across his lips as he could already see something that Buddy couldn't.

"Yes... yes, Daddy," Buddy choked.

"Son, make me a promise," Gary's gaze locked on his, clear and steady even as the color was draining from his face, "when your day comes, you'll be there. Just be there."

Buddy nodded with his head, hearing his father's words, yet panic was beginning to take hold of him.

"I'm gonna go for help now. I love you, Daddy!" Buddy blurted out, the panic and love tingling in his chest. He squeezed Gary's hand once and scrambled up the slope, legs pumping and heart pounding a prayer he couldn't even form into words.

By the time the dust had settled and the help had come, the pillar of their family - and of Grace Fellowship Community - was gone, pinned under the very timber he had spent his life felling. The mountain that had always felt so solid now seemed to tilt under Buddy's feet.

The news hit Eliza like a blow to the chest. One minute, she was stirring gravy at the stove, humming, "Blessed Assurance" under her breath; the next, a neighbor stood in the doorway, hat clenched in his hands, his eyes wet. The wooden spoon slipped from her fingers and clattered to the floor. For a moment, she couldn't breathe.

Then the sound came - low and aching - from somewhere deep inside, a wail she would remember for the rest of her days.

For Buddy, the grief settled differently. It wrapped around him in layers. In less than a year, he had lost his dream, his love, his child, and now the man who had taught him what life was worth. Some nights he lay awake staring at the ceiling, hearing the screech of the metal again, feeling his daddy's hand on his arm again, and that last charge – 'when your day comes, you'll be there'.

Something in him had shifted on that mountain road. Whatever days he had left, they were no longer his to waste.

Chapter 11 –

Eliza's Victory

The house sounded wrong without Gary's boots on the floor. The ticking clock over the stove seemed louder, and the refrigerator hummed more harshly. And the old boards in the hallway were popping like they were protesting every step that wasn't his.

Eliza Holcomb lay in the big iron bed they had shared for over forty years, her body turned toward his empty pillow. The hollow he had worn there looked like a dried-up riverbed, a place where something living used to run strong. Her fingers smoothed the sheet the way they used to smooth his hair when he came home from late hospital calls, and the ache in her chest folded in on itself again.

"Gary," she whispered into the quiet, "what am I supposed to do with all this space?"

Grief had knocked her flat since the day they had put him in the ground up on that hill. At first, she told herself she was 'just resting a spell', but days turned into a low, gray stretch where she found she could barely make it from the bed to the rocker and back again. Her joints screamed louder than ever, and the simple act of sitting up felt like lifting a log soaked through with creek water.

When she closed her eyes, the years rode back like someone thumbing pages fast. She saw Gary as he had been the first night at the dance hall down by the river. Wild grin, his hair too long and his boots muddy from running shine along the backroads. Her modest, homemade dress had hung awkwardly on her, but Gary had looked at her like she was the only person in the room.

"Lord, what a fool I was," she murmured, half smiling despite the tears, "fell for that man like he was the last song on the jukebox."

She remembered the rush of their young love - the shotgun wedding, the way his daddy had cursed and her mama had cried, the nights she had lain awake listening for his truck and praying it was the law's headlights chasing down somebody else. Then the wreck. Gary's broken body in that hospital bed, the preacher leaning over him, and the merciful way God had turned a moonshine-runner into a gentle shepherd.

"First, You nearly killed him to get his attention," she whispered toward the ceiling, "then You gave him to me anew, and now You have taken him home, and I'm the one laid up unable to run."

Her mind drifted to the childless years - the months after months of empty arms, the way she had pressed a hand to her flat belly and begged God for a baby until the prayers felt like they were scraping her raw inside. She saw herself sitting on the same bed in her thirties, her Bible opened on her lap, her tears dripping on the pages while Gary snored softly beside her.

“Do you remember that, Lord?” she asked hoarsely. “I asked You for one little one. Just one. You made me wait. Wait half a lifetime. But when You sent him...” she could see Buddy now, red and squalling in the nurse's arms, and Gary's big hands shaking as he cradled his miracle son.

“You outdid Yourself.”

Buddy's boyhood played like a home movie behind her eyes - the first time he toddled across this very floor, the way his tiny fingers had curled around her thumb, the sawdust kingdoms he built at Gary's feet. She heard his teenage laughter echo in the hallway, saw his gangly frame filling the doorway with cleats slung over his shoulder, and that shy, proud light in his eyes when college scouts started sniffing around.

“I got to be wife and Mama,” she whispered, “a thing I thought You had said no to. I cooked his breakfasts, packed his lunches, and patched those jeans till there wasn't any original thread left in them. I watched him grow into Gary all over again, only more gracious in some ways.”

Her throat tightened.

“And then You went and took his daddy before I was nearly ready.”

The first week after the funeral, the church ladies kept the kitchen full. Casseroles and pies landed on every flat surface, and somebody was always sitting in her rocker when she shuffled out from her room, ready with the tissue and a verse. Now the visits had slowed down. Buddy tried to fill the silence with his soft footsteps and the scrape of his chair, but when he left for town or was out on a job, the house settled into a heavy stillness that pressed against her ribs.

One afternoon, the ache in her chest swelled so sharply that she thought it might split her open. She lay curled under Gary's old quilt, hymns half-formed on her lips, and finally stopped trying to pray politely.

"Lord," she rasped, "You have taken the man I shared my youth and my middle age with. You have left me with empty plates at the table and one boy carrying more weight than his back ought to. I know You are good. I sang that for years. But right now, it feels like You have swung the axe at my roots!"

Her tears soaked Gary's pillow. She gripped the edge of it like a lifeline.

"You could've left him here," she cried, "there were still years left in those hands, still sermons in that throat. Why'd You have to haul him up out of this world before he finished the job?"

Silence answered at first. Then, from somewhere deep in her memory, an old phrase rose up -Gary's voice from the pulpit, from this bedroom, from a hundred kitchen table devotions:

The Lord gave, and the Lord hath taken away; blessed be the name of the Lord.

She turned the familiar words over on her tongue like they were foreign.

"I know what the scriptures say," she was talking to Jesus as if He sat right there with her, "I've nodded along plenty when Gary preached it. It sure sounds pretty in a sermon," her fingers knotted tighter into the sheet, "but it's uglier when it's your own bed that's half empty."

Her heart battled - love for the God who had saved them both, and anger at that same God who had allowed this.

Somewhere in that wrestling, a quieter thread of truth slid in - how many times Gary had told her, she could hear him say the words even now in the very depths of her heart:

"Eliza, faith ain't faith till it goes through the fire. Anybody can sing, "It Is Well" when the pantry is full, and the house is warm."

She swallowed hard.

"All right then," she croaked, "here's my fire." Her voice steadied a fraction.

"I don't like what You've done. That's the truth. It hurts. But I know who You are. That's the truth, too. So I'm gonna hold to these words till mine come back."

With a shaky breath, she forced the old scripture out, each syllable slow as if they weighed pounds:

"Though He slay me, yet will I trust in Him," then again with more vigor, "Though YOU slay ME, yet will I trust YOU."

Something eased, just a hair. The pain stayed, but it lost a little of its teeth.

Down the hall, Buddy hesitated outside her door. He had heard her talking before, low and fierce, and more than once he had to walk away so she could have it out with God without her boy hovering.

Today, he could not bring himself to leave. He knocked gently.

"Mama?"

"That you, Son?" Her voice sounded thin, worn at the edges.

He pushed the door open. The room was dim, curtains half drawn, the air carrying the faint scent of liniment and starch. Eliza looked smaller against the pillows, her braid grayer than it had been even a month ago. But her eyes, when she turned them on him, still held a stubborn spark.

"Have you eaten?" he asked, trying to sound casual and light, as he set a tray down on the nightstand - broth, a biscuit, and coffee, just the way Gary had liked it.

"I'll try a few bites," she said, giving a small smile. "Broth tastes like somebody whispered, 'chicken over hot water'. That your doin'?"

He gave a small laugh in spite of himself.

"Patty brought it. So if you don't like it, you can fuss at her."

From the doorway, Patty came in behind him with her braid swinging.

"I heard that," she said softly, "and I'll have you know I put real chicken in there, Miss Eliza, just boiled the life out of it by accident."

Eliza's mouth twitched.

"Well, bless your heart! Y'all trying to keep an old woman on the earth with weak broth and pity?"

Patty stepped closer, perched on the edge of the dresser like she had a hundred times before as a girl.

"We're just trying to keep you here because we're greedy," she answered, "we're not done needing you just yet."

Buddy moved closer to the bed.

"Mama, you barely been up in days," he said, trying to cover up the worry in his voice. "Your legs are getting weaker. I..." he swallowed, "I'm worried about you."

Her gaze softened.

"You sound like your daddy," she said. "He used to fret the same way when I had run myself ragged canning tomatoes.

'Eliza, take a load off,' he would say. Now look at me - loads off so much I might float away."

The joke came out thin, but it was there. Patty caught Buddy's eye over the bed, and some of the tightness in both their shoulders eased.

"You're allowed to be sad," Patty said gently, "nobody expects you to be up singing and frying chicken like nothing's happened. But you staying in this bed forever, ain't honoring Gary either. He'd have a fit if he saw you not bossing us around in the kitchen."

A ghost of Eliza's old mischief flickered.

"That man never minded me bossin'," she muttered. "Saved him a heap of trouble, at times."

They stayed with her that afternoon - Buddy reading from the Psalms in his low, steady voice and with Patty shelling a bowl of peas by the window just so the sound of home would keep humming in the room. When Eliza tired, she closed her eyes, but she didn't send them away. Their presence wrapped around her like a quilt.

That night, when the house settled and the farm creaked itself quietly, Eliza made a choice. It was a small mustard seed, but it was a choice all the same. She swung her feet over the edge of the bed, every joint complaining, and sat up on her own. The room tilted; she reached for the bedpost and held on till everything steadied.

"Tomorrow," she whispered into the dark, "I'm gonna sit in my kitchen chair, even if it kills me. I will not let this grief turn my bones to stone. Do you hear me, Lord? If I have to trust you with a limp heart, I will- though you slay me, yet I will trust you."

The next morning, Buddy nearly dropped the bucket in his hand when he walked in and found her already at the table, wrapped in her old sweater, both hands hugging a warm mug. Her skin looked papery, and her shoulders slumped more than they had before, but the sight of her upright sent a wave of relief through him so strong that he had to grip the counter.

"Mama," he breathed, "what are you doing out of bed?"

"Drinking coffee," she replied, "trying to remember which one of you heathens moved my sugar bowl. Sit down before your frettin' wears a hole in my linoleum."

Patty bustled in behind him, arms full of fresh towels, fruit, and a basket of biscuits she had brought from home. She stopped short, her eyes shining.

"Well, look who decided not to meet Jesus just yet," she said teasingly, grinning through tears.

Eliza sniffed.

"I figured I owe y'all at least a few more lessons on how not to ruin green beans. Can't leave before my work's done."

Her hands shook when she reached for her biscuit; Buddy quietly slid the basket closer so she wouldn't have to stretch.

Patty poured Eliza more coffee before she asked. Between them, they made it possible for her to be weaker than she once was without making her feel like porcelain.

She tired quickly and needed to lie down again after an hour, but each day after that she pushed a little further - from bed to chair, from chair to porch, wrapped in a shawl while she watched the light move across the pasture. Her steps stayed small, and her breath was shorter than it used to be, yet the old stubbornness burned on.

One evening, as dusk brushed the mountains purple, Buddy eased her rocker onto the front porch. Patty tucked the blanket around her knees. The creek's song floated up faintly, and somewhere down there, stones glinted in the fading light.

"You see it?" Buddy asked softly.

Eliza's eyes were wet, yet fierce.

"Grief can lay me low, but it don't get the last word," she said. "My Gary's fine. He's with the One he has spent his whole life hollerin' about. I'm the one still in the Valley of the Shadow. But I ain't walkin' it alone. Do you hear me, Boy? You hear me, Pattygirl?"

"We hear you," Patty whispered as Buddy nodded, his own throat tight.

Eliza leaned her head back against the rocker, her breath shallow but steady.

"Though He slay me," she said again, her voice barely audible, "yet will I trust in Him." A tiny smile tugged at her mouth. "And if the Lord wants to talk with me about time and when I see Him, well, He knows I never was shy."

Buddy chuckled low. Patty shook her head.

"Now that's the Miss Eliza I know," she said.

"Somebody's got to keep these menfolk straight," Eliza replied, her eyes closing as the rocker crept in its own familiar rhythm. "Might as well be me till He calls my shift over."

The night settled softly around them. Grief still sat heavy in the corners of the house, but it no longer owned the whole room. In the half-light, Eliza's frail frame and fierce faith made a new kind of picture - not the bustling, apron-snapping mother she had been, but a woman who had wrestled with God on her sickbed and had come up leaning harder on Him, and still just feisty enough to keep Buddy and Patty on their toes.

Chapter 12 -

Ashes and Resolve

The months that followed Gary's death were thick with both kindness and sorrow, a bittersweet tide that washed over the Holcomb farm. The people Gary had ministered to throughout the decades of sermons and storms - loggers who had confessed to moonshine sins, farmers who had found grace amid crop failures, and mill hands nursing their Vietnam scars - poured their love back onto his widow and son. The ladies from the congregation continued to send food over with handwritten notes tucked beneath with short words of encouragement, such as, "Praying Psalm 147 for you," and their prayers filled the farmhouse until it felt like the very walls hummed with hymns, the air heavy with the scent of yeast and faith.

But beneath the comfort beat an aching time could not touch, a hollow rhythm where Gary's voice used to steady the dawn. Buddy walked through each day acutely aware of the empty space his father once filled: the steady baritone over breakfast biscuits calling out so many scriptures from memory, his deep laughter booming over the timber road as they hauled pines together, his hymns rising strong at the closing of Sunday service - "It Is Well With My Soul"- drawing amens from packed pews. The loss had stolen more than a man; it had stolen the heartbeat of their home, the predictable cadence of chainsaw mornings and vesper prayers that had marked Buddy's life like rings in an oak trunk.

Eliza's health faltered under the weight of her grief, her body betraying the spirit that had canned hundreds of jars of green beans without pause. Her joints stiffened like old hinges as her steps slowed to a shuffle across the kitchen linoleum. Sometimes it was Buddy's strong shoulder - forged hauling logs since boyhood - that kept her upright through the chores Gary once led: splitting firewood for the hearth, hauling water from the spring when the pump froze, or mending the fence where brambles crept back in. Yet in every small kindness he offered - stacking her chair cushions just so, setting her well-worn Bible open to Psalms by the window seat or brewing black coffee strong as Gary liked it - Buddy saw his father's lessons living on, quiet embers refusing the dark.

He heard the gospel from the Bible his whole life, page corners worn soft from Gary's thumb, but one message rose above the rest now - the one that had guided him since the boyhood meadow clearing days: *Know who you came from, know who gives you meaning, and seek what He desires until you meet Him face to face.* Simple words among thousands, Gary had thundered from the Grace Fellowship pulpit, but it was as if the finger of God had burned them into Buddy's soul with a branding iron, searing through the fog of fresh loss.

Those words lingered deeply in his chest like roots cracking stone, stirring something restless and unnamed. It wasn't pride or ambition, those hollow hungers he had seen claim Atlanta weekenders - no, it was helplessness, the sharp kind that slices a man watching the weak go unprotected, trampled under indifferent boots. The image of that day behind the Peach Avenue clinic never left him: the woman in scrubs hefting bags without a glance, tiny limbs slicking garbage.

Tony's hidden grave by the creek whispered constantly with every rustle of leaves in the Appalachian wind; every dawn fog curling low - *Don't forget. Don't forget.*

He found himself walking before first light, boots damp with dew on the meadow, his spirit wrestling with silent wishes: undo the shock of Donna's pleading eyes, rewind the bin lid's hollow clang - or at the very least, build some dam to keep the flood from claiming more nameless ones.

One chilly morning, as frost silvered the grass and Panther Creek murmured indictment, Buddy made up his mind like a logger sighting the fall line.

He would drive back to Atlanta.

Though part of him ached to see Donna again - to hold her, hear her laugh cut through the city's gray, something larger burned holy fire within him now: *How many others*? How many nameless little ones are waiting for someone - anyone - to give them dignity before the bins swallow them whole?

He packed a dented thermos of Eliza's chicory coffee, black as midnight, and told his mother he had business to take care of downstate; then he fired up the old Ford and headed down the highway. Rabun's curves yielding to straight-line sprawl, billboards rising like false prophets, and exhaust tang thickening the air. By early afternoon, the city skyline loomed ahead: a wall of glass and steel as indifferent as the clinic plaque, swallowing the mountains whole. He pulled into the same small brick building on Peach Avenue, his heart heavy as wet timber but clearer-eyed than grief's first rage.

This time, he didn't storm the door, crutches flying. He parked across the lot in the shadow of a dying sycamore, thermos cooling on the dash, and waited - breath steady, his eyes hawk-sharp. Minutes stretched into hours, a multitude of cars hissing past like indifferent ghosts, until a white, unmarked van rode silently beside the clinic. The driver slid out, heavy-booted, opened the back doors with a rusty groan, and unloaded empty metal bins that clanked together loudly.

Buddy's throat tightened like a vice as the man disappeared behind the side door, re-emerging minutes later, pushing the bins again - now filled heavy and sealed tightly with industrial clasps that mocked any escape. The van rumbled a block down to a small warehouse, tires crunching loudly as it stopped in front of a big bay door that was opened wide beside a red dumpster scarred by years of burdens. Buddy followed at a distance, killing his lights on the shoulder across the street, his truck blending into the dusk.

He watched, his breath held, as the man with a full beard and an unsteady gait and his eyes hollow from too many hauls climbed out and hefted the first two bags that were bulging into the dumpster with grunts that echoed off the concrete. Bag after bag was thrown into the huge bin until the lid slammed shut. After the last one, the man fished out a cigarette from his pocket, cupped the flame against the wind, and leaned against the wall, appearing quite weary as smoke curled into the air. Buddy swallowed and forced his breath and his body to calm and relax - in through the nose, out through the mouth, like Coach had taught him for enduring the game. Then he stepped from the truck, cane clicking on the asphalt, and called across the quiet street. His voice carried in the wind:

"Hey, sir!"

The man looked up slowly, squinting through the smoke veil.

"Yeah?" He grunted, flicking ash.

"You hiring?" Buddy asked calmly, meeting eyes that had seen too much refuse.

The worker scratched his grizzled beard, eyeing the cane, and his logger's build.

"Yeah," he said after a long beat. "Had a guy quit last week. Couldn't handle the work."

His voice was rough as burlap, his words slurring faintly- liquor thick on his breath, and sorrow dripped thicker underneath.

Buddy held his gaze, unblinking. "I can handle it. I got this."

The man nodded once, then stubbed his smoke under his boot.

"Alright. Not much pay, and the route runs from morning into the evening sometimes. Pick up is daily to keep the smell down. Ain't going to make you rich, but you won't starve neither." He spat tobacco juice and jerked his thumb toward his small office door, covered with peeling paint. "Be here tomorrow morning. And wear some old clothes, cause you will get dirty."

"I will."

And he was. Every day after that, like clockwork. An hour-and-a-half grind from the Falls - Highway 441 blurring dawn to dusk - limping fiercely through every shift. He loaded the bins and hauled them steadily and gently.

Radford would poke fun at him: "Boy, them cans aren't going to break," he would say as he set them off the van.

Then Buddy would hose off the concrete slick with bleach as he cleaned without one complaint crossing his lips. The wages were meager - just gas for the Ford, and for the medicines that were stacking up for Eliza's joints and other issues she acquired - but the money was never the chain pulling him back.

Each day, his work fueled something deeper within him: a quiet vow etched soul-deep that as long as breath filled his lungs, whenever he crossed a soul starting its journey earthside in that brick shadow, they would never go unnamed. What the world rejected casually as Tuesday's trash, Heaven accepted with arms open wide - and Buddy Holcomb stood sentinel in that narrow, holy space between, bearing witness one bin at a time. It was as if Tony's creek side grave whispered '*keep going*' with every dawn that dropped.

Chapter 13 – Run to the Store

The late-afternoon light over Panther Creek had turned the ridgeline to gold, but the yard outside the Holcomb farmhouse felt quieter than it used to.

The woodpile was still stacked neatly against the shed. The porch swing still creaked when the wind nudged it. Gary's old truck still sat by the oak tree, the hood catching the sun just so—but the man who'd filled the cab with humming and low-voiced prayer was gone, and the silence he left behind had a weight all its own.

Eliza wiped her hands on a dish towel and stepped out onto the porch. From there, she could see Buddy down by the first gate, lifting a length of scrap lumber into the back of his own truck, his limp more pronounced when he was tired. He paused, hand braced on the tailgate, and stared off toward the line of hemlocks as if listening for something she couldn't hear.

"Buddy!" she called, raising her voice just enough to carry. "You got a minute?"

He straightened, the faraway look fading as he turned toward her. "Yes, ma'am."

She held up a folded list.

"Mr. Hall called. Said my flour is in, and I'm short on sugar and coffee, too. Thought you could run to the store before they close." Her eyes softened. "Give you a break from haulin' that lumber."

He wiped his palms on his jeans and started up the slope.

"I can finish this after supper. Truck's itching to go somewhere anyway."

Eliza smiled at that. He sounded like his daddy for half a second.

When he reached the porch steps, she studied his face a moment before handing over the list. The muscles in his jaw were set a little too tight. The skin under his eyes looked bruised, and had the kind of tired that sleep didn't fix.

"How's that city job treatin' you?" she asked, keeping her tone light as she tucked the towel over her shoulder. "Radford still got you runnin' around for that sanitation outfit down in Atlanta?"

Buddy huffed a small breath that might have been a laugh.

"Radford's fine, Mama. Trash and tanks don't take days off. City makes a mess, somebody's gotta clean it up."

"Hmmm." She tilted her head. "That's not what I asked."

He glanced down at the list, stalling.

"It's work. Honest work. Man can't ask for much more than that."

"That's true," she said. "But a man can still tell his mama if his feet are draggin' more than usual when he comes home on weekends."

He shifted his weight, cane tip ticking once against the bottom step.

"City's loud," he admitted. "Fast. I drive back up 441 and feel like my bones can finally breathe. Then I get here and..." he trailed off, his jaw working, feels like I'm just passin' through both places. Like, I don't quite fit in either one anymore."

Eliza heard the small catch in his voice but didn't push for the reasons. She didn't know what all sat heavy on him these days - she only knew it went deeper than long hours and Atlanta traffic.

"I know it's different," she said softly. "I know it's not the life you and your daddy once laid out on napkins and scrap paper." Her mouth curved sadly. "But I'm proud of you, Bud. You keep showin' up. You take care of what's in front of you. That's more than most men do."

"Some days I feel like I'm just driftin'," he said, the words low. "Atlanta, then home, then back again. Station yards and dumpsters by day, trying to figure out my calling and daddy's chores by night. Circles 'round the same hill."

"Circles ain't always wasted," Eliza replied. "Sometimes the Lord uses 'em to wear a path where somebody else can walk easier later."

He looked at her then, his eyes dark with things he hadn't yet put into words, and she saw what she could see - the grief for Gary, the strain of the city, the way burdens had settled into his shoulders since the funeral.

She patted his arm once and straightened.

"Now. You standin' here jawin' with me ain't gettin' my flour in the pantry."

There it was - the shift back to ordinary that she knew he needed.

"Yes, ma'am," he said, the corner of his mouth quirking. "You ridin' with me?"

Eliza's eyes flicked toward the sky. Clouds were starting to stack in the west, blue-gray and low.

"Might as well. Mr. Hall will give me fresher gossip if he sees my face." She paused, mischief glinting. "And I want to make sure you don't come back with half the store in that truck just 'cause it was on sale."

Buddy snorted. "You're the one who taught me to watch for bargains."

"I taught you to watch for needs," she corrected, reaching for her pocketbook. "Not to haul home three sacks of candy because they were two-for-one."

They walked to the truck side by side, the old gravel crunching under their feet. Buddy opened the passenger door for her, just as Gary had always done. For a second, as she climbed in, she had the oddest sense of the past and present overlapping – her young husband's eager hands, her grown son's careful ones.

On the ride into town, they talked about small things.

Eliza pointed out Mrs. Tate's new clothesline and wondered aloud if the woman had finally given up on her old wringer washer. Buddy mentioned that Radford was talking about picking up a couple more commercial accounts, given the state of the business. They both agreed that Panther Creek's water had been higher than usual and that the trout were lazier this year.

She didn't ask what else was turning over in his mind. He didn't offer. Some things, she knew, a man had to bring to the Lord before he could bring them to his mama.

Tallulah Falls' main street slid into view, just past the old depot, a handful of stores crowded together like old friends – post office with its new flag out front, the barber shop with the striped pole that hadn't spun in years, and Mr. Hall's general store with its faded Coca-Cola awning. And a hitch post left over from many decades ago.

Buddy parked out front, then he killed the engine and came around to help Eliza down from the cab, sticking close at her side.

“You want me to get it all, or you comin' in?” he asked. “Or you want to sit here on the porch?”

“I’ll come in,” she said. “I aim to keep Mr. Hall honest about his egg prices.”

The bell over the door gave its usual tired jingle as they stepped inside, cool air wrapping around them along with the familiar scents of coffee, candles, motor oil, and penny candy.

Eliza peeled off toward the shelf with the dry goods. Buddy headed for the counter to settle up the special order.

Two boys near the drink cooler went stiff as fence posts.

They had been arguing in whispers over Nehi versus RC Cola a second before, but the moment Buddy’s shadow slid over the scuffed old pine floors, both pairs of eyes snapped to him like he was a bear that had just walked in on two raccoons raiding feed bins.

Travis’s hand froze on the cooler handle. Tommy stood there with a Moon Pie halfway to his mouth.

Buddy tipped the brim of his cap, a polite habit. “’Scuse me, Fellas.”

They flattened against the cooler as if trying to merge with the glass.

For half a heartbeat, their faces were clear in the dusty light – Turnerville boys, jeans still damp at the cuffs from creek banks and puddles, their eyes wide in a way that didn't match the harmless errand of buying soda and sweets. Something about the set of their shoulders tugged at the back of Buddy's mind, but the thought skated off before it could find a name.

Tommy swallowed hard, his Adam's apple bobbing. The Moon Pie thudded back onto the shelf.

"Come on," Travis hissed under his breath. "Let's... uh... let's go. Mama said we got chores."

"You ain't even paid," Mr. Hall called from the counter.

"We, – we changed our minds," Travis stammered, already backing toward the door. "We ain't thirsty."

Buddy reached past them for a sack of feed stacked by the cooler. The boys flinched in unison as if the bag might bite.

He paused, brow furrowing just the slightest, then hefted the sack onto his shoulder as if it weighed nothing at all.

"Y'all all right?" he asked.

"Yes sir! No sir!" Tommy blurted the words, tripping over each other. "We gotta go – Travis, move!"

They bolted.

The bell above the door didn't so much jingle as screech when they hit it, the frame rattling in their wake. Bikes clanged off the rack out front, followed by the ragged sound of two boys pedaling like every dog in Rabun County had just been turned loose behind them.

Mr. Hall snorted.

“Turnerville kids,” he muttered, shaking his head as he rang up Eliza’s flour and coffee. “Act like they've seen a ghost.”

Buddy let out a puff of a laugh, though his expression stayed puzzled.

“Reckon the hills spooked ’em.”

Out on the sidewalk, Eliza watched the boys shoot past like arrows and then turned her gaze to her son as he stepped out with the feed sack and brown paper bag tucked under his arm. Her smile for him was steady and warm, but her eyes followed the disappearing bikes down the street a second longer than usual, a little line forming between her brows.

“Everything all right in there?” she asked as he shifted the weight to his good leg.

“Far as I can tell,” Buddy said. “Some Turnerville boys just realized they were late gettin’ home, I guess.”

“Hmmm,” Eliza murmured. “Some folks get an itch between their shoulders when they wander too close to things they don’t understand.”

Buddy held the truck door for her.

“You talkin’ about them or us?”

"Both, probably," she said lightly, climbing in. "Come on. Let's get these groceries home before the ice cream turns to soup."

The truck pulled away, leaving behind the little store, the rattling bell, and the faint echo of two boys whose nerves were fraying over something they couldn't have put words to if they tried.

Chapter 14 –

Assembly Line Mercy

Buddy had never liked downtown after dark.

By the time Radford slammed the office door and killed the last fluorescent light within the warehouse, the sun had already slipped between the Atlanta high rises, leaving the warehouse lot in a dreary and lonely setting. The trucks sat in a crooked row like tired old mules, streaked with the mud and the grime of the city. Somewhere beyond the chain link fence, the traffic hummed like a distant hive.

"You lock up," Radford called over his shoulder. "I'm late as it is. And don't forget to drop that list at the office in the morning. I get cranky if I lose paperwork."

"Yessir," Buddy said.

The office door banged shut. Silence rolled in.

He finished the last of the paperwork at the scarred desk in the corner, flipped the lights off, and stepped outside. The chilly air hit his lungs - sharp, almost clean after hours of diesel and disinfectant. He closed the padlock on the warehouse door, slipped the keys into his pocket, and stood a moment, just listening.

Out past the warehouses, a side street opened into a little run-down neighborhood - narrow houses with sagging porches, one brick apartment block, and a patch of dirt that passed for a park. When he had first started running the routes near the clinic, he had stumbled on it one evening and had heard the kids before he ever saw them - laughing, arguing, the slap of a rubber ball on cracked pavement.

Tonight, he turned his feet that way, same as he did most nights, when he could bear it.

He told himself it was just to stretch his legs. The truth was, after a day of hauling black bags stamped with the word 'medical', he needed to see somebody that was still breathing - on purpose. He needed to hear a child's squeal that wasn't trapped in his chest.

The further he walked from Radford's warehouse, the less the city sounded like sirens and brakes and more like people: A radio playing soul music from an open window, someone arguing on a stoop, a baby crying and then quieting again. As he rounded the corner by the little park, he heard a boy shout, high and fierce:

"Go long!"

Under the yellow wash of a streetlamp, five kids were playing football on the patchy grass – the two older ones against the three younger ones - with their jackets on the ground for the goal lines. The ball wobbled through the air and skidded across the sidewalk, bumping against Buddy's boot.

"Hey, mister," one of the boys called, his breath puffing white, "Can you toss it back?"

Buddy bent and picked up the ball, feeling the familiar weight settle into his palm. The leather was scuffed, the laces loose, but it sat in his hand as if it belonged there. For a second, his muscle memory tugged at him - Friday nights, clear eyes in the stand, Coach hollering his name across a high school field.

"Y'all ready?" he called.

"Yeah!" the smallest one yelled, already taking off down the park, his legs pumping and his arms churning. The others turned to watch, half laughing and half curious, as to how far their friend would run.

Buddy stepped back once, set his feet, and let the ball fly.

It left his hand in a clean spiral, cutting through the frigid air, sailing higher and farther than any of them expected. The kid was under the next streetlamp, having stopped running and just standing there, staring with his mouth open, as the ball gently dropped into his arms halfway down the street.

"Whoa! You should play for the Falcons!" one of the kids exclaimed.

"Man!" the one who caught the ball crowed, still clutching it to his chest, as he came running back to join them, "Did you see that?"

The oldest boy squinted up at Buddy. "Do you play for somebody?" he asked.

"Used to," Buddy answered him, shrugging one shoulder, "long time ago."

They all looked at him like he had just stepped out of a game on TV. For a moment, their eyes were full of nothing but wonder and the thrill of a good throw - not fear, not shame, not the heaviness that he had been hauling around all day.

"Thanks, mister!" the smallest one shouted.

Buddy tipped two fingers off his cap.

"Ya'll stay out of trouble," he said.

As he walked on, their laughter and the shouts followed him, warm as a campfire in the cold. He let it soak into the cracks in his heart.

"Thank you," he said under his breath. "For this. For them."

By the time he reached the end of the block, the sky had gone full dark. Neon sign glowed ahead - BEER, as another sign flickered, OPEN, over a corner bar he had never paid much attention to. He meant to turn back, head for the truck, grab his thermos, and make the long drive home.

Then he saw her.

She came out of a side street near the clinic, coat collar turned up, her hair yanked back in a tight clip. He recognized her gait before he placed her face - the brisk, efficient stride of somebody who had walked past him a dozen times in a white coat without seeing him. One of the nurses. He had watched her across the alley with tied-off bags more than once, her head tipped away like she didn't want to smell what she was carrying.

Tonight, she walked straight to the bar door and slipped inside like she had done a thousand times before.

But he stopped.

He had no business going in there. Places like that had never sat right with him. His daddy had taught him what the bottom of a bottle could do to a man, and he vowed years ago - long before the clinic, long before the meadow - that his own kids would never have to drag him home that way, reminding him of his mom when she had talked about dragging Gary home more than once - years past.

Still.

Something twisted in him. Curiosity, maybe? Or the raw need to understand how a person could walk out of that building with hands that had held death all day and then go laugh like it was Tuesday.

Before he thought it through, his feet were moving.

He pushed the door open and stepped into a fog of cigarette smoke and old music. The place was narrow and had a low ceiling. A long wooden bar filled one side, and a row of battered booths was on the other. A jukebox in the corner hummed out an old Skynyrd song. Glasses clinked, men in work jackets hunched over their drinks.

He felt out of place at once - too clean in his flannel, and too sober in his skin.

"Can I help you?" the bartender grunted, sliding a rag down the counter.

"Just a Coke," Buddy said quickly. "In a glass, please, with ice."

The man's brows twitched, but he grabbed a tumbler, filled it from the gun, and set it down without saying a word.

Buddy laid a couple of crumpled bills on the bar and took the drink, grateful for something to do with his hands.

The nurse sat three stools down, her back half-turned, talking to a man in a loosened tie and another woman in a nurse's uniform. Her white clinic badge was tucked into her pocket now, and the lanyard hung like a secret. They already had a small pile of empties in front of them.

"... I swear," she was saying, her voice too loud in the small room, "if I have to listen to one more girl tell me, 'Oh, but he said he would marry me', I'm going to start handing out flyers for common sense."

The man in the tie laughed. "But you'd be putting yourself out of a job."

“Oh, honey, don't you worry,” the other woman said, swirling the amber liquid in her glass, “they just keep on coming.”

They clinked their glasses together.

Buddy stared at the brown fizz in his own cup, his jaw tight.

He had not thought about what they might say to each other after hours. In his mind, the people inside those clinic walls were either quiet, clinical professionals or complete monsters. These look like... regular folks. Tired. Irritated. Yet laughing too loudly because it was easier than saying they were sad.

The nurse - he had called her name now as the other woman addressed her: Elena - took another drink and wiped her mouth with the back of her hand.

“You should have seen the one today,” she said. “Fourteen weeks, the first one I've seen that far along in a while. I told the doc, if you don't get it all with the first pass, I'm not fishing in there all afternoon.”

The man in the tie winced but kept grinning. “You're terrible.”

“Terrible is when they don't listen the first time,” the other woman said, tipping back her glass. “They come in at ten weeks, twelve weeks, swearing up and down they had just missed a period. Honey, by then it's all arms and legs in there. Makes the tray look like somebody's dropped a baby doll down the disposal.”

They both laughed.

Buddy's stomach lurched. His mind snapped back to the split bag on the truck - the tiny hand he had seen once through torn plastic, limp, and wrong. He had tried not to picture how it got that way. Now, without wanting to, he saw it: metal, suction, something twisting, and pulling a child to pieces before it ever saw daylight.

"Don't say it like that," the man said, half laughing and half shocked. "You'll kill my buzz."

"Oh, please," Elena said, swirling the ice in her glass. "It's just tissue. Have you ever seen the machine work?" She made a swishing sound as she twirled her finger. "A couple of passes, and you're done. Clean up what's left, count what you need to count, and the next one is on the table. It's assembly line mercy."

"Mercy," the other nurse snorted. "That's what we're calling it now?"

"Cheaper than college," Elena shot back. "We ought to get thank-you cards."

Their laughter grated like metal.

Buddy's hand clenched around his Coke so hard that the ice popped. *Assembly line. Count what you need to count.* He thought of the way they talked about making sure they had, 'all the parts' so nothing got left behind. *Little hands. Little feet. Pieces.*

Not cells. Not formless. Not babies. Little ones taken apart like junked engines.

“Yeah, but what if...” the man stopped, then his voice dropped, “what if they're not just... you know. Tissue?”

Elena lifted her chin, and she smirked.

“Then I hope whoever's in charge has a good pension plan, because he's gonna owe me hazard pay!”

The others howled.

Buddy felt cold from the inside out. It wasn't just what they did. It was how easy they said it. Like you might talk about a rough day at the factory. Like pulling apart a child was no different than pulling apart a carburetor.

The other nurse caught his eye and smirked, saying, “Well, lookee there, Elena,” she drawled. “You've got a fan.”

Elena turned, following her friend's gaze. Her lips curved when she saw him - a slow, appraising grin.

“Don't think I've ever seen you in here before,” she said. “You with one of the guys from the warehouse?”

Buddy shook his head.

“Just off work,” he managed.

“Hmm.”

She slid off her stool and took a step closer, her gaze flickering up and down, over him. Up this close, he could see the faint indention on her nose where a mask had rested all day.

"You looking for company, Handsome, or you just like drinking your Coke alone?"

Her hand tipped toward his glass, her fingers brushing his for a second longer than necessary.

Heat rushed to his face, not from the touch but from the wrongness of it all. This woman spent her days handling the smallest and most fragile gifts on earth like they were medical waste. Now she was leaning into him like he was just another way to forget.

"I'm married," he heard himself say.

She blinked, then she laughed. "Ring's on the wrong hand."

He glanced down, realizing too late that he wore no band. He swallowed.

"I'm not interested," he said, gentler, but was no less firm. "Thank you, kindly."

Her smile flickered, then hardened.

"Suit yourself," she said, turning back to her friends. "Guy's probably scared of a little fun."

"You do work in a scary place," the man with the tie said.

"Oh, please," she said again. "You wanna talk scary, come stand in the alley with me when the truck comes. That's when it hits you - just how much of this city is just excess."

"Here we go," the other woman muttered, but there was no real protest in it.

Elena leaned on her elbows on the bar, talking with her hands now, warmed by the drinks and the company.

"You start your day with coffee and a cigarette, and end it with a margarita, and in between you listen to sob stories and scrape out mistakes. After a while, you either grow a sense of humor, or you lose your mind."

Buddy's grip on his glass was so tight his knuckles began to ache. He set it down slowly, afraid his shaking hands would send it flying, and slipped off the stool.

Outside, the frosty night grabbed him. He braced one palm against the brick, his head bowed, breath coming in quick, ragged pulls. Sweat prickled down his back despite the chill.

"God," he whispered, his voice cracking. "God, have mercy."

The city noise rolled past - sirens in the distance, a bus groaning through a turn, and a couple arguing somewhere up the block. Here, in this little pocket of a shadow by the bar's back door, he felt the weight of a nation's sins pressing down, funneled through one alley, one dumpster, one truck.

"Lord, I can't unsee this," he choked. "I can't unknow what they're doing in there, what I've been hauling like it was nothing."

The images crowded in - white tile, bright lights, the hum of a suction machine, a nurse counting parts on a tray while a girl sobbed into a paper gown, and black bags thumping into the truck bed. Then a quick vision of the meadow at home - just quiet and green.

“I don't know how to fix it,” he said as the words began tumbling over each other. “I am just one man with a shovel and a trash route, but I'm asking You. I'm begging You. Please stop this. Shut it down, however, You have to do it. Laws, hearts, clinics, I don't care. Just... don't let us keep on going like this. Don't let us keep killing our babies and calling it mercy.”

His voice dropped to a hoarse whisper.

“And don't let me go numb,” he prayed. “Please. Don't ever let me get used to this. If my heart’s gotta break every time so I remember they're Yours, then break it. Just don't let me start thinking of them like trash.”

He stayed there a long minute, his forehead resting against the rough brick as the cold began seeping through his jacket. Finally, his breathing slowed. He straightened up, wiped his face with the back of his sleeve, and turned his steps toward the warehouse lot where his truck waited.

The city kept humming, lights blinking, and people going on with their nights. But something in Buddy had shifted, settled into a fierce and aching resolve.

As long as God gave him breath, he would keep carrying what others threw away. He would keep putting little bodies in the ground with a name and a prayer instead of just a number on a schedule, and he would keep begging Heaven to do what one man with a shovel never could - end the killing altogether.

Chapter 15 -

Frozen Creek Grace - 1980

It was near the end of 1980, with light snow tracing the edges of the fence post and glimmering blue beneath the pale dawn. Buddy Holcomb's old Ford coughed twice, rattled, and finally came to life - the engine humming steady as a song. Beside him, Patty tugged her hat down and grinned around the steam rising from her thermos.

"You sure about this?" she asked for the third time, her voice sleepy but laced with anticipation. "You turn twenty-five, and your big plan is to wake up before sunup and drive two hours up to Gatlinburg?"

He smiled, his eyes keeping on the road ahead.

"You said once you always wanted to see the Christmas lights up there. I'm just fulfilling a seven-year-old wish."

"Hmm. I said that back when I thought twenty-five was old!" she taunted him, then took a sip of her coffee, its heat fogging the window. "Good thing you remembered."

The heater sputtered, offering little warmth. Early morning light filtered through the bare trees. Patty reached for the radio and tuned it between the static until a bluegrass gospel song found them. They drove in easy silence a while.

“You could have spent your birthday with anyone,” she said gently.

“I could,” he answered simply. “A great way to end 1980, don’t you think?”

That stopped her for a moment. She turned to look at him - the strong line of his jaw, the way his eyes stayed soft even when the rest of him seemed worn down. Seven years had passed since Donna's visit to the clinic. And in all that time, Buddy had never taken to another woman. Not really. He had kept to work, to duty, to the quiet that made folks mistake reserve for peace.

If there was peace in him, it had been hard-won.

She had been the only one he had confided in - how Donna's parents had pushed him out, how fear and silence had taken the place of courage. Only three people had ever known the whole truth, and two of them had not spoken since that day. Patty carried it with him, a shared hurt wrapped in years of understanding.

By the time they rolled into Gatlinburg, the sun was flooding the mountains. The streets shimmered with patches of snow, the shopkeepers sweeping their stoops, wreaths hanging from every lamp post and every doorway trimmed with garland. When Buddy parked near the Smoky Mountain Diner, the air smelled like cinnamon and sweet smoke.

Patty jumped out, her scarf fluttering. “Breakfast first! My treat!”

He smirked as he followed her inside.

“I planned this just to have you feed me.”

Inside, warmth and chatter filled the diner. Alabama crooned faintly on the jukebox, and a waitress with bright red hair poured coffee before they even ordered.

“Two coffees,” Patty told her with a grin, “and hubcap-sized pancakes for the birthday boy.”

But he shook his head, trying not to smile. “Eggs and sausage will do.”

“He's being humble,” Patty teased, “load him up, honey.”

The waitress laughed, scribbling down the order. When she walked away, Buddy gave Patty a narrow look.

“You are determined to make folks talk.”

“Let them,” she said, stirring sugar into her cup, “you could use some good gossip for a change.”

He laughed - quietly but real - and Patty thought it was the best sound she'd heard in years.

“It's good to hear that again,” she had to say, yet softer than she meant to.

He looked down into his coffee, his smile still easing across his face.

“Forgot what it felt like.”

“Well,” she said, raising her cup to him, “let's start remembering.”

They spent the morning meandering down Main Street, the snow fluffing the rooftops, and all the shops dressed in holiday color. He bought her a caramel apple; she bought him a tiny wooden keychain carved into a bear. They wandered into craft booths and tourist traps, mocking each other's taste in souvenirs. The air was full of laughter and fiddle music spilling from street corners. For the first time in a long while, Buddy walked with ease.

In a little woodworking shop, the smell of cedar hung thick and sweet, and it lured him in. Buddy's fingers lingered over a hand-built table.

“You like that,” Patty stated as she observed him.

“I'm taking to it a little.”

“Well,” Patty said, “Gary always said you should be proud of your work. It's so neat that they are selling your pieces at the store.”

“I’ve got a couple here. It is neat to see it displayed.”

Patty said, “You do make beautiful pieces. Your daddy really taught you about wood.”

He shrugged.

“Wood makes sense. You learn the grain, work with it, and if you take care of it, it stays fixed. People aren't that simple.”

“Maybe not,” she said thoughtfully, “but they come together the same way – slowly and carefully - in the right good hands.”

He met her eyes, and for a lingering heartbeat, something passed between them - warm and fragile, like light caught in glass.

By that midafternoon, the snow had started again, tiny and flurry soft as sifted flour. They took the lift up the mountain, their boots brushing the top of frosted pines. They gazed upon the town, it appearing like a sparkling diamond necklace below them.

Patty leaned close to the rail.

“Would you look at that?” she whispered. “Feels like Heaven's reaching right down to touch Earth.”

He smiled faintly.

“You have always seen the light before anyone else.”

She nudged him with her shoulder.

“And you've always needed draggin' into it!” she retorted.

He laughed, low and free.

“Maybe so.”

When they reached the top, they stood side by side at the lookout, their breath clouding the freezing air.

"It is something, isn't it?" he said in wonder.

"Yeah," she answered, a little breathless, "everything looks smaller from here. All that heavy stuff we carry around, it shrinks when you see it like this."

He nodded, the wind reddening his cheeks, but he said nothing.

They headed back toward town later, the headlights carving gold across the snow. Patty suddenly leaned forward.

"Pull over! See that bridge? That old wooden one?" she almost shouted with excitement.

Buddy sighed. "What now?"

"Remember playing there when we were kids?"

He smiled despite himself.

"Barely," he said jokingly, then added, "You dared me to hop the rocks, and I fell in. Mama made me hold a hot brick to my feet, so I wouldn't catch pneumonia."

"Then you ought to try again," she said, her eyes glinting, "you could redeem your honor."

"Patty - no!" he said firmly. "That water's icy."

But she was already grabbing at the door handle, intent on her mischief.

"Oh, come on, Buddy Holcomb. You used to be brave! Where's your sense of adventure?"

"Used to be smart, too," he said under his breath, watching her dart out of the truck.

She ran toward the creek, her laughter echoing off the bridge timbers. Her boots crunched through the thin crust of snow as she leaped onto a stone midstream.

"See? Not so bad!"

He moved down the bank slowly, muttering under his breath.

"Every fool stunt we ever pulled started with you saying that."

The next second, she slipped.

A small gasp, a big splash of icy water - and she was gone under.

"Patty!"

He didn't think. He just ran towards her. His bad leg screamed as his boots hit the water, but somehow he managed to grab her coat collar and pull at her with all his might. The creek soaked them both thoroughly before he could haul her upright.

"Good grief," he said, his breath ragged, "are you trying to scare me to death?"

She sputtered, the water running from her hair and eyelashes.

"I guess I found the deep part..."

She was still laughing with her face flushed red from the cold. Buddy grabbed her hand and began dragging her up toward the bank.

“You will freeze solid.”

“You too,” she said through chattering teeth, “you are shaking worse than me.”

“Truck,” he gritted. “Now!”

By the time they tumbled into the cab, the heater’s weak blast felt like heaven. Steam rose from their jeans and coats.

“Well,” she said between gasps, “that was... stupid.”

“Accurate statement,” he said, running a hand through his dripping hair.

“Still, we've had worse birthdays,” she stated, ever the optimist.

He gave her a look.

“You nearly drowned.”

“Oh, now you're being dramatic!” she piped back.

“Patty...”

She cut him off with a sneeze and a laugh. “I'm fine, Buddy, honestly.”

She tugged off her soaked sweater and shivered before he even realized what she was doing. He jerked his gaze to the windshield.

"Hold up!" he said hoarsely.

"Relax," she said lightly, turning her back as she wrung out her hair.

"You've seen worse and more at the river baptisms."

He still faced forward, his jaw tight. His reflection caught her half-bare shoulder in the fogged glass, and for a heartbeat, every repressed part of him came clamoring awake. He squeezed his eyes shut and prayed under his breath.

"Lord, don't let me wreck what you've built."

She caught the sound of his whisper and smiled faintly to herself.

"Your turn," she said casually, "get warm before that leg seizes."

He pulled off his coat and shirt, trading them for a blanket from behind the seat, the cab filled with the hiss of the heater and the smell of wet flannel and skin. Patty elbowed him gently.

"You realize if the church folks see us right now, we'll both be on the prayer list next Sunday."

He barked out a laugh, half shock, half amusement.

"You really are impossible."

"I call it being adventurous!"

"You call everything adventurous."

“Because it is,” she teased.

Her smile softened. “You laughed, I'll count this whole trip as a success.”

“I've been laughing since you hit the water,” he said, hiding his grin.

“You missed your calling as a comedian, Holcomb.”

“Only when you're around,” he admitted.

She fell quiet at that, a slow smile rising as she pulled the blanket tighter.

“I miss hearin’ that kind of talk from you. You've been... quiet for far too long.”

He stared at the dashboard, his voice low. “Hard to talk much when your memories start screamin’ louder.”

Patty turned toward him, her eyes kind.

“Seven years is a long time for a man to walk under the same cloud. Maybe it's time you looked up instead and seek the sunshine.”

“I've been tryin’”, he said. “Some nights I even manage.”

“And you did today,” she proclaimed to him. “You laughed! Really laughed. That's a start.”

He looked at her, something in his chest loosening for the first time in years.

"Yeah," he murmured with a soft smile, "it's a start. Thanks to you."

They found a thrift store still open near the edge of town, the type that smelled of cedar shavings and someone's past. Patty picked out a mismatched sweater and a plaid skirt; Buddy grabbed a flannel shirt half a size too big. When they came outside, their breath puffed white in the dim light as the sun began falling behind the mountains.

"Well," she said, shaking her head, "not exactly high fashion, but I at least got new clothes out of this deal."

That pulled out another full, and rare laugh from him - deep, genuine, echoing across the quiet lot. The sound startled even him.

Patty smiled, satisfied.

"There it is. I told you it was still in there."

He let out a long breath, his eyes shining. "You make it sound simple."

"Grace usually is," she said softly, "we are just slow to believe it and grab hold of it."

They rode home under a sky salted with stars, the thawed hum of the heater filling the cab. For the first time in years, Buddy did not press down the guilt when it tried to rise. He let the warmth and thoughts spread through him instead, like forgiveness might – quietly and slowly - melting the cold corners of a weary heart.

When the lights of Rabun County came into view, Patty broke the silence.

“You know,” she said, smiling at him through the dim glow of the dash, “you might have just had your first happy birthday since you were seventeen.”

He thought about it, and he chuckled low.

“Maybe so.”

“And next time we go out,” she added with a gleaming smile, “I'm stayin’ on dry ground.”

He grinned. “And miss all this excitement?”

She glanced at him, that familiar sparkle back in her eyes.

“You keep me laughing, Holcomb. And I will risk the creek again.”

He laughed softly, the sound carried with the hum of tires on asphalt, a sound that felt like grace, breaking the long silence between them.

Frozen Creek Grace - a day of laughter found through icy water and mercy, when old shame thawed just enough to let joy reach its way in.

Chapter 16 –

Mama Knows

Buddy's boots sounded softer these days, Eliza thought. Maybe it was that he had grown gentler on purpose, like he was afraid a hard step might jolt her bones loose. Maybe at eighty, it was just that her ears were not what they used to be. Either way, by the time she heard the back door ease shut, he was already in the kitchen.

"Mama?"

"I'm in here," she called, one hand braced on the edge of the counter, the other reaching for the dishcloth she had dropped on the floor.

"Don't go sneakin' up on an old woman like that. I nearly met Jesus."

His low chuckle rolled through the room.

"I am in no hurry to rush that meeting, but I hope you are not as feisty with him."

He crossed the worn linoleum in a few strides and relieved her of the damp plate in her hand, then bent down and picked up the dropped dish towel from the floor for her.

“What did I tell you about these dishes?” he asked. “You tryin’ to put me out of a job?

“You already have two jobs, as far as I can see,” Eliza responded back to his tease, “hauling for Radford, and then comin’ home and fussin’ over me like I am made out of spun glass or somethin’. A woman's got to keep her hands busy, or she'll forget what they're for.”

“I'd rather you forget dishes than steps,” Buddy said mildly, “you nearly took a spill this morning, remember?”

“That throw rug had it comin’,” she muttered. “I told it who was the boss.”

She reached into the drawer for a clean dishcloth, and he proceeded to take it from her, his fingers brushing hers.

“Sit,” he commanded gently, “then you can tell me all about you and the rug from that chair.”

“I can stand,” she protested, though her legs still felt like weak twigs.

“I know you can,” he said, “but you don't have to.”

There was not much to say to that. She let him steer her to the kitchen chair by the window, the one where the light used to pour in bright and sharp enough for her to shell peas without squinting. Now it came in blurred at the edges, the shapes outside more of a suggestion than a clear line.

She could still make out the pasture, though - the pale strip of fence, the dark slash of woods beyond, and if she leaned exactly right, she could glimpse down the hill towards the creek.

“You smell like diesel and sawdust,” she said, watching Buddy move back to the sink with his sleeves rolled up, displaying forearms that were brown and strong, “and something else I can't place,” she added.

He grinned a little.

“Radford had me helpin’ old Mr. Lewis move some scrap lumber behind his place after the route,” he said. “You're probably smellin’ that cedar stacked back there.”

“Hmm,” she smiled faintly. “Your daddy would have liked that part, at least.”

Buddy's shoulders appeared to sag just a bit.

“Yeah,” he said quietly, “I think he would have.”

He worked in easy silence for a few minutes, the plates clanging softly as the water ran down the drain. Eliza folded and refolded the edge of her apron in her lap, listening to the familiar sounds of her own kitchen in a way she had not when her eyes had done more of the work.

“How's Radford?” she asked. “He still fussin’ at you about keepin’ his trucks cleaner than his language?”

"He fusses a little. But I don't see him as much anymore. He does allow me to be my own boss, so I can live with that," he replied.

"You always could," she said. "You were born old, you know that?"

He glanced back at her with half a smile.

"So you tell me."

"So everybody tells you," she corrected. "Thirty-five years old and act like you're fifty-five!"

He shrugged, turning back to the sink.

"Somebody's got to," he said.

She let that sit. Outside, a bird was building a nest in the hedge. The clock over the stove ticked steadily. Her left knee throbbed; her right hip pulsed a dull complaint each time she shifted. She pressed her palm over the ache and prayed it would behave till Sunday.

"Buddy?" she said after a while.

"Yes?"

"How long are you plannin' on ridin' on that sanitation truck?"

He went still for half a second, then rinsed another plate.

"Till the Lord says that's enough," he said matter-of-factly.

“Hmm,” she cocked her head, “and you think that’s your calling, hauling waste? Seems you come home a little too heavy from just picking up bags.”

He turned off the water and set the last plate in the rack.

“We do more than waste,” he said, “Miss Jenkins had me patching her porch this afternoon. Might even let me charge her if she doesn't pay me with pound cake again.”

“Don't play word games with me, Buddy Holcomb,” she said, firm but kindly. “I changed your diapers. I know when you're answering around a question instead of at it.”

He dried his hands on the towel, then leaned against the counter across from her, his arms loosely folded. The light from the window caught the new threads of gray at his temples, the ones she pretended not to see.

“What do you want to know, Mama?” he asked.

She studied his face, softening at the lines she could still make out.

“I know you're helpin’ Radford,” she said. “I know you work hard down at the shop. I am proud of that. But I also know you, boy. You come in quieter these days than you ought to from ‘just’ liftin’ cans and makin’ furniture.”

He looked away, his jaw working.

“You think I don't notice when you wash your hands a little longer than normal?” she went on, gentle but with some firmness. “That you stand out there on the porch some nights like you're tryin' to leave the entire world on the steps before you come in. You forget how many years I've listened to your boots across this floor."

He let out a breath that sounded a little like surrender.

"It's nothing for you to worry about," he said, "not yet."

"I'm your mama," she said, "my job is to worry. You can't retire me from that. But I won't push you if you're not ready."

A muscle jumped in his cheek. He dropped his gaze to his hands, big and scarred and - as far as most folks in Rabun County knew - only stained with oil and varnish.

"Eliza," he said suddenly, switching to her given name like he did when something sat heavy on him, "can I ask you something?"

"That depends," she said, a small smile easing the sternness from her tone, "is it about why you ain't married? Because I got a whole drawer full of answers for that one."

He let out a huff that was almost a laugh.

"Not today," he said, "it's about you."

She lifted her brows. "About me?"

"About... now," he said, gesturing vaguely at her, at the house, at the way she had shuffled instead of walked this morning.

"Your eyes. Your legs. The way you act like the mop weighs a hundred pounds but still try to sneak it out of the closet when you think I'm not lookin'."

"Eliza Mae Holcomb does not sneak!" she declared.

"You hobble with intent," he allowed. "Call it what you want."

She tried to swat at him, but her reach wasn't what it used to be. He caught her hand midway and held it, his thumb rubbing over the paper-thin skin on the back.

"How bad is it?" he asked quietly. "Really. And not what you tell the church ladies. What's the truth?"

The fierce retort rose: *Fine. I'm fine. I'm just old, not dying.* But it stuck somewhere between her teeth.

"I don't see as I did," she admitted, surprising herself with the ease of it. "The sun's too bright, letters are too small, and people look more like shadows if they are across the room. My knees holler when I stand, and my hips fuss when I sit. Half the time I feel like I'm arguing with my own bones."

He flinched, his grip tightening.

"But I'm here," she added quickly, "I get up. I make biscuits slower, but I make them. I can still find my Bible. I can still hear you comin' up the drive. That's more than some mamas my age can say."

He nodded, and he swallowed. "You tell the doctor all that?"

"I tell him what he needs to know," she gave a little snort. "He tells me what I already know – 'You're not twenty anymore, Mrs. Holcomb.' I told him I already noticed that - when I bend over and need help getting back up."

He almost smiled, but his eyes were wet now, and it undid her.

"Hey," she said softly, "look at me."

He did.

"I am not porcelain," she said tenderly, "I am not a piece of that fancy china we never use. I am more like one of these old chairs - creaky, scratched up, a little wobbly on one leg, but still holdin' more than I was ever built for."

"You are not a chair," he murmured.

"And I am not done, either," she said robustly. "The Lord decided my eyes would dim and my steps would slow. Fine. He didn't say I had to sit in a corner and collect dust! You hear me?"

"Yes ma'am," he said automatically. Then, softer, "I just... I don't wanna see you hurt."

"Oh, Buddy," she reached up, cupping the side of his face, "you can't walk me around all the hurt in this life, no matter how big your shoulders are, that's not your job."

He leaned into her palm and for just a second – thirty-five years old and still her little boy.

"What is my job, then?" he asked, almost like he didn't mean to say it out loud.

She smiled, feeling the weight of his question reached further than the kitchen.

"Your job," she said slowly, "is to walk with Him where He leads you, and to love who He puts in front of you while you're there. Sometimes that's me, needing help to the porch. Sometimes it's Radford, needing a pair of steady hands. Sometimes it's folks nobody else wants to look too closely at. Trust what the Lord has planted in you, even if you never eat of that fruit here on Earth."

Something flickered over his face at that last part - guilt, maybe, or the shadow of a secret. He looked away.

"You've been doin' that a long time," she said gently. "Long before you ever climbed up in one of Radford's vans."

She squeezed his hand. "I don't need to know everything," she said, "not yet. The Lord knows I know more than most mamas, and I wish I didn't. But I know this: whatever you're carrying that you think you've got to keep from me, you're not carrying it alone. Don't you ever lie to yourself about that."

He let out a slow breath.

"Sometimes I wish you didn't see so much," he said.

"Sometimes I wish you'd stop thinkin' I can't handle what I see," she countered, "between your daddy's wild years and raising you and tending to half the county at their bedsides, I've seen about all there is to see."

The mention of Gary hung between them a moment, both tender and sharp. Buddy's thumb moved over her hand again, like he needed the reassurance that she was really there.

"You think your daddy would be proud of you?" she asked quietly. "Makin' furniture and ridin' that route, pickin' up people's messes, doin' whatever else it is that you do?"

He gave her a humorless little huff.

"He always said, 'Boy, don't miss your calling today, while wishing the Good Lord would use you tomorrow.' Yeah, I think he'd be proud if he knew."

"He knows enough," she said in quiet reflection, "the Lord don't keep His children in the dark about the good things He's doin' through their people. I believe that."

He absorbed that, his eyes far away.

"You are a good son," she said, with the kind of firmness that didn't leave room for an argument. "Whether the whole county knows what you're doin' or thinks you're just haulin' trash or buildin' a table every now and then, whether you ever marry or if you don't. And whether my eyesight goes or my legs give out."

He swallowed, his throat working. "You sure you're not just sayin' that cause I do your dishes?" he managed.

"That's at least half of it," she said, a smile tugging at her mouth, "the rest is because I've watched you since you were the size of a sack of meal, and I know what you're made of."

He looked back at her then - really looked - like he was trying to memorize her face before the years blurred for him too.

"I don't know how much longer you're going to be able to see me clearly," he said softly, "but I want you to know... if you wake up one day and all you get is shadows and shapes, I'll still be right where you expect me to be. Boots on these floors. Hands on this land. Doing what He tells me, the best I can."

Her eyes stung.

"You just make sure one of the things He tells you is to get me to church on time," she said thickly. "I don't care if I have to sit in the front row with dark glasses on, I am not missing my pew."

He laughed, swiping at his own eyes with the back of his wrist.

"I'll get you there, Mama," he said finally, "even if I have to carry you in."

"You try to carry me, and I'll pinch you so hard you'll drop me," she joked.

"Then I'll just have to build you a ramp," he said, "and a pew with arms so you can push yourself up and hymnals with big, huge print."

"Now you're talkin' some sense!" she laughed.

He bent and kissed the top of her head, the way he had when he left for the first game he started, for his first trip without them, and for Gary's funeral.

"Rest those eyes," he murmured, "I'm goin' to run down to the store and then work in the shop for a bit."

"You tell Pattygirl, I said 'hello' and to come see me, and don't you work so late past dark again, or I will be coming' down there with my cane," she said.

"Yes ma'am. I'll try not to," he said, smiling.

She listened to his boots fade down the hall, then across the porch, and then out into the yard. The world outside her window was softer now, the lines fuzzed, and the colors bleeding into one another, but she could still see enough to know which way he had gone.

Down toward the road. Towards town. Toward whatever work the Lord had placed in his hands, hidden in plain sight until it was time for folks to know.

Eliza rested her hands over her apron and closed her eyes.

"Thank you," she whispered, "for these years. For that boy. For letting me watch him be gentle when the world is so rough."

Her knees ache. Her eyes burned. But her heart swelled.

She couldn't see every detail anymore, but she could feel the shape of something good being carved, slowly and faithfully, in the hands of her son - and in the hands of the God who had never once wasted a hard day.

Chapter 17 –

Shadows of the Bin Man

Radford, Buddy's boss, had spent the last twenty years staring down at the bottom of a bottle, chasing ghosts in the amber swirl. Warehouse air hung thick on one Tuesday afternoon, bleach biting sharply into their hands as they hosed off the concrete pad, water was slushing silver under the bare bulbs overhead. Buddy killed the nozzle, wiped the sweat beating from his brow with a forearm grimed and nasty, and finally asked straight out,

“Radford, what's eatin’ you? That shadow in your eyes - it's the same one doggin’ me every dawn.”

Radford froze mid-scrub, water pattering off his beard like reluctant rainwater on a tin roof. He scratched at the grizzle slowly, as if pulling thorns.

“Was a farmer once. Had a big spread down Pike County way – six hundred golden acres rolling with corn and soy, whispering in the breeze with a big red barn standing tall and proud like a deacon's promise. I had six sons - strong as mules, and three pretty daughters bright as sunbeams and eight grandbabies tumbling wildly through the tall grass - their laughter chasing dragonflies." His voice was dry and smoky; his cigarette dangling, almost forgotten, and the ash lengthening like a lie about to drop.

"You sell it off?" Buddy asked while coiling the hose with hands that knew rope and regret alike, calluses snagging hold to the rough, green rubber tightly. In his chest, compassion stirred - a familiar ache for a man trying to outrun his own story.

"Nah. Just walked off. Ain't mustered the grit to go back. Land is still in the family, I guess. My boys still run it, I reckon." Radford's eyes went distant, tracing ridges that weren't there anymore, lost hills folding into memory's haze.

Buddy leaned on the wall, rag twisting slowly between his scarred fingers that had gripped bins heavy with the world's leavings. One of Radford's other workers had said his sons were holding the acres together, even through many hard years, and even keeping the red barn from falling to ruin.

"What spooked you bad enough to run?"

Radford flicked his lighter, fresh smoke blooming with an orange glow against the warehouse murk, and he exhaled a breath like a confession uncoiling.

"Thanksgiving morn'. Breakfast was steaming on the table, the house alive with the young'uns hollerin' and all the grandbabies with sticky fingers from their jelly biscuits - just the pure chaos I craved like air. Needed to turn the ground early, the fields behind schedule, and the frost nipping at our heels. I backed the old, snarling tractor out of the shed, and... I should've thought... my mind was somewhere else... Spud usually scrambled up the step like a puppy...every time..."

His voice cracked as tears hacked clean trails through the day's grime caked deep on his face.

"Then I saw her face, my daughter-in-law's- twisted in agony, her screams tearing the sky open."

No, God, no! He could still hear her as it had just happened.

"The wheels pinned him down flat, my little Spud, six years old, and Papa's faithful shadow on every chug across the field. Crushed him down in the mud."

Radford's frame shattered like a felled oak in the aftershock; the lighter began trembling in knuckles that had gone white.

"Couldn't look them in the eye after that. Couldn't stand my own reflection staring back... hollow. I walked away from the fields and from the God I thought was always watching. Been hauling other people's garbage ever since, like maybe if I moved enough of theirs, I wouldn't have to feel the weight of mine."

He ground the cigarette butt fiercely under his boot heel, then mustered a crooked grin.

"Boy, you're fixing to make a career out of this bin work, aren't ya? Steady as they come."

The pivot was clumsily done but hooked deeply. Pain's grip was universal. No loners in its cold clasp. The riddle of suffering - tangling life's bright thread with death's black knot - hung over them. Buddy's heart ached for the man beside him; Gary's sermons whispered through his memory about a God who stayed even when his children ran.

Fifteen years had rolled by since their paths had crossed, Buddy's raw first shift as Radford eyed the limping man through a hangover fog and a coffee-ringed clipboard. They saw each other on payday mostly now; the envelopes slid quietly to him. Radford had handed off routes wholesale, banking on the silent logger-turned-hauler who clocked in faithfully, rain or bone-ache.

Thirty-eight now, Buddy's easy charm was etched hard by labor's chisel - temple thinning with a little silver-shot; hands mapped with callus and scars from bin bites and bleach scalds. But his eyes held fast, carrying the stubborn spark Gary Holcomb once thundered from his pulpit: his faith a candle guttering fiercely against the gale, unquenched. Some evenings, to ease the pain of the daily route, Buddy would take a break and walk through the surrounding neighborhood – there he would find himself watching children on the playground – their laughter a healing sound and yet bittersweet in the midst of such dealings with death. Some nights, when the work felt too heavy and the memories pressed too closely, he would remember his daddy saying, “The Lord won't waste a hurt, Son,” and him always singing that old gospel song ‘I Feel Like Traveling On.’

One day at the shop, Gary had encouraged him to start, Buddy didn’t notice his tears at first. He only knew the light was changing. Late-afternoon sun pushed through the high barn windows in the slanted bands, catching the floating dust so it looked like the whole shop was full of slow, golden snow. The planer had gone quiet a few minutes back, leaving only the tick-tick of the cooling metal and the soft rasp of his sanding block moving in circles.

He worked the edge of the tabletop, his bare forearms covered with sawdust, and his hands had gone numb from the years of the same motion. Oak under his palms - solid, true, the kind of board his daddy would have smiled over. He paused, turned it to catch the grain in the light exactly right, and saw how the darker streaks curved and crossed through the lighter heartwood, like scars that had healed into a rare harden beauty.

His thumb traced one of those dark lines.

“Naughty, ain't you,” he murmured, hearing Gary’s laugh in his memory. “Storm-beaten. Still holdin.”

Something in his chest tugged.

The shop smelled of cut wood, varnish, and the faint sweetness of Eliza’s stew drifting from the house. Shelves lined the walls and clamps by the dozens, a variety of special woods stacked neatly, drying in bundles and jars of screws sorted by size. On one beam, near the door, he had hung an old, rough-hewn cross he had made as a teenager for a sunrise service. The pine had darkened with age, edges rounded by time, but the shape still spoke clearly - a rough beam laid across another, the place where Heaven bent down to meet a world that didn't deserve it.

Buddy's gaze snagged on it and didn't let go.

He looked down at his hands. Big, blunt fingers, nails rimmed dark, knuckles scarred white from saws and falling chains. These were the same hands that had gripped a shovel at Panther Creek, the same hands that had eased black plastic bags open and lifted tiny, weightless bundles against his chest. The same hands that had chiseled names carefully on little, white stones and set them in a meadow of witness.

His thoughts carried him into deep reflection: My Savior's hands were in wood from childhood *to the cross.*

His throat tightened.

He heard Gary's voice as clear as if his daddy stood there beside the workbench, preaching in the little clap-board church: "A man's life with his hands in wood - from a carpenter's shop to the cross. That was His message, Son. His hands were always in it. He saw a world that couldn't rescue itself, and He willingly laid His hands into that wood for a people who hated Him. 'Forgive them, Father, 'cause they know not what they do.'"

Buddy thought to set the sanding block down. It fell instead with a soft thud on the bench. He pressed his palms flat on the tabletop, then turned them over, staring at the scar lines crisscrossing his flesh. For just a breath, he saw another pair of hands layered over his - nails driven through, blood on rough grain, fingers spread wide in surrender.

"Like me," he whispered, his voice catching. "Oh God... like me."

The words came in a rush, torn from someplace deep.

"I was one of those people," he choked. "Got caught in the moment. Turned and transgressed your design. They... like me... didn't see you, Lord. Didn't see the cost. Now I see. I see the cost..."

The memory of the alley slammed back with it - the dumpster, the smell of bleach and metal, the first time he had reached in and touched skin that would never be warm. And all the times after. The mother's faces, some hard, some just empty, and some soft with painful regret they didn't have words for. The way the world hurried on, horns and sirens, never stopping long enough to know what it was throwing away.

He saw again these small torn bundles, the tiny fingers no bigger than matchsticks, the curve of a shoulder that would never shrug into a schoolbook strap, and the outline of a foot that would never feel creek water. He heard the rustle of black bags, the hollow bang of metal lids, and the soft thud of dirt falling over cloth in the meadow.

He leaned his weight onto his hands, head bowing over the newly-made table as the first sob punched through his chest. It hit so hard his knees went weak. He caught himself on the bench edge, shoulders shaking.

"Lord, I never knew this would be the work you'd call me to do," he said, the words rough with grief. "Daddy used his voice to spread the good news of the cross. How are these hands ever gonna amount to that?"

He lifted one hand, turning it in the light and seeing every scar anew.

"I know you saved me down on that creek bank," he went on, softer now. "I know you're workin' somethin' out in me. But I'm tired now, Father, so tired, I just want to be where you are. I feel your presence with me daily when I'm drivin' them highways and laying these little ones down with dignity. But all that talk in your Book - no more death, no more pain..." his voice broke again, "There's such... a longing in me, Lord."

He slid his hand from the table and pressed his palm against the old pine cross, fingers splaying over the rough surface. Splinters pricked his skin, sharp and real.

"Jesus, you finished your ministry in perfect timing with the Father's will. Lord, give me strength to finish what you want me to do," he whispered. "My hands just lift what sin, and hard hearts have produced and try to lay it gently in the ground. The enemy likes to blind hearts, as I have been.

He drew a shuddering breath.

"I never thought these hands would be in bins and in dumpsters and in dirt," he said. "Never thought this little shop would feed Mama and me and buy cloths for the little ones. But it's enough, Lord. You've put my hands in this wood, and you've drawn me downtown and to Radford so I might bring back and give a name to what you have made. I can't wait to see them all, Lord, and hear their laughter, playing on your streets, where no one will ever harm that which is helpless, anymore."

The shop was very still. Even the dust and the light seemed to hang quietly, as if they were listening.

"I just want to be where you are," he repeated, voice barely more than a whisper. "If this is where you stand - in the places nobody wants to look, with the little ones nobody claims - then I reckon I'll stand here with you. As long as you'll have me. As long as these hands hold out."

A quiet knowing rose in him: every board on his bench, every table he had built and sold, that money had moved like a current, carrying him back and forth between this shop and those hidden places where nobody else wanted to go. Wood to fuel. Fuel to mercy.

He wiped his face with the back of his wrist and looked down at the damp spots his tears had made on the oak. They would dry. Maybe leave a faint mark, maybe not. Either way, the table would be strong.

“These trees took storms,” he murmured, hearing Gary all over again. “Lots of character comes out when things face storms. It strengthens them and reshapes them.”

He managed a tired, crooked smile. “I reckon I have too.”

He picked the sanding block back up and ran it in slow, even strokes along the edge, following the line where the light met the shadow.

“This one might get Eliza and Patty a surprise trip to Gatlinburg,” the thought warmed his spirit.

He continued with his talk with the Lord.

“You keep on forgiving them, Lord,” he whispered, eyes on the cross. “And I'll keep bringin’ them home best I can. They don't know what they're doin’. But you do. And you know what you're doin’ with me. Til that day there ain't no more death and no more pain.”

Outside, a wind came down off the ridge and rattled the barn boards, like some great hand passing over the hills. Inside, a man, a piece of wood, and a Carpenter-Savior stayed together in the quiet, hands, grain, and grace, work, and worship, woven so tightly that it was impossible to tell where one ended and the other began.

Chapter 18 -

Missing

A week later, Monday felt especially heavy because the truck was running a little warm at the crawl's speed. He already had the day's collections strapped securely in the back. Atlanta baked in the heat that shimmered like a devil's brew. The exhaust was thick enough to choke you when the traffic began to slow down suddenly, as lights and loud sirens pierced the horizon - police cruisers were pulling in right and left as other officers began moving quickly out of their vehicles. There was already a frenzy of reporters pressed together at a yellow tape line, shouting and causing a scene like a hound after a bone - multiple cameras flashing toward some fresh carnage.

Buddy feathered the brake while the parade crawled - strobes of blue, faces gone pale, sirens wailing in the distance. The snarl stretched for endless miles, twisting his northbound haul into a drag. As he waited, he whispered a quick prayer for whoever's world had just been split wide open - knowing too well the feel of a life broken - before and after.

He finally rolled into the farm's gravel drive as the evening presented itself, robed in purple across the meadow. He parked the truck, walked down the hill, and submitted four more names to the Father.

The next morning, downtown Atlanta still crawled with reporters. The yellow tape fluttered at every intersection Buddy passed on his route, bright as dandelions against the concrete and steel. Patrol cars idled at the curb, blue lights turning slowly in the already thick heat, and clusters of men in uniform stood talking in low, urgent voices; their faces drawn in the washed-out light of another too-long night. The radio crackled with static and coded chatter, a constant backdrop of tension he could feel in his bones, but Buddy kept his hands steady on the wheel of his old '62 Ford pickup as he threaded through the city traffic.

The truck rumbled beside him like an old, patient friend, the years having etched its shape to match his own - a little dented and a little weary - but still running on faith and habit. The dash rattled over every pothole, and the fan squeaked in time with his breath; it was the kind of truck that remembered every road it had ever been on.

As he slowed near one of the checkpoints, an officer stepped out from among a cluster of people standing by a cruiser and lifted a hand, motioning for him to stop. Buddy eased the Ford to a halt, rolled down his window, and let the heavy air and the sirens wash in.

"Good morning, Officer," Buddy said, tipping his chin. "What's happening?"

The man leaned in close, one hand on top of the door frame. Buddy could see the fatigue in his eyes - the kind that came from too little sleep and too many bad possibilities.

"We're looking for a little girl," he said, his voice rough. "Five years old. She went missing last night. Blonde hair, blue eyes, red shoes."

He reached into the folder tucked under his arm and handed Buddy a flyer. On the front, above the word *MISSING*, a grainy photo showed a smiling child with tangled, blonde curls and eyes that sparkled with a joy the city didn't deserve. Someone had caught her mid-laugh, chin tipped up as she had just heard the best secret in the world.

Buddy's throat tightened. For a second, he couldn't make his fingers move. He stared at the picture, then down at the red block letters, and felt like the air had been sucked out of the cab.

"Lord, help her," he murmured, bowing his head as if it were the most natural thing in the world to pray over a steering wheel in the middle of an Atlanta highway. He paused long enough to whisper a few words only God could hear, then, lifting his gaze, added louder, "I'll keep my eyes open. If I see anything, I will certainly let you know."

The officer nodded, some of the tension in his shoulders loosening a fraction.

“I appreciate it,” he said, giving the side of the truck a slap. “Drive safe.” He waved Buddy through, and the Ford rolled on.

For the rest of the day, Buddy couldn't shut the image of the little girl's face from his mind. At every stop, as he stepped down from the truck and wrestled with lids and levers, her picture hovered at the edge of his vision - blonde curls, red shoes, that wide open grin. He prayed under his breath, prayers so soft no one else could have heard them, but surely Heaven did.

“Lord, put your hand on her,” he whispered as he rolled one big bin back to the curb. “Bring her home,” he breathed while he hefted another. “Be with her mama,” he added, the words rising from his chest like wood smoke in the hot Georgia air.

Stop after stop, street after street, the same silent plea threaded through his work. The city's heat pressed down hard, shimmering above the black top, and every siren in the distance made his heart lurch and his palms sweat.

The search dragged on throughout the week. News vans crowded the sidewalks and curbs, their satellite antennas jetting toward the sky like accusing fingers. Cameras flashed as volunteers in bright T-shirts combed alleys and vacant lots, forming lines across scrubby patches of ground where the weeds grew through broken concrete. Faces from television stood in front of microphones, mouths moving with words like “developing situation,” “possible leads,” and "community effort". None of it quieted the fear that hung over the city like a storm cloud.

Buddy worked his route as normal, but in every move, he slowed: his eyes were sweeping every corner, every side street, and every shadow between the buildings. He checked porches, fire escapes, and dumpsters behind greasy-spoon restaurants and even the narrow gaps between fences and walls. Every time he turned the truck down a new block, he found himself searching for a flash of blonde hair and a pair of red shoes.

"Lord, let someone find her," he prayed as he drove. "Don't let her be alone." He clenched the steering wheel until his knuckles ached.

Late one afternoon, with the sun sagging low and the sky turning the color of burnt peach over the city skyline, Buddy pulled into a tired-looking gas station on the north side before the long drive to the Falls. The concrete was stained with years of oil and grease, and an old Coke machine hummed miserably against a brick wall. He eased the Ford up to the pump and climbed out, his muscles aching after a very long day.

A weary attendant came out of the office, wiping his hand on a rag that had seen better decades. He nodded a greeting as Buddy took off the gas cap and set the nozzle in, and the pump rang to life.

"How you doin' today?" asked the man, voice casual but eyes taken in more than he said.

"Can't complain," Buddy answered. "Just ready to point this whole thing North and head for home."

Attendant's gaze drifted toward the bed of the truck out of habit more than suspicion, the way people's eyes do when they see a work truck - curious what story the cargo might tell. His gaze landed near the tailgate and stopped. There, shoved against the side, sat a shovel and a black bag from the day's route. It was sealed tightly, edges cinched and knotted, but the canvas was worn through at one corner. And in that frayed spot, a few dark stains - of some type of liquid it appeared - had leaked out onto the metal bed and had dried into a shadow.

The attendant's brow knitted tightly, his hand still holding the old rag as he followed his own line of sight. Buddy saw his focus shift and felt a short, guilty jump in his chest, even though he knew what he hauled. He stepped closer, craning his neck.

"Old bin bag," he said quickly. "Been there since my last stop. I'll get it to the yard in the morning," he tried to make his voice steady, even light. "Probably just some kind of kitchen mess."

Atlanta was full of dirty secrets.

The attendant didn't answer right away. The pump clicked off, and Buddy replaced the nozzle, then walked inside to pay. He bought a cold Coke from the cooler, the glass sweating in his hand, then he paid the man in cash. He tipped his cap as he headed back out.

The attendant watched through the smudged office window as Buddy climbed into the driver's seat, the old Ford coughing twice before the engine caught. Then the truck pulled away, the taillights glowing faint red against the lengthening shadows until it was back on the road and disappeared into the traffic.

For a minute, the attendant stood there, staring at the empty space the truck had left behind, his mind imagining the worst, but hoping he was wrong. Finally, he walked into the small station office where his boss sat behind the counter with a half-finished crossword puzzle in front of him and a fan turning slowly overhead.

"Hey," the attendant said in a low voice. "Did you see that truck just now? That old Ford?"

His boss glanced up, then looked toward the window. "The greenish one with the rusted tailgate?"

"Yeah. That fella," the attendant paused before continuing, "he had something in the back. A black bag. And a shovel. Looked like something might have leaked through. Dark. It almost looked like..." he hesitated, the word catching in his throat, "like blood." Silence settled between them for a beat. "You think maybe..." The attendant's voice trailed off and pointed a thumb back toward the newspaper article pinned behind the counter.

The bold headline screamed across the front page: *MISSING GIRL- FOUL PLAY FEARED.*

The boss followed his gaze; his eyes narrowing. He reached back and took the paper free, scanning the picture - the same blonde-haired girl Buddy had prayed for - the same red shoes, and the same smile that hurt to look at now. He rubbed his chin uneasily.

"You get that tag number?" he asked.

"Sure did," the attendant replied. "Just in case - wrote it down as soon as he got back in his truck."

The boss sighed, the sound heavy.

"Alright. Call it in. Let the cops decide what it is and what it ain't. Better they see it than we sit on it and find out what should have been done too late."

By sundown, the tag number was scribbled in the margin of a detective's notebook downtown - one more line of ink in a day filled with questions and not nearly enough answers. Another thread in the city's widening web of fear, tucked tight by hands that didn't yet know whose life they were weaving into the center.

Meanwhile, Buddy drove north toward the Falls, unaware of the storm gathering behind him. The highway opened as the city slowly fell away - buildings giving way to trees, billboards to ridgelines. The air cooled by a few degrees as he climbed, and the first stars blinked overhead shyly in the distance. His mind stayed in Atlanta, though, circling the same image: blonde hair, red shoes, gap-tooth grin. He kept praying, words quiet but constant, a thread tying his heart to a child he had never met.

"Lord," he softly said, hands resting on the worn steering wheel, "You see her. You know where she is. Don't leave her alone tonight. Be with her mama. Be with whoever's out there searching for her. Turn somebody's head at the right time. Let dark things come out in the light."

The old Ford hummed along, the engine steady; the tires singing their own, low song against the pavement. Pines rose black against the deepening blue. Somewhere behind him, men in suits and uniforms were already tracing his tag number across papers and screens, already seeing his name in rooms lit by fluorescent buzz and fear. But he didn't know any of that. All he knew was the road, the truck, the feel of the wheel under his hands, and the edge of a prayer that wouldn't let him go.

The little girl's face stayed with him, hovering on the edge of his thoughts like a photograph taped on his skull. It would follow him long into the night, into his dreams and restless turnings, long after the last light at the farmhouse went dark. North of Atlanta, summer held its breath over Rabun as Heaven listened to a tired man in his truck whispering the same plea for a child they were scrambling to find.

Chapter 19 –

River of Lights

The sky over Duluth was just awakening with streaks of red and silver over Stone Mountain as a fog blanket settled at its base. Buddy sipped his coffee from his thermos that had been resting on the seat. With the windows down, the fresh morning air was rushing in, and an AM talk show crackled on the staticky radio.

He heard his daddy's voice saying, "Red sky in the morning, loggers take warning."

He chuckled.

Light traffic allowed time to meditate. His mind turned to Patty, his faithful childhood friend. She had been so good to Eliza after Gary's passing. Buddy whispered a prayer of blessing for her.

He rounded the next bend. Flashing blue lights reflected across the windshield like lightning ahead of a storm. Patrol cars swarmed the shoulder, lights spangled off concrete and glass. Buddy's first thought was courtesy: pull off and let them pass - saying a prayer for whoever was in trouble. He slowed and steered to the side.

The nearest patrol car pulled in behind him; another swung across the front bumper. Within seconds, half a dozen cars surrounded him as doors flew open, and officers began shouting commands. His hands rose on instinct as confusion began to tighten in his chest.

"What's this about?" he asked. His voice stayed steady. But his heart hammered.

A trooper yanked open the door, pulled him out, and cuffed his wrists before he could speak again. They tore through the truck with mechanical precision - under the seats, behind the cab bench, under the tarp in the bed. Nothing to find. It was early; his route had not begun yet. No mercy seemed written into them this morning. The officers kept their faces square and their movements precise. One radioed in,

"The suspect detained, vehicle cleared, we're bringing him in."

Minutes later, Buddy sat in the back of a patrol car. Strobing lights washed over his pale hands and the cracked dashboard ahead. His mind spun. *Suspect of what?* He tried to speak, the engine's hum drowning him out.

The convoy headed south - a river of flashing blue lights as downtown rose in the distance, the city's skyline dancing in the morning sun. Before long, they pulled beneath the stone archway of the county jail. Reporters were already crowding the steps, their microphones and cameras jostling for a view as the car door opened.

"Is that him?" someone shouted.

"Can we get a name?" came from another.

The uniformed officer answered as Buddy was led past the cameras. "Gary Holcomb, from Rabun County."

Questions, shouts, and camera flashes sparked madly.

"Was he arrested in connection with the missing girl?" a voice called.

"No comment at this time," the officer barked, pushing through the doors. The cuffs bit into Buddy's wrists. The weight of misunderstanding pressed deeply into his chest.

From the edge of the crowd, Channel 3's Donna Chambers pushed forward, not hearing the full name, her notebook clutched tightly.

"Can we see a picture?" she called after the detectives.

The reply came from the PR Sergeant near the door. "Later this evening, there will be a full release once we have finished questioning."

The cameras turned on her as she repeated the report live, unaware of how close she was to the story as the man was ushered inside - a man who once loved a girl who had also vanished years ago, who now stood branded by the world's worst suspicions.

The police hall buzzed under cold lights. They uncuffed Buddy at a bolted table.

"I'm Detective Harris. Gary Holcomb, correct?" the plainclothes gentleman stated.

"Gary Holcomb Junior is my full name, sir. I've always gone by Buddy, though."

The detective dropped a folder with a flyer on top, showing the blonde curls and the bright smile. "Know anything about this?"

"I heard about it a few days ago," he responded. "I've been praying for her."

"We have witnesses that say they saw your truck in the area where the little girl went missing," he said.

"What area is that?" Buddy asked simply. "I work for a small sanitation company downtown."

Detective Harris leaned in close, coffee-tainted breath warm. "Witnesses say they saw what appeared to be blood in the back of your truck. Can you explain that?"

"Where exactly do you live?" he also asked as he continued to hammer him with questions.

Buddy answered him directly, "I live on my family's farm on the Habersham-Rabun County line."

The detective's jaw tightened. "You mean to tell me you drive over an hour and a half for a minimum wage job? I don't buy it."

The detective took a breath and quickly continued, “Do you live alone? Are you married?”

“No,” answered Buddy. “I still have my mama, but she doesn't get around very well. Lost my dad some time back.”

“Why don't you move closer to your job?” asked the detective.

“I guess memories give more to a man than money,” Buddy quietly uttered.

The hours dragged. The questions looped. The flyer stared as Buddy remembered Daddy's hymns: “Precious Lord, Take My Hand.” In the interrogation room, Buddy’s legs grew numb as his prayers rose quietly so that the truth would become known.

Chapter 20 - Shadows of the Lake

Once, Donna Hargrove was a young, unknown field reporter who humbly began working at Channel 3. Now her name rang across Georgia as the station's lead evening news anchor. But Buddy Holcomb never knew. The Holcomb home TV sat dark, gathering dust - no screens lit up their quiet woods.

Years had carved poise into her sharp edges. Money had bought a Buckhead home that included a pool and several fine cars. Her handsome pilot husband, who was absorbed with making his own mark on the world, was gone more than he was at home. To viewers looking at her on live TV, her life looked charming and glamorous. But a quiet emptiness had trailed her for decades - the shadow of the lake, a promise made, and the boy she once loved with every young heartbeat.

That morning in the newsroom, footage rolled across the monitors. Police cars with flashing lights and a small-town Georgia man led through the jail crowd. Donna leaned closer. The world began to narrow. She knew that tilt of the jaw, and the shape of those shoulders bowed under strain.

She froze.

"Buddy?" she exclaimed under her breath.

All noise faded: reporters talking over each other, phones ringing sharply, and the hum of the bright studio lights. All she heard was her own heartbeat thundering in her ears.

Married or not. Success or unknown. One glance pulled her back - moonlight on the water, his laughter warm in the summer air, a name whispered softly against her skin, and a promise sealed in young love.

"I have to get there," she murmured, half to herself.

The news chief frowned. "Donna? You okay?"

"Fine," she lied, already grabbing her credentials and heading for the door.

By mid-afternoon, the jailhouse steps churned with questions and camera lenses. Inside, Buddy sat under harsh lights, his shirt rumpled and his eyes hollowed from hours of questioning. The detectives pressed again about Atlanta's missing child - days gone now with no sign of her, no hope left unspoken.

Each time, he gave the same answer, quiet and steady. "I don't know anything about that little girl. I've been praying for her - same as you."

His sincerity only muddled their confusion. By late day, the press clamored outside for a statement. Street interviews buzzed. Public condemnations flew. Judge and jury already.

“You know he did it,” one said. “Fits the profile.”

When the metal door swung open, Buddy stepped into the glare. The crowd surged forward.

“Mr. Holcomb! Did you know her?”

“Connected to the search?”

“Where were you that night?”

He said nothing, only shielded his eyes from the flashbulbs popping like gunfire.

Then he saw her.

Standing just beyond the police tape with a notebook hanging loosely in her hands. Her eyes were wide.

Donna Hargrove.

Time unfolded slowly. The lake shimmered in memory with echoes of laughter, then heartbreak bloomed fresh. Their eyes locked through the storm of lenses and shouting voices. Her breath caught. Tears welled until the world blurred.

“That's my Buddy,” she whispered, her voice trembling too softly for cameras.

An officer guided him to the squad car. But he turned once more - the faintest nod passed between them - recognition, forgiveness, grace unnamed, and flickers of time lost.

The door slammed. And the engines began to roar. The convoy pulled north toward the Falls. Blue lights faded into the evening hush.

Donna stood rooted behind the barrier, the press swirling around her. For the first time in years, her practiced words deserted her. She simply watched until the last taillight disappeared down the highway. The ache in her chest felt both old and new.

Buddy rode silently in the patrol car. The cuffs chafed his wrists, yet he barely noticed the discomfort. As fields began to roll past, his mind recalled the look on her face.

Donna.

She was still just as beautiful to him as if no years had passed since he last gazed at her. He wondered how she came to be there. A thousand thoughts began to cross his mind. He closed his eyes as pine scent began slipping in through the vents. Then Buddy felt a calm peace come over him, and he began to hum a familiar hymn - knowing God was with him.

The detective in front glanced back. "You got friends in high places. That reporter looked ready to cry."

Buddy stared out the window. "Just old memories."

Back at Channel 3, Donna's hands shook as she gripped the desk.

Chief leaned in. "What's going on with you? You are not acting like yourself."

"That man. Buddy Holcomb. The one they have in custody..." she started without blinking.

She was still lost in her memories, her face having gone pale.

"You knew him?"

She nodded slowly. "From... before. Tallulah Falls. A lifetime ago."

"Conflict?" he asked, concerned.

"No," she said firmly. "The Truth? I know his heart."

The evening news aired her report - her voice calm and steady, but viewers saw something more: a flicker in her eyes; faith and innocence amidst a storm.

Chapter 21 –

Night at the Farm

"I know where they're going," Donna whispered to herself, shoving her press badge deep into her purse. With the broadcast completed, she could no longer wait- she had to get there. She hurried past the camera crew, who were shouting after her as she made her way to the parking lot and slipped behind the wheel of her sedan.

Lord, give me strength, she prayed silently, her hands trembling at the ignition. Atlanta's skyline faded in her rearview mirror, soon replaced by the silhouette of boastful ridges.

As she made her way back to Buddy's mountains, she felt a haunting echo of grace calling her home. For two hours, she followed the ribbon of highway back to the past - to sleepy, small towns and winding mountain roads where headlights carve brief tunnels through the mist. Fog clung to the valleys like a layer of cotton candy. She didn't dare call ahead. No.

She only knew she had to see for herself what they were accusing the love of her life of.

When her car veered onto the gravel track marked Holcomb Lane, her chest tightened like a vice. The long, familiar smells of pine and the damp earth began flooding through her cracked window, causing a rush of memories, previously tucked away in the recesses of her mind - pulling her back twenty years. *This place,* she thought. *God's quiet cathedral.* So different from the chaos of her own childhood home, where shouts drowned out love and doors slammed on dreams.

The memories seemed so real as they took over her mind: the long talks with Eliza on that very porch, rocking slowly as fireflies danced, where she shared Buddy's boyhood favorites, like whittling sticks by the creek, precious Bible verses memorized under Gary's steady gaze, and the way he prayed over injured birds before letting them fly free.

"*That boy's got a heart like David,"* Eliza always said. "*Tender under the fight.*"

Gary's absolute peace had wrapped them all - a peace that passed everything Donna had ever known in her polished, empty world. She saw Buddy's long walks by moonlight; Panther Creek singing its song beside them and its wild rhythms pulsing like God's own heartbeat. And covenants whispered between two young hearts under the stars - lying shoulder to shoulder in the grassy meadow, their hands linked and staring up at the miracles of their Creator - shooting stars streaking like promises kept.

"Oh, Buddy," she breathed. "Did we lose our way?"

At the farmhouse, the convoy that had arrived much earlier had piled into the yard and had parked without any set pattern or order - cars seemed to be everywhere - on the grass and the gravel road. Donna parked far down the drive, killed the engine, and sat barely breathing - her heart hammering. From the shadows, she watched the porch lights flickering warmly against the night, the shadows stretching long across the yard like faithful sentinels.

Inside, Eliza Holcomb sat propped in her rocker, her frail hands gripping the quilt over her lap - stitched by those same hands through decades of Holcomb winters. The fireplace crackled steadily, even on this mild night, because its glow chased shadows and its warmth remembered Gary's laugh. The commotion at the door startled her - a heavy knock that rattled the quiet like a thunderstorm. She tried to rise anyway, her bones protesting softly.

"Can I help y'all?" her voice quivered, laced with gentleness of almost eighty-three years.

"Ma'am, we're here on official business," the lead officer said softly, tipping his hat as a gesture of respect and then giving her a paper that gave them the authority to enter, while others stepped past into her sanctuary.

Heavy boots thudded across worn pine floors. Flashlight beams sliced sharply through the corners of the tiny rooms, hunting for secrets in places where only grace had ever lived. They rifled through every closet and cabinet with an urgency she did not understand, then tromped out to the shed. Eliza never realized that her son was waiting out in the yard in the back of a police car. Relentless and irreverent - yet the farm yielded nothing but sights and sounds of simple, God-filled living: neat stacks of split firewood under the eaves, mud-caked boots by the back door, and a family Bible sitting on the kitchen table beside Eliza's half-knit shawl. Bread dough rose slowly under a clean cloth, yeast scent mingling sweet with turpentine drifting faintly from the barn where Buddy carved gospel truths into wood.

Eliza sat quietly, rocking with a prayer steady on her lips. “Lord, let your light shine here.”

After half an hour, the detective exhaled heavily, wiping sweat from his brow.

“Nothing here but country,” he murmured to his team, his voice thick with the weight of empty hands. “We'll regroup at sunrise - sweep the property completely when there's more light. Y’all get a little shut eye in the meantime.”

Outside, flashlights were shut off, one by one. The officers began climbing slowly back into their cruisers that were previously exited in a rush in front of the house - their headlights on bright, the beams cutting foggy ghosts through the pines and their police radios fading out as they each watched the moon rise over the farm. The night settled into an easy, waiting quiet, as dew beaded heavily on the leaves.

Down the gravel driveway- hidden deeply in the long tree shadows- Donna stayed put in her car, watching every move.

Her heart pounded not with fear, but with iron certainty. The answer she had run from for twenty years waited somewhere on the farm, wrapped in the same love that had driven her to Lake Rabun's dock all those summers ago - young promises sealed in moonlight -unbreakable. It pulled her now toward the warm, clap-board house glowing at the lane's end, a beacon through her prodigal years.

She whispered again into the velvet darkness, "Hold on, Buddy. Hold on, I am here."

A tear traced her cheek; prayer rising unbidden. *Father, protect what's yours.*

The mountains stood peacefully back in silence, broken only by a distant hoot owl's call - lonesome, then gone.

Dawn hovered just hours away with gray light promising truth on the horizon.

Chapter 22 -

Stones in the Morning Light

The first colors of dawn broke across the ridgeline - strong streaks of pink and violet. Mist drifted up from Tallulah Gorge, softening the edges of the pines. The officers had been there before sunrise - they began to stir in their cars with the majority of them rubbing sleep from their eyes.

“All right, men,” the lead detective called, stepping into the cool morning air. He looked out at the expansive forest that seemed to stretch toward heaven. “Let's find this girl. It's going to be a long day.”

Engines coughed to life. Radios began to crackle. Men laughed low, shaking off the night.

Buddy said silently in the back seat of the patrol car, his wrists still cuffed and his face drawn, but calm. His breath fogged the window as he stared up toward the hillside that crowned the Holcomb farm. Beyond that rise lay the creek - the same creek where he had buried Tony so long ago.

Down the gravel road, Donna parked her sedan and began to walk. The air was a bit sharp and clean. The gravel crunched loudly under her toes. She moved slowly, keeping close to the fence line as she heard several car doors open ahead, and voices scatter through the trees.

“Buddy?” she whispered toward the house, barely daring to breathe.

No answer at first. Woodpeckers rang through the trees. An early crow cried out sharply. Then, finally, through the gray light, his voice came low, but certain.

“Donna? Is that you? My love... you're here.”

Her eyes filled as she reached the car window where he sat. For a fragment of a second, the past unfolded. Lake Rabun shimmered.

“Buddy, are you all right? What is this?” she whispered.

He looked at her, tears cutting clean streaks through the grime on his face.

“I did it for us. For them. To make it right.”

“Did what, Buddy?”

A sharp shout sliced through the quiet behind him.

“Hey - what are you doing over there?”

An officer jogged down from the hill, coming closer. Donna straightened, her hands trembling.

"Mrs. Chambers?" The man stopped short - instantly recognizing her from TV.

"What are you doing here? We're not giving interviews yet. Please - you'll end up working on this story from inside a jail if they find you here. And me too. Come on up with us, but don't talk to him again."

Donna nodded gently, feeling guilty and afraid, and followed as the officer led her up the hill beyond the barn. The rest of the search team had already climbed halfway up.

Then, as the sun crested the ridge, a shimmer spread across the ground. Silver, white sparkles flickered through the dew and wildflowers. The men stopped walking. A hush fell over them.

"What on earth?" one muttered.

Donna caught her breath.

Hundreds - maybe thousands - of small stones dotted the slope. Smooth, round, flat river rocks, each one chiseled by hand with a single name and a single date. Some so faint they could barely be read. Morning light struck their granite faces until they gleamed like a field of stars spilling down to the water at the base of the hill at Panther Creek.

Way on southward, its bed was almost bare of any rock, except for some large boulders too heavy to tote. But Buddy had taken them all. Each stone a story. Each grave was a silent prayer for a child the world had thrown away.

"Dear God," Officer Ray whispered, his hat pressed to his chest. "What are we looking at here?"

No one said a word. The wind moved through the trees, stirring dandelions to their puffs, seeds floating farther than anyone had imagined.

Down below, in the cruiser, Buddy closed his eyes and let the sunlight touch his face - for the first time in years without shame. He felt no need to explain. The evidence spoke for him now. One grave, and then another, and then another. His truth was shining quietly in the new day. His calling was revealed.

The sun climbed higher, gliding over every carved name.

Baby Grace, 1978. Little Hope, 1980. Samuel, Beloved, 1983.

Each stone a marker Buddy had hauled from the creek bed in moonlight hours and then chiseled with calloused hands and whispered Psalms. No fanfare. No fame. Just a man doing God's quiet work for the least of these.

Donna knelt by the nearest stone; her fingers tracing the faded letters.

The detective paced slowly among the graves; the radio had gone silent in his hand.

"This changes everything," he murmured, his voice thick.

One officer knelt and began reading names aloud like a litany. Another crossed himself - his eyes lifted heavenward.

Chapter 23 –

Atlanta at Dawn

“Better get a hold of the Chief on this one,” the detective stated flatly, staring at the hillside shimmering with the white stones. “And get the old woman's statement. No sign of the little girl alive here- only the dead.” His voice carried like a heavy weight as his eyes scanned the graves and the names edged in granite.

The team moved quickly. Orders crackled through the radios like dry lightning. Officers went back to their cars and began gathering shovels, gloves, and cameras. Buddy watched from the patrol car, his face steady through the window, as the sunlight caught the silver in his hair.

Lord, let them see, he prayed silently.

“Let's get him back downtown. We're going to need a recorded statement,” another officer said, his voice edged with procedure. Gravel spat beneath tires as one by one the convoy threaded down the hill.

Donna stood off to the side of the drive, clutching her notebook but writing nothing - pen limp in her hand and her heart full. She couldn't look away from Buddy's silhouette: head bowed and shoulders proud in the back seat, like David bowing before giants. The same love that had pulled and reached her heart so long ago now anchored her here.

Theodore McCall sat at the scarred oak table with his elbows planted on both sides of the morning paper, though he stopped reading hours ago. The ink had blurred where his thumb kept rubbing the same corner, smearing the headlines about the missing girl into a gray, meaningless haze. His granddaughter's preschool picture from last year - the only one he had framed- stared back at him from a side table. The gap-tooth smile mocked the silence that had swallowed the house.

Down the hall, Clara's room sat untouched. The pink bedspread lay smoothly, stuffed animals lined in their usual row, and her favorite doll on the pillow as if waiting for small hands to return. Ever since he had heard Lydia's screams, and she had come running into the house with tears streaming down her face, clutching that same doll in her hands where she had found it lying in the backyard, as Clara did not go anywhere without it, Theodore could not look at that doorway without something hard and unforgiving rising in his chest. A man's home ought to ring with children's laughter, not police radios and whispers.

His son paced the kitchen like a restless hound; his boots were wearing a dark track on the linoleum.

"They're not doing enough," Ronnie murmured for the tenth time, his fingers dragging through his hair. "The sheriff, the deputies - they just talk, no action."

"Sit down, Ronnie," Theodore said, though his own legs itched to move. "We've got to keep our heads."

Across from him, his wife clutched a dish towel in both hands, ringing it until the cotton appeared faded, and twisted it as tight as a rope. The coffee in her cup had long gone cold. She hadn't even noticed.

"Maybe she's just..." Lydia's voice trembled. "Maybe somebody got the story wrong. Maybe her mama knows where she is. Maybe she..."

"She doesn't know!" Ronnie snapped, his voice cracking. "She would be over here screaming my name. You know how she is." Hurt and pride flared across his face, old resentments rising. "She doesn't care about her. She hasn't even called to check on her lately. And she won't give me her number. I hate that woman."

Theodore studied his boy. Thirty-one years old, shoulders as broad as his own, but right now he looked like a wild-eyed twelve-year-old again, desperate. It was the same look he had worn as a teenager when Theodore had tried to discipline a son who wouldn't listen, a son too much like himself. He had failed then; he told himself, but he would not fail now.

"The sheriff says they've got people looking by the river," Theodore said. "They'll find her."

The words felt thin, like tissue paper stretched over a hole.

Ronnie stopped pacing. His palms slammed flat on the table.

"You heard what folks are saying," as his voice dropped to a hoarse whisper. "They saw that truck near our house. And something's wrong with that fella. He's... off."

Lydia flinched. "Ronnie, you don't know that. His truck comes by here all the time. It could be anybody."

Theodore's jaw tightened. He had watched Buddy come and go into the warehouse for years now, carrying metal bins to and from the van. He had seen the hollow stare on certain days, the way the younger man lingered at the edge of the street, his eyes tracking children with a sadness that was hard to read - guilt, grief, or something else. Theodore had never been sure.

"He seems like he's had a hard life," Lydia said more softly. "What may have happened to him, what he might have lost - we don't know what's going on inside his head."

"We know enough," Ronnie shot back. "He was there. People saw. And my little girl's gone."

The last word broke on a sob he tried to swallow.

Theodore's gaze drifted to the open Bible near his elbow. Lydia had laid it there at dawn, its pages fluttering until they settled somewhere in the Psalms. His eyes skimmed lines about enemies, about God being a shield, about deliverance. Other words rose from memory instead - ones his own father had liked to quote, standing tall and stern over a younger Theodore:

A man who won't protect his own ain't worth the boots he's standing in.

He could almost hear his father's voice now. That old shame burned in his chest, tugging him back to the night a neighbor's boy had gone missing when he was a boy himself. Men had gathered on porches, talking big and doing little. Fortunately, the boy was found a few days later, and every man in town had carried the weight of "could have" and "should have".

Not this time, he thought.

Across the table, Lydia spoke again.

"Hasn't she called, Ronnie? Didn't she say something about wanting to see you last month - when she called then?"

Ronnie looked away. "She just wanted money. I told her I'm cutting her off. No more."

"She might know something," Lydia pressed.

"Mom, she's in New Jersey now. With another man. She doesn't care about Clara."

"She might be acting foolishly now," Theodore said quietly, "but she loves that child."

Ronnie's shoulders sagged, guilt flickering and gone. He didn't correct his father. He didn't mention the conversation with Susie last month when she asked to see Clara. It had felt, at the time, like just one more way for her to use their daughter to get under his skin. Now, with the town whispering and the thoughts of abduction closing in, that same choice sat on his chest like a cinder block. But he said nothing.

“I've got to get back out looking for her,” Ronnie said.

“You're going to have to eat something and sleep,” Lydia answered.

“I will. Later.”

Theodore pushed back from the table and stood. His knees popped in protest, reminding him he was no longer the young man who could run the hills from dawn to dusk. But something in him rose taller than his years - a stiffening born of anger and love braided together.

“I'm not gonna sit here while some twisted soul does God knows what to my granddaughter!” he stated passionately.

The dish towel slipped from Lydia’s hands onto the floor.

“Theo, don't,” she pleaded. “The sheriff said...”

“The sheriff said he'll follow up on leads,” Theodore snapped. “Leads don't keep a child warm at night.”

He jerked his chin toward the side table, toward the smiling picture.

“That little girl can't fight for herself. She deserves somebody to stand for her.”

Ronnie's eyes flashed. "So, what are you going to do? Go after the man yourself?"

"You said it yourself - he tried to talk to your mama and Clara the other day. You want me to wait until we get a call from Atlanta saying they found her in a ditch?" Theodore almost yelled.

The words tasted like iron on his tongue.

"He was just being friendly," Lydia said weakly. "Wait. Be patient. They'll find her."

Silence settled heavily over the kitchen. A clock ticked in the living room with each second landing like a hammer. Lydia's lips moved in a silent prayer.

"Theo," she tried again, her voice shaking, "What if you are wrong? Talk to Old Man Radford, see if he knows anything, see if he's seen anything."

"I haven't seen Radford around in years," Theodore muttered.

He looked at Lydia - the woman who had stood beside him through war, funerals, lean years, and good ones. He saw fear in her eyes, and for a heartbeat, doubt knocked at his own heart.

What if...

Then he pictured Clara's empty bed. The stories he had heard all his life came rushing back - children taken, families ruined, men wringing their hands and saying,

"We never thought it could happen here."

Heat surged back through his veins.

"If I'm wrong," he said in a muffled voice, "I'll answer for it. But if I sit on my hands and I am right, I won't be able to look at myself in the mirror."

He crossed to the cabinet in the hallway, the one he kept locked since the boys were young. The key hung high, exactly where it had been for decades. His hands didn't shake as he took them down. The click of the lock sounded too loud in the quiet house.

"Daddy," Ronnie whispered, some of the bravado gone, "This isn't like putting down a dog that's got rabies."

Theodore slid the gun from its place, the familiar weight settling into his hands.

"If a dog threatens your family, you don't wait for paperwork," he said. "You do what needs to be done."

"Please," Lydia pleaded, tears beginning to spill down her face. "At least wait on the Sheriff. Or talk to the Reverend. Pray with somebody before you decide your judge and jury."

"I have prayed," Theodore answered, and he believed it. The words he had thrown toward heaven in the dark hours of the night - pleas, bargains, half-formed verses - felt like prayers to him.

He took Lydia's hand for a moment and squeezed.

"God put this family in my care. You may not like how I do it, but I will not stand aside."

He put on his jacket - the old denim one he wore for serious business - and stepped toward the door. The screen made a loud protest as it opened, then banged once when he let it fall behind him.

Lydia followed to the porch, stopping at the top step. The cold morning air rushed in, carrying with it the distant wail of sirens somewhere across town.

"Theodore McCall," she called after him, her voice breaking, "God help you if you're wrong."

He did not look back.

The convoy hit the main road where the reporters had already gathered behind barricades - word of what was discovered in the mountains was spreading like wildfire through the Georgia pines. News vans hummed. The crowd swelled into a relentless sea of microphones and flashbulbs popping like judgment hail.

As the lead car rolled to a stop, voices rose sharply, and overlapping questions began pelting the police line:

"What about the graves?"

"Were there remains?"

"Where's the girl?"

The uniformed officer stepped from the first cruiser, his hand steady on the gun in his holster, and opened the back door where Buddy sat. He had spent the whole night cuffed - his hands raw from the metal bites in his wrists and his body stiff from the lack of movement. Now, sun in full light, he stood straight and tall again. Unbroken. His eyes were calm and held a warmth that was drawing.

Donna, having parked just behind the last patrol car, pushed through the noise and called out to him anxiously,

"Buddy!"

Cameras swerved hungrily.

"Sir, over here!" a reporter yelled. Chaos tore the morning in half, voices exploding at once.

Then - a man broke from the crowd, his face twisted in anguish and rage, his pistol shaking wildly in his weathered hands. His granddaughter's name burned unspoken in his eyes. His shout came hoarse and raw:

"That's my granddaughter, you son-of-a-..."

Two sharp cracks split the air like heaven being torn. Buddy staggered back, the shots flashing white across his eyes as crimson bloomed across the front of his faded shirt. He fell to his knees, his eyes wide in shock, his breath escaping in a hard gasp as pain began to sear through every part of him, and he hit the pavement as if in a final prayer.

Donna screamed - raw, primal, the sound of Lake Rabun summers shattering. Time slowed to fragments: the echo of gunfire bouncing off courthouse steps carved with justice words, officers shouting orders lost in the roar, reporters diving for cover behind their vans, and people crying out in frozen horror. The shooter stood stunned, then Theodore McCall lowered his pistol to the pavement like a man waking from a fevered dream, his hands trembling and empty now.

Donna shoved past the wall of bodies - press, police, strangers - and dropped beside Buddy. Her pink blouse became darker by the second, his blood warm and accusing, as she tried to lift his failing weight.

“Buddy, talk to me,” she pleaded, her tears spilling hot. “You're going to be all right. Stay with me, please!”

His lips trembled, his eyes finding hers through the pain’s gathering fog - knowing his love had never faded for her - even after all the time that had passed.

“Tony,” he whispered faintly, his voice growing weak. “My love... I named him Tony. We loved him. All of them. You loved them, didn't you, Donna?”

“Yes my love, yes.” Her words choked on sobs, her hands cradling what years had stolen.

She kept his face in both hands, blood slick against her palms, her thumbs tracing the jaw she had memorized under moonlight.

“Don't go! Don't go, my angel. We...” with her sobs and words interrupted.

Sirens wailed closer now, an ambulance crawling through the chaos. Officers pushed the crowd back, batons firm. But Donna couldn't hear them - only his slowing breath, a quiet between heartbeats. The echo of a life spent hauling river stones and whispering Psalms over tiny graves the world forgot. His hand fell gently against her shoulder, his hair damp against her neck.

"God help us," someone murmured nearby. Followed by a few soft *Amens.*

Paramedics swarmed in and began prying her away.

"Ma'am - we need you to move!" Monitors beat frantically. Needles flashed.

Pulse thready. BP dropping.

They lifted him onto the stretcher, the oxygen mask fogging with shallow draws. Donna stumbled back, her eyes full, her shirt ruined, and her hands a stained witness.

Donna was oblivious to the massive group of microphones and cameras that had captured the whole scene- many cold and unfeeling lenses - that were fixed on the woman in a blood-soaked blouse as she cradled the love of her life - that the entire world seemed to hate.

Chapter 24 -

The Meadow

Headlines screamed across Georgia the next morning, dividing the state in two:

One Man Dead. One Arrested. Mystery Deepens in Rabun County.

Reporters camped from folding chairs outside the county jail, their microphones hungry for scandal. A grandfather sat shattered in a holding cell - grief twisting his murder charge into regret's cold cage. Another lay cold in the morgue, name flooding the broadcast:

Buddy Holcomb, 38, a logger turned sanitation driver, was shot to death by the grandfather of a missing child.

Donna Chambers - once Hargrove - wandered the edges half-conscious with blood-stained hands scrubbed raw, but the memory clinging: his final 'Tony' whisper, their eyes locking for one last time.

Guilt gnawing her hollow.

Back at the Holcomb farm, the investigation had turned solemn. Morning mist clung damply to the grass as deputies crossed the five-acre meadow. Eliza testified that Gary Sr. and Buddy had cleared decades ago. They had deeded it to Grace Fellowship as a Potter's Field - a tithe of ten percent from Gary's fifty blessed acres. Strangers passing without a home church might rest there. Little did Gary know it cradled his own bones now, alongside thousands more. He always felt kin to the lost, the poor, the helpless - Jesus' least, always etched in his callous prayers.

Wet earth scent mingled with diesel and cooling coffee. Everywhere their eyes turned was fresh soil patched neatly, squares made deliberately as stitches on a quilt or the mending of a vast wound.

"Start here," the lead detective ordered, pointing to a smaller mound that appeared to have been made recently. *Within a year, the soil whispered.* The shovels bit softly.

Silence held but for metal scraping on clay. Then a deputy knelt, brushing dirt gently from a chiseled rock that was no larger than a man's footprint. A faint name surfaced.

Date etched thinly:

1975- Joanne.

"Found one," he called, his voice catching.

More were yielded up quickly. The ground between the pines surrendering stone after stone, each guarding disturbed earth. Under some, fabric lingered - woven cotton wrapped tightly like swaddling clothes - with soil clinging to it like a final embrace.

A young officer, academy-fresh, crouched low at another.

“Sir, a cloth blanket here. It's hardened, and there’s something dried and stiff on it.”

The detective exhaled heavily, and his head began shaking slowly.

“Don't force it open. Bag a half dozen or so for the lab. Be gentle,” his muddy fingers pressed his temple. His eyes swept the field. “Long week ahead, men.”

They labored until late in the evening, the tally climbing in a surreal way.

“Ten... two-hundred... 10,201, sir,” the deputy announced finally, his back stiff, yet humbled to have witnessed mercy's math.

The shovels stilled. Sunlight danced over the pale stones - an ocean of names, dates, and prayers dotting the ridge where Panther Creek kissed the hill. Senior detectives in rumpled suits and officers with earth-stained uniforms all stood frozen. Some shook their heads with disbelief - the scene cracking through the toughest shell of each man. Others murmured curses softly or prayers under their breath.

Crime scene? Cemetery? Testament? Words failed the sacred.

The lead detective tugged off his hat and wiped his brow slowly.

“10,201 graves,” he uttered, feeling overwhelmed at the site. “I thought I had seen everything.”

Beyond them, the mountains stood sentinel with a hush. The creek whispered through rocks Buddy had left untouched - a steady song of grace, unbound. The sun dipped behind the ridge, washing the meadow golden like heaven's own gleam - like stars carved deeply into Earth's tender heart.

Chapter 25 -

Patty Hall's Visit

Sunset spilled across the Holcomb porch as a woman made her way up the gravel path with her arms full - a basket and a poke sack full of food. Her brown hair was pinned back neatly, and her steps were sure despite the slanted boards on the old porch. Near the driveway, a young deputy stood guard.

“Ma'am. I’m sorry, ma'am. You can't go in there right now.”

But she was already gently pushing past him.

“You hush, Son,” she said with a smile more commanding than with any request, “I've known these folks all my life. Ain't no better people on God's green Earth.”

The deputy hesitated, then let her by. The door opened with a shoulder nudge.

"Hey, Mrs. Eliza," she called, her voice bright and familiar, "brought your bananas and peppermint sticks, just the way you like."

Eliza's face lifted from the rocker, lighting softly as if seeing her own daughter.

"Pattygirl," she whispered, "I've been waiting to see you all week."

Patty Hall set the baskets on the table and looked around at the strangers filling the house - wires, cameras, and lights cluttered in all corners.

"Mercy," she said softly. "What's all this?"

"These men have been swarming around whispering about stones down by the meadow. I can't see from where I am. I ain't been able to get down there for about fifteen years now... Where's my Buddy?" Eliza blinked, confusion softening her eyes. "He'll be home soon, I suppose," she said more to herself, her voice wavering somewhere between comfort and wonder.

The deputy gave them a few quiet moments before clearing his throat at the door.

"Ma'am," speaking to Patty, "when you have a moment, the officer in charge would like a word with you."

Patty gathered her now-empty baskets after visiting Eliza and stepped outside.

"All right, young man," she said as the lead detective approached. "What can I do for y'all?"

"Ma'am," he began, "have you seen the news lately?"

"I have," she said simply, though her eyes began to fill.

The detective adjusted his hat. "How long have you known Gary Holcomb?"

"You must mean Buddy?" she corrected him gently. "Known him since we crawled under the pews together at Grace Fellowship. His daddy preached there till the day he passed."

"Have you seen Buddy lately?"

Patty nodded. "Every week since Gary Sr. died several years back. Eliza has been my closest neighbor and my friend, so I bring by a few goodies - dry goods, fruit, and such - from my store, but she and Buddy appreciate it."

"So you say her and Buddy..."

"Of course," she said brightly, "he's usually right here with me on the front porch till dark -sometimes we'd talk about faith, the weather, price of lumber."

The detective scribbled notes, trying to keep up with a life that seemed simpler and deeper than his notebook lines could hold.

"Did he mention to you where he worked in Atlanta?"

She frowned a little. “Well, he drove downtown most days. He said it was some kind of dirty sanitation work, but it was steady pay. He was mighty particular about the cloth he bought - had to have the best cotton. Always demanded the best kind. I always thought he would log full-time and take on the pulpit like his father. And he had the ability, but something drew him toward the city.”

“Ever ask what for?”

“Oh yeah, and he'd smile and say, ‘For work’,” she shook her head, a small smile touching her lips. “Never pushed more than that.”

The detective closed his notebook. “Miss Hall, would you be willing to answer a few more questions in the morning in Atlanta?”

She gave him a strange look. “The truth doesn't make any difference between counties.”

“We record our interviews down at the station, Ma'am.”

“You driving? I don't do too well in all that busyness.”

“Yes ma'am, and we'll bring you back,” he added thoughtfully.

“Okay. I've got to look after Mrs. Eliza in all this,” she said, glancing back toward the farmhouse, where grief and holy memories mingled in every room.

The detective managed a slight smile.

“Yes ma'am. We appreciate you helping us all.”

“Miss Patty,” she corrected him with her basket on her arm like always.

“I will pick you up in the morning.”

Patty checked on Mrs. Eliza early the next morning and met the detective on the porch.

As the patrol car pulled away from the house, Eliza was inside, slowly rocking and humming to herself, and began lifting silent prayers only Heaven heard. The fresh peppermint smell drifted into the kitchen, a small sweetness in the middle of so much sorrow.

Outside, beyond the meadow, the stones stood quietly after all the commotion from the city. The wind shifted through the white pines where Buddy’s spirit still lingered - as if watching over the two women who had loved him - both, like their own.

Chapter 26 –

Looking Back

When the patrol car rolled up to the marble steps of Atlanta police headquarters, it felt as if the entire city had gathered to watch. Reporters pressed against a barricade, their questions ricocheting off the glass doors and the stone walls. Flashbulbs burst with every movement, freezing faces in harsh white light.

Patty Hall stepped out first, guided by the detective who had driven her downtown from the mountains. The moment her head appeared out of the passenger side of the car, voices erupted from the crowd:

"Who is this, and where did you find her?"

"Is the girl alive?"

"Was it the Holcomb man?"

The crowd had gathered at the headquarters for a new police release. The detective raised his hand for silence.

"The child is safe," he said firmly. "The mother had taken her on a trip without the father's knowledge. The parents are separated, going through a difficult divorce. But the girl has been returned unharmed. There was no connection whatsoever to the Holcomb man."

"What about the graves?"

"Is this now a murder investigation?"

A rush of murmurs swept through the crowd - relief, confusion, disbelief all tangled together. Cameras caught every angle: officers straightening their hats, weary detectives wiping their brows, and Patty blinking under the bright lights as questions flew at her that she never tried to answer.

She was led inside the building and then to a plain room with an old tape recorder on the table and a microphone pushed towards her. An officer poured a paper cup of water, her hands gentle as she took it from him as if afraid she might break it.

"Just tell us what you know about Mr. Holcomb," started the same detective who had driven her there, his voice softening a little. "Say it like you're sitting on your front porch back home."

Patty nodded, folding her hands in her lap. The brown braid down her back caught the fluorescent light. There was city dust on her shoes, but a mountain calm in her eyes.

"I don't know much about all this city business," she began. "I just know Buddy."

The tape hummed quietly as it rolled.

“He loved the hills,” she said, her voice was strong and sure through the microphone static, even as her heart was breaking. “The rivers, the tall, strong trees. Things pure. I swear that man was like lookin’ at a compass of truth. Somehow, he always pointed you back toward bein’ a better you.”

“As to the meadow,” she continued, “I’m not sure what’s going on there. But maybe he kept it in his journals. He’s got years’ worth of them stacked out in his daddy’s old logging truck. But I am sure, whatever our Buddy was doing out there, he had a good reason for it.”

The detective's pen slowed.

“I spent most of my time helping his mama,” Patty went on, “bringing casseroles, sittin’ with her when her legs got bad. I never followed him out to the barn or out in the fields. I just saw the kind of son he was - he was very gentle with her, quick to fix what was broken, and quick to bow his head when the pastor prayed.”

She hesitated and then added. “Every so often, he'd stop by my place in town and buy up bolts of cloth. White, mostly. Said he needed it for somethin’ out at the farm. I figured maybe for Eliza's quilts, or for staining wood in the shop. I never asked right out. It wasn't my business. I surely didn't know it had anything to do with little ones or graves.”

The detective glanced up.

"You've never seen the stones yourself? The field?"

Patty shook her head.

"No sir. I'm not much for trompin' out past the house these days. I usually sit on Eliza's porch and look down toward the creek, but the meadow - Buddy kept that mostly to himself. I knew he liked to walk and pray down there. That's all. I didn't know what he was building, not really, until you all found it."

She swallowed, her eyes shining.

"What I did see," she said with conviction as her eyes pierced each person in the room, "was a man carryin' a heaviness he didn't name. He never bragged on any of it. Never once tried to paint himself a hero. He just... took the hard things the world handed him and tried to meet them with kindness. With work. With faith. There was hardly a day that went by, just like his daddy, that Buddy didn't seek to lift somebody up."

The questions continued with the detective seeking details-sanitation routes, cotton towels, the pull of the city.

Patty answered simply, with porch talk honesty.

The detective tapped his pen once on the pad.

"You mentioned journals earlier, Miss Hall. Can you tell us more about that?"

Patty nodded slowly.

"Buddy wrote a lot," she said. "Always has. Little spiral notebooks when he was young, then the bigger ones later on. He kept them out in his daddy's old logging truck."

"The truck by the field?" the detective asked.

"Yes, that would be the one. That old truck's been sittin' there for years now, since Buddy had it pulled up from the ravine where his daddy was killed. He never did haul logs with it after Gary passed. He started turning all the logs into furniture and sold some beautiful pieces. But he'd go down there with his Bible and those notebooks, climb up in the cab, and write. Said it helped him to think. To pray. Sort things out in his mind."

"Did you ever read them?"

She shook her head again.

"No sir. That was between him and the Lord. All I know is he kept them stacked in the passenger seat and up under the dash. If you're looking to understand his heart, that's where I'd start. But don't expect to find any ugliness there. Knowing him all these years, I'm bettin' you'll find scripture, and people's names he was prayin' over, and maybe some of the reasons he did what he did. Just... no darkness like the folks have been saying."

Questions came again, one after another - about the clinics, the bins, the long drives back and forth from the city.

"Yes sir, he drove for the medical waste company, as they now call it," she answered. "Yes, he stopped by my shop for towels and cloths time to time. No, sir, I never heard him speak unkindly about babies or women. If anythin', his eyes went far away when folks mentioned such things, like he was prayin' a prayer he couldn't say out loud."

The detectives exchanged glances. The tape rolled on.

When they finally clicked the recorder off and thanked her, Patty felt the tightness in her chest ease just enough for her to breathe. She hadn't explained every mystery. That wasn't hers to do. But she had pointed them toward the truth as she knew it - toward Eliza's boy, steady as a rock, tender as a flowering bud, and the silent stack of journals in a truck that hadn't run in years.

In a city full of half-told stories, that felt like a holy thing.

Outside, the reporters were still lined three deep, their microphones raised like a forest of black stems. Word of Clara's safe return had spread from newsroom to newsroom and from office to office. The city's shoulders had dropped an inch.

Behind them, Donna remained where she had started, just beyond the reach of the cameras. The Channel 3 logo shone brightly on the side of the van. Her name was taped neatly on her microphone.

It suddenly felt like it belonged to someone else.

Patty's words drifted out through the open doors, caught by halfway microphones, and fed to speakers on the steps.

"He had hauled grace where the world dumped shame...He was like looking at a compass of truth."

Donna closed her eyes. That was Buddy. Not the graphic picture portrayed on the evening news. And not the mug shot they had leaned on for days. The boy from Tallulah Falls, the young man willing to lay down football glory for a baby they never held. The driver who had spent his nights in the dark, burying what the world had thrown away and whispering scriptures over graves and giving them a name and a date.

His choices had been for the Kingdom of God. Quiet, costly, aimed at the least and the lost.

Hers had not.

She had told herself otherwise, of course. She had wrapped her ambition in churchy phrases - "using my gifts," "being a light in media," "going where God opens the door". The truth, standing here under Atlanta's hard light, was plainer and far less flattering.

She loved the sound of her own name.

Story by story, year by year, she had built a life with herself at the center. She had chased the bigger market, the later slot, and the lead story. She had learned to lean into lines that made viewers lean in closer, even when it meant tilting a story to make it sharper, darker, more frightening, and enticing.

The danger of a destroying tongue, Gary had preached more than once from the little pulpit at Grace Fellowship, was that with only a small spark, the thing could set a whole forest on fire.

In the station's breakroom, they had joked about that - about "lighting up the phones," about "setting the town buzzing". Now, with Buddy's blood still a memory on her hands, it didn't feel like a joke at all.

She thought about Theodore McCall, sitting at his oak table in the center of the city with Clara's picture on the side table near the kitchen, the television humming in the corner. Night after night, he had listened to her voice, along with others, talk about clinics, waste, and risk. He had heard the radio men call Buddy "The Clinic Body Man," and her station put on words like "POSSIBLY DANGEROUS!" and "Clinic Driver Under Question" beneath his face.

He had heard the accusation long before any judge heard any evidence.

When he finally walked up those courthouse steps with a gun in his hand, he carried not just his grief, but all the words they had spoken over Buddy.

It wasn't just a broken system. It was an imbalance of justice in the very way they used their tongues. Men and women accused by cameras before they ever saw a jury. Innocent people were dragged through the mud because their pain made a delightful story.

And she had been good at telling those stories. Too good.

"Lord," she breathed, so low that no one around her could hear, "I've been so wrong."

The words came from somewhere deeper than embarrassment or career regret. They rose from the same place that had cried out on the courthouse steps when Buddy's body had sagged in her arms - a place that knew, without argument, that the road she had walked for years had been leading her in the wrong direction.

"Repentance," Gary had said once, *"wasn't just feeling bad - it was turning. Changing roads. Putting your feet where your mouth said you believed."*

Slowly, Donna unclenched her fingers from around the microphone and held it out to the nearest cameraman.

"I'm finished for today," she said, her voice steady in a way that surprised her. "Maybe for a while."

He blinked, startled. "Donna? The 6:00 news..."

"Find someone else," she said gently, "please."

He hesitated, then took the mic and turned back toward the crowd, already scanning for another familiar face to slide in front of the lens. The machine would move with or without her. And for the first time in her life, she was willing to let it.

Donna stepped back from the knot of cameras and cables until their voices blurred into one distant roar. The courthouse loomed behind her; all glass and stone. Ahead, the city streets stretched out in a maze of concrete and lights.

She turned away from the steps and walked into the stream of Atlanta's morning.

Taxis honked. Buses stopped at the curb. People hurried past with their briefcases and coffee cups, chasing meetings, paychecks, and promotions. Once, she would have been right there with them, rehearsing her lines for the new update, her mind racing ahead to the next big story.

Now, with every step, a different kind of prayer rose under her breath.

"Jesus," she whispered, "I've spent so many years lifting up my own name. I've used this tongue to wound when I should have been trying to help heal. I don't want to live like that anymore. Show me how to spend what's left on your work, and not mine."

She didn't know yet what that would mean. Whether it would lead her back to a newsroom one day with a changed heart, or into some entirely different work she couldn't yet imagine, that she could not see. The future beyond the next corner was foggy.

But one thing was clear.

The girl who had left Tallulah Falls years ago had been running toward her own glory. The woman who walked away from the cameras just now was turning back toward the God she had left behind.

Buddy's steady faith had become a mirror that she could no longer ignore. In it, she saw the weight of her sin, and just beyond it, the wide mercy of the Savior who still welcomed prodigals.

She lifted her face briefly toward the strip of pale sky between the buildings.

“I'm coming home,” she whispered - not yet to the mountains, but to the Lord who had waited there all along.

Somewhere beneath the rumble of the city, she could almost hear Panther Creek’s song and Eliza's soft voice humming a favorite hymn. The memory rose up around her like a promise: even wasted years could be gathered, even misused words could be redeemed, and even a heart that had chased its own glory could be turned, one small, surrendered step at a time, back toward the Kingdom of God.

Chapter 27 - Holy Writ

The old Holcomb truck sat where it had sat for years, half-swallowed by tall grass at the edge of the meadow. Rust had chewed through the fenders. One headlight was clouded white, and the other was gone altogether. A fine layer of pollen dusted the cracked windshield, soft as ash.

The detective paused a few feet away and took off his hat.

"Hard to believe this thing ever ran," the younger officer beside him muttered. The top of the cab looked sunken in like a boulder had dropped from the sky as a result of the accident.

"He ran long enough," the detective said quietly. "Miss Hall said this is where he kept his notebooks."

They had driven straight from Atlanta after Patty's testimony, listening to her chit-chat as they made their way toward Rabun County - past subdivisions and strip malls, onto roads that had narrowed and curled along ridges, then onto a gravel lane that crackled under their tires. The city's noise had fallen away behind them like a dropped signal. Here, the only sound was Panther Creek rumbling somewhere below, and the wind moving through pines like a low choir.

He reached for the driver's door handle. It stuck, then it gave way with a groan, hinges protesting as if reluctant to open up about what the cab held. The smell of old leather and dust rolled out, mixed with something else - a faint trace of cedar, maybe, with some ink left too long in the summer heat. Sunlight slanted through the dirty glass, catching on the edges of stacked notebooks lined up on the passenger seat and floorboard.

“Here they are,” the detective said.

He picked up the top one carefully, as if it might crumble. The cover was cheap cardboard, the corners softened, and the edges darkened where fingers had worn them smooth. On the front, in square, neat letters, someone had written simply:

Journal 1992

“Bag them”, the younger man said automatically.

“Not yet,” the older, seasoned detective interjected quickly as he slid a thumb along the edge, “let's see what we're dealing with.”

He eased it open and began to read.

“January 3rd

Route #4 - Southside clinic. Cold morning. Frost on the van windshield. Prayed over every car as it pulled in. A young girl in a red coat sat in the passenger seat a long time before she got out. Could see her daddy's knuckles white on the steering wheel. Asked the Lord to give him courage to turn that car around. And he did. They left before the doors opened. Thank you, Jesus."

The handwriting was plain, unadorned. No flourishes. Just pressed into the paper like he meant every word.

The detective turned the page and continued.

"January 10th

Same clinic. Group of ladies with signs out front, shouting loudly. Some of their words sounded more like stones than prayers. Try to keep my own words aimed higher. Ask God to speak where my tongue would only get in the way. Two women went back to their cars today. One went in. Lord, hold them all. The ones who turn and the ones who don't.

February 2nd

rain. Parked the van and sat awhile. Didn't want to crank it yet. Watched folks go in, huddled under umbrellas, heads down. All colors. All ages. Sin and sorrow don't care about skin color. Prayed over each one by what I could see - blue dress, green jacket, tired eyes. Felt helpless and somehow useful at the same time."

The detective exhaled slowly.

"These aren't rants," the younger officer observed, peering over his shoulder, "they are...what... devotionals?"

"Prayers," the detective answered. "And records."

He flipped forward.

"March 18th

One of the protest fellows said today, "We're here to talk to men about God." Felt a check in my spirit. I reckon more days I'm called to talk to God about men. He can reach where my voice never will. Still, there's a time to speak. Asked Him again to show me when to stay quiet and when to open my mouth. Don't want to be a divider or the loud Pharisee. Want to be like Daddy - firm and kind.

April 7th

Another little one in the dumpster. Could not drive off this time without stopping. Brought him home to the creek. Named him Danny. Wrote the date. Carved slow till the letters looked like somebody loved him. My hands shook the whole time. Ask the Lord to forgive this land. Asked Him to forgive me if I ever grow numb."

The younger officer looked away, his jaw tight.

"Chief needs to see that," he said.

"He will," the detective replied. His thumb moved to the next journal in the stack - 1980. He opened somewhere in the middle. His voice was somber.

"August 3rd

Bought more white cloth from Patty's shop. She asked what it was for. Told her “work”. Couldn't bring myself to say I was cutting burial shrouds in the barn at night. Maybe one day she'll understand. For now, better to let that weight stay here. Sewed edges by hand so they won't fray when the clay settles in around them. Mama thinks I'm fussing with wood down at the shed. Some things a mama's heart don't need to carry.

September 10th

Another long day on the route. Fell asleep sitting in this old truck, journal in my lap. Dreamed Panther Creek was running red, then cleared up again. Woke up with Daddy's voice in my head: ‘You know a society by what it does with its young and its old’. Sometimes I feel like I'm standing between the two, one stone at a time.”

The detective turned another page and stopped at a line where the handwriting went softer, almost hesitant, as if he paused long between the words.

A tear tracked down from the young officer's eye, and he wiped it fast away as if to say I can handle this job.

“September 21st

Swung past the lake house road today on the way back north. Couldn't help it. Thought about Donna. Wondered if she still swims with her dark hair loose like she used to. Wondered if she ever stands at the Falls and remembers. Tried not to let my heart go there, but it did anyway. Told the Lord again I forgave her and her folks. I meant it. Still hurts like a bone healed crooked. Asked Him to bless her wherever she is. If she's got other children now, pray to give her the courage that we were both too scared to grab hold of back then. I still love her. Don't know what to do with that except lay it down at his feet."

The detective glanced at the officer, then back to the page. He turned a little farther in. The words turning on his tongue.

"November 3rd

Patty brought soup to Mama today - chicken and rice, with those little carrots she grows herself. Stayed and sang a hymn with us after supper. 'Great is thy faithfulness.' Her voice shakes on the high notes, but it sure does land strong on the last line. Thank the Lord for a friend who sits in the quiet and doesn't ask for explanations. I told her I was tired from work. She patted my arm and said, "You rest, Buddy. The Lord sees." Those words carried me longer than she knows. Sister in Christ, through and through.

December 12th

Church was full this morning, even with the cold. Pastor Davis preached on 'whatever you do for the least of these.' Thought about that all through the service, sitting in the second pew where Daddy used to sit before he got up to preach. Looked around at our folks - farmers, mill workers, Ole Mrs. Fain pinching sleeping children to wake, a few fresh faces from down by the lake. Tallulah Falls and Rabun and Habersham all meeting under one roof, singing, 'Just As

I Am'. Thought, Lord, this is where I learned what life is worth. If you want me to keep doing this quiet work with the babies, keep my voice soft like these saints' hands. Don't let me turn hard."

The detective closed the journal; his thumb pressed in the middle to hold his place. The weight of the little book felt larger than its size.

He looked at the stack still waiting - years upon years, scribbled in the same steady hand.

"Holy Writ", he said under his breath, almost to himself.

"Charlie? Sir?" the younger officer asked.

"Nothing." He opened a different one, a later date, 1977 - a page that had been dog-eared.

"May 6th

Long day. Too many bags. Too much red. Sat in the van afterward and told the Lord I didn't think I could do it again. Felt Him nudge my spirit: you weren't meant to carry it alone. So I brought three of them home. I gave them names - Grace, Michael, Hope. I marked their stones with verses Daddy loved: Psalm 139 and Matthew 5. Cried until my eyes swelled shut. Then I slept like a man who had laid bricks on the right house, even if nobody else ever sees it."

The detective shut the journal gently and rested his hand on the worn cover.

For a long moment, neither man spoke. The creek's steady roar rose from beyond the trees, and somewhere a hawk cried high and thin.

"This is not the writing of a monster," the detective said at last.

"No sir," the younger officer agreed.

"It's the writing of a man who believed every life mattered and acted like it, even when nobody was watching."

The detective slid the journal into an evidence bag with a care that felt more like reverence than procedure.

"Whatever happens with the case file, this needs to be read. By the chief. By the DA. By that woman from the news. Maybe by a jury someday. Somebody needs to see what was really going on in this man's heart."

He reached for the next notebook.

"Bag them all," he said. "Top to bottom. We'll call them exhibits if we have to. But between you and me, Son..."

He glanced out toward the meadow, where the tops of the white stones shimmered faintly in the morning light.

"... this might be the truest record we get."

The younger officer nodded, swallowing hard.

They worked in silence then, lifting each journal as if it were fragile as glass, sliding them into plastic bags - one by one.

Outside the cab, the world would go on arguing about Buddy Holcomb - the headlines, the talk shows, the half-knowing neighbors. But inside those thin cardboard covers, his days lay written in a different ink.

Prayers. Names. Places where Heaven and red clay had met.

Holy Writ- from a man the world had never truly known.

Chapter 28 – Mr. McCall

The cell was smaller than Theodore McCall's garage and colder than he could have imagined.

The cinder block walls sweated with a faint, clammy dampness. A metal cot clung to one side, its thin, old mattress sagging like tired shoulders. Overhead, a fluorescent light hummed constantly, a poor imitation of daylight. The only window was a narrow-slit high on the wall, a square of colorless sky that never quite warmed the room.

He sat on the edge of the cot, elbows on his knees, hands hanging heavily between them. The skin across his wrists was cracked, red, and raw from the handcuffs that had bitten in when they pulled him off the courthouse steps.

He could still feel the weight of the gun.

A television out in the hall murmured over the echo of footsteps with a news channel always on. He had tried to tune it out at first, but here there wasn't much else to listen to, besides his own thoughts, and those were louder than any anchor.

“The child is safe,” a man's voice said now, carrying thin through the bars. “Authorities confirmed there was no connection whatsoever between the girl's disappearance and the now deceased, Mr. Holcomb.”

Theodore flinched.

“Say that again,” he murmured, pushing himself up off the cot. He shuffled toward the bars, fingers curling around the cold steel.

The volume came up a notch, a guard somewhere twisting the knob.

“Clara McCall, the five-year-old who was at the heart of yesterday's courthouse tragedy, was never in danger from the man who was shot there on the steps,” the anchor repeated. “According to police, her mother had taken her on an unscheduled trip without advising the father. Her parents are in the midst of a difficult divorce battle. She has been returned home to her father, unharmed and safe. Again, this does not appear as an abduction, though the investigation continues to see if the child’s mother has violated any existing court order. But, there’s definitely no link to the driver involved with the Rabun County graves.”

The room tilted.

No danger from him.

Theodore's hands tightened on the bars until his fingers began to ache.

He saw it all again - the dark hair threaded with a few gray flecks, the bewildered calm on Buddy Holcomb's face as the cruiser door swung open and he began to step out onto the courthouse steps. The way Theodore's own arm had lifted, with the gun shaking in his hand. The look on Donna Chambers's face when she had screamed.

He had told himself, even in the chaos, that he was protecting Clara. That he was doing what any Atlanta grandfather would have done when "The Clinic Man" walked free and a little girl was missing.

Now the floor seemed to fall away beneath him.

"Clara..."

His voice cracked on his granddaughter's name. He had stepped back from the bars, then sank to his knees on the concrete, his hands dangling, useless, at his side.

She did not need saving from Buddy at all.

He had killed an innocent man.

A shadow moved across the bars, blocking the weak light from the hallway.

"Theodore," came a soft voice, "you want some company for a minute?"

He lifted his head.

A guard stood there with a woman at his side, her gray hair pulled back, and her eyes swollen from the storm sweeping the McCall household.

Lydia. Her hands were clenched around the strap of her purse.

"Lydia," he croaked.

The guard unlocked the door to the small visiting room instead, the one with the pane of scratched plexiglass.

"We'll put y'all in there," he said. "Five minutes."

A few minutes later, Theodore sat on one side of the cloudy barrier, a phone pressed to his ear. Lydia sat on the other, her eyes older than they had been a week ago.

She held the receiver as if it might burn her.

"You've seen her?" he blurted, his voice rough with emotion. "Clara? Is she..."

"She's home," Lydia said, the words coming out flat from too little sleep. "Shaken some. But whole. She was never with that man, Theodore. Her mother was the one who had taken her. Fool that she is. But we told you this already, but you wouldn't hear it."

He swallowed hard.

"I thought..."

"I know what you thought," her eyes filled, but her voice stayed hard. "You sat in that recliner every evening and listened to the radio or watched the news. Letting those people in Atlanta tell you a story till it was the only one you could hear. Clinic driver. Dangerous. Monster. You let their words get louder than God's."

He flinched.

"I was scared for her," he whispered, "for our baby."

"We all were," Lydia said. "But there's a difference between being scared and being blind, Theo. You were so busy listening to those loud, wrong voices."

He closed his eyes. He could still see Clara's small bed, the worn stuffed bear on the pillow, the spot on the wall where she had banged her toy truck one too many times. Panic had eaten him alive that morning, gnawing every inch of sense he had left.

"Did they tell you about the field?" Lydia asked quietly.

He blinked.

"What field?"

"The one behind the Holcomb place."

Her gaze dropped to her hands, her fingers twisting the purse strap nervously.

"They found it, Theo. A meadow full of stones. Little ones. That's what he's been doing all those days you swore he was up to no good. Burying babies properly when nobody else would. Praying over them."

The words landed like blows.

"He was... what?!"

"Praying," she repeated simply. "They have been talking about it, and that reporter woman, Donna Chambers, and his pastor, Pastor Davis, from up near Tallulah Falls. The police found a bunch of his notebooks. He wrote down what he did every day. Prayed over every woman walking into that clinic. Then took and named those discarded babies from the clinic and gave them a decent burial on his farm."

The phone slipped in his sweaty hand. He gripped it harder.

"That doesn't make any sense," he rasped, "the station kept saying..."

Lydia's expression hardened.

"The station was wrong," she said, "and so were you. So was I, for keeping quiet while you worked yourself into a rage. But you're the one who pulled the trigger, Theodore McCall. You shot a man who was on his knees, asking God to help little girls like our Clara."

Tears stung hot at the corner of his eyes.

"I didn't know," he choked. "Lydia, I swear before God, I didn't know."

Her face softened then, years of marriage and shared grief rising up between them like a bridge.

“I believe you,” she said, “he might, too. But not knowing doesn't make the bullet any lighter.” Her voice trembled. “Our girl's going to grow up knowing her granddaddy killed the man who had prayed for her.”

He bowed his hand, his shoulders shaking.

“I have ruined everything,” he whispered. “I honestly thought I was saving her. I thought I was doing what God wanted. Turns out I was just... angry. And those loud men on the radio and the TV fed that anger till I couldn't hear anything else.”

On the other side of the scratched plastic, Lydia’s palm flattened, as if she could touch his cheek.

“Pastor Davis is down from Tallulah Falls,” she said after a moment. “He came to sit with Clara. Says he wants to come talk to you if you'll let him.”

Theodore's throat closed.

“What's a preacher got to say to a man who shot one of his own?” he asked.

“Maybe he's got something you need,” she answered.

The words lodged somewhere deep, where his pride and his shame had been wrestling.

Lydia’s eyes began to fill again.

“Let him in, Theo,” she whispered. “You can't undo what you've done. But you can decide what you will do with what's left.”

A tear broke free and slid hot down his cheek.

"Tell him to come," he managed.

The guard tapped the glass; time was up. Lydia pressed her hand there one last time.

"I love you," she said, her voice fraying, "but I don't excuse you. You hear the difference?"

He nodded, unable to speak, and watched her go.

Time blurred after that - minutes or an hour, he could not tell. The door at the end of the block opened again. Footsteps, slower this time. A figure in a worn suit stopped outside his cell.

"Theodore?" Pastor Davis' voice was like it always sounded on Sunday mornings, just quieter. "Mind if I sit a spell?"

Theodore sat back on the cot, wiping his face with the palm of his hand.

"Don't reckon I can stop you," he muttered.

The pastor gave a faint, sad smile and lowered himself onto the bolted-down chair on the other side of the bars.

"I came down from Tallulah Falls this morning," he said. "Stop by your place first. Lydia walked me through what she knows. Then I sat with Clara a little while. She's holdin' tight to that little stuffed bear of hers, says her granddaddy's going to talk to Jesus."

The words broke something loose in Theodore's chest.

"I've talked to Jesus plenty," he said hoarsely. "Shouted, even. Don't know as I've ever really listened."

Pastor Davis nodded.

"That problem seems to be going around," he said wryly. "Whole lot of us talkin' at God and at each other without listenin' much at all."

He leaned forward with his hands folded loosely.

"You know they found his notebooks," he said. "Buddy's. I've read some of them. The man spent his days talking to God about people, Theodore. Men like you and me. Girls like Clara. Women the world didn't make room for. He prayed over that clinic lot like it was an altar."

Theodore stared at the floor.

"I heard," he said. "Lydia just told me. I didn't want to believe it, but I can't unhear it now."

Pastor Davis let the quiet sit for a moment.

"You thought you were stopping a monster," he said gently. "Turns out you sent a faithful servant of the Lord home. You didn't know what you were doing."

"That's supposed to make me feel better?" Theodore snapped, then winced at his own tone. "I'm sorry, Pastor. I just... that sounds like an excuse."

"It's not," Pastor Davis said, his voice firm. "Ignorance doesn't erase consequences. You'll live with those, and you'll answer for them in court. But I came here to talk about a different kind of court."

He opened his well-worn Bible and turned the pages by feel.

"You know the story," he said gently as he continued, "when they nailed Jesus up, the world thought it was doin' right. Protecting order, protecting children, protecting the nation from a troublemaker. And from that cross He said, 'Father, forgive them, for they know not what they do."

He looked Theodore in the eye.

"That prayer was big enough to cover Roman soldiers and religious leaders and the scared, blind crowds shouting, 'Crucify him!' You don't think it's big enough to cover a scared granddaddy from Atlanta who believed the wrong story and pulled a trigger?"

Theodore swallowed hard.

"I don't know," he whispered, "part of me thinks I deserve Hell. Part of me...wants to crawl out into that field y'all are referring to and lie down between those stones and never get up."

"Both can be true," Pastor Davis said softly. "You do deserve judgment. So do I. So did Buddy. That's what the cross says. But that same cross says Jesus took that judgment on Himself. The question now isn't whether you deserve forgiveness. It's whether you're willing to ask for it and let it change you."

Theodore's hands trembled in his lap.

"I can't bring him back," he almost sobbed, "can't give that mama her boy. Can't give that woman her husband," pointing towards the hall.

"No," the pastor agreed. "But you can stop pretending you were justified. You can take ownership of your mistakes. You can ask God to cover what you have broken with a mercy you can't earn. You can spend whatever days you've got left telling the truth about that man instead of the lie you believed."

He closed the Bible, his fingers resting on the cover.

"Lydia told me you've been hearing voices real loud lately - talk radio, TV, evening news, the fear. I'd like to pray that you begin to hear another voice over you, if you let me."

Thedore's eyes were closed. He simply nodded.

"Go ahead," he whispered.

Pastor Davis bowed his head.

"Father," he said, "this is Theodore McCall. You know he's a stubborn man. You know he loves his little Clara. You know he let fear and anger drown out your voice. You heard every word he shouted, every bullet he fired. And You heard Your son, hanging on that cross, saying, 'Father, forgive them, for they know not what they do.' I'm asking you to let that prayer land on Theodore today."

Tears slid, unchecked, down Theodore's face. He sat through a lifetime of altar calls, but this one felt like it had his name carved on it.

"Help him see the truth about his sin," Pastor Davis went on, "no excuses. No blaming the news or the neighbors. Just truth. And then, Lord, show him the truth about Your grace - bigger than his crime, deeper than his shame. Give him the courage to say, 'I was wrong,' to you and to Clara and to anybody else who needs to hear it."

He was quiet for a moment, then finished.

"In Jesus' name, Amen."

The cell seemed to expand and contract around Theodore's heartbeat.

Slowly, he slid off the cot onto his knees, the concrete biting into his bones. He gripped the edge of the thin mattress with both hands like a drowning man catching a rope.

"God," he rasped, his voice breaking, "I killed your man. I opened my ears to fools and closed them to You. I trusted angry people more than I trusted Your word. I was wrong. Lord, I was wrong."

The words tumbled out, ragged and real.

"I don't know how to fix what I broke," he sobbed. "I can't. But if there's any of that cross left for a fool like me, I need it. I need You. Forgive me. Please."

He wept then, his shoulders shaking. The sound echoed down the block like a wounded animal's cry. He didn't care who heard.

When the worst of it had passed, he felt a hand, warm and steady, close around his through the bars. Pastor Davis had knelt too, one knee on the hard floor.

“That's the first true thing you've said to God in a long time,” the pastor said quietly, “and He has heard you.”

Theodore leaned his forehead against the cold metal.

“You think Buddy would forgive me?” he whispered.

Pastor Davis thought of the journals, the entries about men who yelled in the parking lot, about enemies he prayed for by description rather than by name.

“I think,” he said slowly, “that the man who prayed over your Clara before he ever knew her name, would be the first one to ask Jesus to show you mercy now. And I know this - if you walk in that mercy, if you tell the truth from here on out, the field he left behind would speak louder than the shots you fired.”

Theodore nodded, tears still falling, but something in his chest looser than it had been since the sirens wailed.

He would still face a judge. He would still receive a sentence. He would still carry Clara’s questions and the weight of one man's blood on his hands - forever.

But for the first time since the courthouse steps, as the words, “Father, forgive them, for they know not what they do” echoed in his mind, he believed there might be a way forward to the truth instead of from the law.

Chapter 29 –

Rough Landing

Steve Chambers set his flight bag down by the door and stood still a moment, listening to the quiet of the Buckhead home. No TV. No music. Just the faint tick of the kitchen clock down the hall.

Donna was at the table when he walked in, shoulders a little hunched, her hands wrapped around a mug she wasn't drinking. The morning light poured through the big windows, making everything in the room- granite, chrome, framed travel photos - look cleaner than it felt.

"You're home early," she said.

"Swapped a leg," he answered a little short, "didn't feel like watching my wife hold another man on the evening news from a hotel room while he bled out."

She flinched. The mug clicked softly against the saucer as her fingers tightened.

"I forgot about the cameras," she softly stated. " I wasn't thinking about that."

"I know you weren't," he retorted. "That's what's got me."

He pulled out the chair across from her but didn't sit down; instead, he rested his hands on its back. Pilot calm sat over something harder in his eyes.

"They ran it on every channel," he went on, "Courthouse steps. Shots fired. Local... whatever he is... goes down, and there you are right in the middle of it. On your knees with his head in your lap, like..." he shook his head once, "like he was yours."

Donna stared at the coffee in her cup, watching one tear fall and disappear into the dark surface before she spoke.

"His name is Buddy," she said quietly. "Buddy Holcomb."

"Yeah, that's what they kept saying on the news," Steve said. "Gary "Buddy" Holcomb, Rabun County, carpenter, controversial figure - all of that. Question is, who is he to you?"

She nodded, her throat tight.

"I knew him a long time ago," she began slowly, "before college. Before the newsroom. Before any of this."

"How well?" his voice roughened enough to show through the smooth.

Donna lifted her eyes to meet his.

"He was my first," she barely whispered, "first love. First... everything."

The admission sat heavily in the air. Steve let out a breath through his nose, not quite a laugh.

"Ten years," he says matter-of-factly, "ten years of marriage and this never came up?"

"I tried to put it all in a box and shove it to the back of my mind," she responded, "pretend Rabun, Tallulah Falls...all of it... had never happened or was another world I had just dreamed of."

His fingers tightened on the chair.

"The news said you were out at his farm when they took him in," he pressed, "that you followed the police from downtown. Is that true?"

She drew a shaky breath.

"I went out there thinking maybe I could talk to him," she explained, "get his side. That was my plan. But when I saw him, they had him in the police car, all he said was, 'I did it for us. I did it for them.' I didn't know what he meant."

Her gaze drifted past Steve, as if she were back on the farm.

"Then an officer came over and pulled me away from the car," she went on, "and said it wasn't safe to stand there. We walked down toward the creek to this little meadow. And I just...stopped."

She swallowed.

"Across that meadow were stones," she said, lost in the feel of what she had seen and felt.
"White creek stones with single names and a date carved into each one of them. I don't know how long they had been there. But the field was full. And it glistened in the early morning sun like a Psalm." Her hand moved to her chest. "Something in me, that morning - my heart - felt like it had melted right into that field."

"The reporters are calling it a burial ground," she added, "they are talking about tiny graves. But standing there, I couldn't move. I just kept seeing those stones and hearing him say, 'I did it for us. For them.'"

Steve's fingers dug into the wood.

"And what about 'us'?" he asked. "Who is 'us' in that little sermon?"

Donna swallowed even harder.

"I was seventeen," she softly began again, "back before I ever heard of the 'press' or 'newsroom'. I sat under Gary Holcomb's preaching back in those days. I heard him preach the gospel - and it hit my heart - how life is in the Lord's hands, how He knitted us together in the womb. When I found out I was pregnant, I heard it in all my bones."

She drew a breath that came out jagged.

"I told Mama I did not want to do anything to my baby," she remembered bitterly. "I told her Buddy would stand by me.

She called me foolish. She said I was throwing away everything for which "they" had worked. Daddy wouldn't even look at me. He just signed where she told him to. The clinic papers had his ink on them before I could even catch my breath."

Her eyes went distant.

"Next thing I knew, I was staring down a long hallway, being led by them," she whispered, almost to herself, "the nurse put a clipboard in my hand. They all started talking over me about dates, procedures, 'getting this taken care of'. I was crying, and no one was listening. I said, 'I don't know! I'm not sure.'"

She looked back at him as the tears began to rise.

"Mama squeezed my arm so hard it bruised," she said. "Then all she could say to me was, 'Hush now. This is what has to be done!', so she claimed."

Her eyes flooded.

"I didn't want to do it, Steve!" she cried. "I was scared. I was frozen. I didn't run. I couldn't run. I didn't call Buddy. I let them steer me down that hall while I went quiet. And my quiet... it was just a quiet yes, but it might as well have been shouted."

She wrapped her arms around herself, feeling suddenly cold.

"I walked out of there and told myself they had made the choice, not me!" she said defiantly, "That I did not get one. I buried it deeply and went off to school. I met you. Then we built this life. I called it - moving on."

She looked back at him then, her tears shining.

"Then I found out that while I was running away from it all, he was running to them," she said. "To those clinics. He lifted those little bodies out of the bags and took them back to Panther Creek. In his truck. He gave them what I never gave ours - a name, a home in that field, a prayer, a place."

Her voice broke.

"So when he looked at me over that car door and said, 'I did it for us... for them,' I know now exactly who 'us' was," she whispered. "The child I let them take. And all the little ones like him. I have a son, Steve. His name is Tony."

Steve stared at her as if he had stepped into a turbulence that he couldn't chart.

"We had an understanding," he said at last, "back in school. Do you remember? We said no kids. No guilt. No letting anybody - including God or our parents - run our lives. We were going to live light and free. Fly high. And not look down. Do you remember?"

"I remember," she finally said. "I clung to that speech like a life raft. I told myself I had already done the hard thing once; that I had paid my dues. I grabbed for anything that looked like life and tried not to think about what I'd left under the wheels."

She glanced around at the gleaming kitchen - at the tasteful art, and the table full of framed photos of them smiling on faraway beaches.

“All of this looks like living,” she said softly, “but it doesn't touch what's under my skin and deep in my heart. It doesn't wash the past that I tried to forget.”

Her gaze steadied on him.

“Steve, all this that we've been doing - it's been just to live,” she whispered carefully, “but I need to be alive so I can do what's right. I can't unsee that meadow. I can't unhear Gary's sermons. I can't pretend I didn't watch Buddy bleed out on those courthouse steps - because he was doing what the world wouldn't do - giving the helpless and the innocent dignity. He made sacrifices. The only thing I've ever given Tony is a myth. That day was by fear, not faith. No more. I can't go forward without help from above.”

“So what now?” he asked. “You'll throw away the life we've built and run back to some little mountain community, some little mountain church? Let a bunch of Holcombs tell you who you are? Light candles, and cry over babies you've never met in the middle of a field?”

“It's not about the Holcombs,” she stated strongly, “not at the center. It's about the Lord I've been running from since I let my parents walk me down that hallway instead of falling on my face and saying no. It's about a child I never mourned and all the little ones like him. I don't know exactly what obedience is going to look like, but I know the first step isn't lying anymore."

He looked away, toward the window, at the slice of skyline they had paid so much for.

"I fly people above thunderstorms," he said quietly, "give them smooth air so they can forget what's underneath. I thought that's what we wanted. Smooth. No regrets. And no judgment."

"I don't want judgment," she said. "I want and need grace. But you don't get grace without truth first. I've been dodging truth a long time."

He was silent for a long while.

"I've got a London rotation next week," he said finally. "I'll stay at the crash pad till then. Maybe longer. You can figure out how much of this, 'doing what's right,' you really want. I'll see if there is a version of it I can live with."

He took a step toward the hallway, then stopped with his back to her.

"For what it's worth," he said in a faint voice, "the woman I saw on the courthouse steps? I don't recognize her. I'm not sure I ever will."

The door softly clicked a minute later. The house swallowed the sound.

Donna stared at the empty doorway until her vision blurred. Then slowly, she slid out of the chair, onto her knees, onto the cool tile, with her hands empty.

"Lord," she whispered into the quiet, the word feeling both rusty and right.

"I don't know how to fix any of this. I only know I've been wrong for a long time. I know, Jesus, you can make me alive again. Gary said so. I am so sorry. Take my thoughts, my heart, and let my actions reflect you."

The prayer was small. But it was the first one in years that sounded like the girl who had once stood on the banks of Panther Creek, listening to a mountain preacher talk about the Carpenter who had laid his life down for people who didn't know what they were doing.

Chapter 30 –

Meadow of Witness

Reporters still gathered that morning at the courthouse steps, their questions rising in a desperate storm:

What about the graves in Rabun?

Who were the children?

Is Mr. McCall charged with murder?

And who exactly was this Mr. Holcomb?

The police chief stood behind the podium, his face drawn.

“We're still investigating,” he said, his voice firm but weary, “what we can confirm is that the child from Atlanta is safe, and the events in Rabun County are still being looked at beyond yesterday's tragedy. Mr. Holcomb's body will be held for a few days while we collect statements and finalize reports.”

Cameras flashed, but the answer satisfied no one. Their hunger for a story could not grasp the man behind the mystery.

Out in the parking lot, Patty Hall stepped from the building after giving her testimony. The waiting squad car would take her home when a familiar voice called softly from the sidelines,

"Patty."

She turned. There stood Donna Chambers - formerly Donna Hargrove, whom she had not seen in years - her face pale from exhaustion and sleepless nights.

"Mind if I ride back with you?" she asked.

The officer in the car hesitated, then gave a quiet nod.

"Ok ma'am. Just keep it civil."

The door shut behind them, sealing the world out. For a few moments, only their breathing and a few interruptions from the police radio filled the silence.

For the ninety-minute ride north, neither spoke much at the beginning. But as the hum of tires met clouds drifting over the Blue Ridge Mountains, they finally spoke in low voices. They talked about Buddy - how he had carried everyone's pain, and how he had hidden his purpose beneath callous hands and a quiet faith.

Patty shared the small kindnesses: Sunday visits, light porch talks, and peppermint sticks tucked in a paper sack. Donna confessed her love - lost to time, now immortalized in heartbreak and headlines.

“He was our best friend,” Patty said softly, “our salt till the very last, our strength whether we knew it or not.”

Donna nodded, her eyes glistening.

“He gave everything to make wrong things right,” she whispered, staring out at the ridges that once held all their dreams.

By the time they reached the Falls, dusk had settled over the ridge. Together they agreed Eliza must never know the full story - not the arrest, not the gunshot, not the way the world had misunderstood her boy. Only that he had gone to meet his Father - both earthly and heavenly.

“Better she ages in peace,” Patty whispered. “Let's tell her it was a car wreck.”

Donna swallowed hard, then nodded. Sometimes mercy was found in what a heart was spared from knowing.

Words from the journals, the lab results, and Radford’s testimony of Buddy’s desire and devotion to give others dignity had made their way through the media. The news had spread fast. Pastor Davis at Grace Fellowship rallied the congregation behind Eliza Holcomb. And the girls continued to protect her.

On the morning of the burial, the tiny church overflowed with locals, strangers, camera crews, and avengers who had never heard of Tallulah Falls until the news had carried the story of the logger with the shovel and a calling.

Inside and outside, they stood, with the heat pressing down heavily, like even the July sky was grieving. Folding chairs stretched in neat rows and were packed with faces Buddy had known since before he could spell his own name. Down front, the casket lay draped in flowers - white lilies, wild daisies, and a few scraggly sunflowers somebody had insisted on adding because Buddy would have liked them.

Two young men in pressed shirts and borrowed ties stood near the front of Grace Fellowship, just to the left of the pulpit, hymnals closed in their hands.

Most folks knew them now simply as Travis and Tommy Stewart from Turnerville – the brothers who sang at little churches up and down the back roads, and who were called on when a service needed harmony more than polish.

“Thank y’all for bein' willing to sing,” the pastor murmured as he stepped aside.

“Yes, sir,” Travis answered. “It’s an honor.”

Tommy only nodded, his fingers tight around the hymnal.

They turned to face the packed sanctuary.

Buddy’s casket rested at the front, the wood gleaming softly under the lights. Eliza was in the front row between Patty and Donna, her handkerchief clenched in one hand, and her other hand pressed over her heart.

Travis opened his hymnal, though he didn't need the words.

"Amazing Grace," he said quietly.

His tenor carried the first line, sure and clear. Tommy slipped in under him, harmony wrapping around the melody.

"Amazing grace, how sweet the sound..."

As they sang, their eyes slid once – not to the crowd, but to the side window where the dark line of the hills rose beyond the glass. For a heartbeat, Tommy saw rain again, and a shovel, and a man in a coat standing in a wet meadow with a small bundle at his feet. A night they had never spoken of in full, not even to each other.

He swallowed and sang a little stronger on the next phrase.

"That saved a wretch like me..."

In the front row, Eliza's eyes closed. The old hymn rolled over her like a familiar tide. She heard her husband's voice in memory, and her boy's cracking along beside him in the old days. She did not recognize the young men at the front as anything more than kind singers lending their voices to her grief, and that was mercy enough for now.

By the final verse, half the congregation had joined in, some steady, some wavering, all carried by the brothers' blend.

When the last note faded, Travis shut his hymnal with careful hands. As they stepped down to an empty pew along the side wall, Tommy leaned in, his voice barely more than breath.

“Think he ever knew we saw him?” he whispered.

Travis watched Eliza dab at her eyes, then watched the pastor lay a rough palm on the casket.

“No,” he said quietly. “I don’t reckon he did.”

They fell silent, two men whose boyhood fear had long since settled into a different kind of ache – one stitched now with something like gratitude that grace could reach even the heaviest places the hills had once tried to hide.

His boys stood off to the side, a loose knot of broad shoulders and bowed heads. They were men now - turnout boots scuffed, work shirts damp at the collar, hands rough from lumber, diesel, and years of shift work - but in the tilt of their caps and the way they kept glancing toward the casket, their teenage selves flickered through.

Big Jim shifted his weight; the black band of his Rolex watch stood stark against his sunburnt wrist.

“Feels wrong,” he muttered, his voice hoarse, “Buddy's supposed to be here jokin’ about the preacher taking so long. Not...” he trailed off, swallowing hard.

Mark nodded, his jaw tight. He owned the hardware store now, had since his daddy's stroke, but all he could see was

Buddy at seventeen, leaning on the counter and spinning some wild story while they sorted nails by size.

“He'd be making fun of how we clean up,” Mark said quietly, “telling us we look like we're about to take prom pictures instead of burying our brother.”

A couple of the guys huffed out soft, broken laughs. The sound hung in the thick air, a small rebellion against the weight of the day.

Back when Grace Fellowship was their world on Sundays, these same boys had lined up with Buddy in ill-fitting ties, their hair slicked down for youth choir and Christmas plays. They'd shoot hoops on the cracked asphalt behind the fellowship hall, where the grass was poking through, while Buddy would be calling plays like he was coaching the state champions. They'd pile into old pickup trucks after Wednesday night service and head to Dairy Queen for cones they could barely afford.

“He's the one who taught me to block,” Jared said suddenly, his voice muffled. He was a firefighter now, the badge on his chest catching a glint of light as he stared at the ground. “I kept dropping my shoulder wrong, remember?” He glanced up, his eyes shining. “Coach was about done with me. Buddy stayed late. Put his hands right here,”- he thumbed his own shoulders - “and said, ‘You plant your feet, J-Rod. You decide you're not moving, and you don't. The world hits you, you hit it back with love and leverage.’”

A tear made a trail down his cheek. "Didn't know he was giving me life lessons at seventeen," Jared whispered.

"He did that," Leroy said, "slipped wisdom in like you were just swapping jokes."

Around them, chairs scraped as people settled. Someone's baby fussed, then quieted. The funeral director caught Eliza's eye and gave a tiny nod, indicating it was time to move the casket soon.

"Y'all remember that youth retreat?" Mark asked, his voice lowered. "Up at the camp near Clayton? The one where the cabin door wouldn't latch, and the skunk tried to move in with us?"

A couple of the guys chuckled, their heads ducking.

"You screamed like a girl," Danny said, a ghost of mischief crossing his face.

"I did not," Mark protested automatically, then gave in with a shaky grin, "Okay, maybe a little. But Buddy... he just stood there, holding that broom like it was a sword, telling that old skunk, 'You ain't coming in here, friend. These are my boys."

"He always called us that," Big Jim finally chimed back in. "My boys."

They fell quiet again, each man tumbling through his own reel of memories.

Buddy grinning across the line of scrimmage, mud on his jersey, and a light in his eyes. Buddy in the church foyer, holding the door for old Mrs. Tate, his callous hand gentle on her elbow. Buddy in turnout gear alongside Jared, his face streaked with soot, his grin white as they stepped out of the house they had helped save. Buddy leaning against Mark's truck, listening more than he talked as Mark spilled his fears about the store, the mortgage, and the baby on the way.

He wasn't perfect; they all knew his temper and his stubborn streak. But when life hit hard, he was the one they called - the steady voice on the other end of the line, the truck that showed up in the driveway, the man who'd take a shift, lend a hand, or just sit and say, *'You're not doin' this alone, you hear?'*

A breeze stirred the edge of the pavilion outside the church, fluttering the spray of flowers through an open window. Somewhere around the back, the ball team's old banner - faded maroon and gold - hung on a makeshift stand, Buddy's number taped a little crooked in the middle. Somebody had dug out their senior team photo and propped it against a vase: a cluster of lanky boys in uniforms, arms thrown over each other's shoulders with grins wide, and the fall leaves a blur behind them.

"We were kids," Mark murmured, his eyes fixed on the picture, "thought Friday nights were the biggest thing we'd ever face."

"But he knew better," Danny said.

"Yeah," Jared added, "but he still made those nights feel like they mattered. Like we mattered."

The funeral director stepped closer, his voice gentle. "Men? It's time."

The knot of them straightened their shoulders as they had on the fifty-yard line under stadium lights. A quiet understanding passed through them as old as their first huddle: whatever came next, they'd do it together.

They moved to the casket, each one taking his place. Hands that had once gripped footballs, swung hammers, turned wrenches, and worked levers on fire engines, now wrapped around cold brass.

As they lifted, the weight settled heavy and real across their palms and into their bones. Nobody spoke. They didn't have to. Every step down that aisle was a testimony - steady, measured, soaked in years of shared dust, sweat, and prayer.

From her seat in the front row, Donna watched the men carry Buddy, her tears slipping freely. She recognized them all - the hometown boys who had filled the bleachers and the youth group photos, now grown into the backbone of the town. Patty watched also, her hands clenched around a damp tissue in her lap, her heart aching at the sight of the line of them, at the way their faces seemed older than the day before.

Eliza pressed a hand to her chest, a silent 'thank you' rising in her heart for the circle of men around her son, though her vision was severely failing her now that she could not make out their faces anymore, she still recognized each voice of these same boys who had eaten at her table, tracked mud through her kitchen, and had called Buddy their captain long before life ever got this hard.

At the back of the pavilion, under the shade of a maple tree, Buddy's old coach stood with his cap pressed against his chest. As the boys passed, he whispered more to himself than anyone else,

"He led them out on that field a hundred times." His eyes were almost overflowing, though he tried to hide it. "Now they're leading him on home."

The sun beat down as the pallbearers stepped out from under the pavilion and into the brightness. Ahead of them, the path to the graveyard, behind the Holcomb house, cut through the Meadow of Stones - field grass swaying around smooth, scattered rocks that caught the light like diamonds, like memories. The ground here was uneven, yet familiar; they had run this way as boys, cutting through after church, tossing those same stones at fence posts and at tree trunks, Buddy always out front.

Now they walked slowly, carefully, boots whispering through the grass. The casket rode steady on their shoulders, every shift of weight reminding them why they were here.

"Watch that hole," Danny murmured, instinctively, like he had a hundred times before on late-night walks home.

The crowd made their way from the little church to the Potter's field, as Gary had named it. No one dared to step on the small stones.

They threaded between the stones - some natural, some marking graves so old the names had worn smooth. The granite shimmered pale against the summer green, little monuments to lives that had come and gone under this same blue Georgia sky.

Jared's eyes flicked down as they passed the flat marker where Gary Holcomb already lay. His throat tightened, but he kept his steps evenly. This family had already walked through one valley of the shadow. Now here they were again.

At the simple marker for Gary Holcomb, *1907-1973*, four people gathered close: Pastor Davis, Eliza in her chair, Patty Hall, and Donna Chambers.

Donna looked down through tears and noticed a small stone just left of his father's - letters faint, but clear:

TONY, 1973.

Her fingertips traced the carving, the date aligning perfectly with the first forgotten chapter of her youth. A quiet sob rose in her throat. When she lifted her gaze, the entire hillside shimmered - thousands of stones catching the light, each one a testimony carved from the faith of a man the world would never understand.

At the far edge of the meadow, under a spread of oaks, a rectangle of new earth waited. The open grave yawned dark and square. The tent above it did little against the heat, but it cast a soft shade over the place where they would leave their friend's body and all the plans that would never be.

Carefully, the men shifted as the funeral director guided them into a position beside the lowering straps. Their arms burned; a couple of them could feel sweat trickling down their shoulder blades, making their dress shirts cling. No one complained. This was the last weight they would ever carry for Buddy, and they meant to do it right.

On the count, they eased the casket down into the braces. When their hands finally let go, fingertips tingling, it just felt wrong - like they were turning loose of something they ought to hold forever.

For a moment, they just stood there at the head of the grave, staring into the Meadow of Stones, the sweep of grass and rock and the shimmer of the heat. In their minds, scenes overlapped: Buddy sprinting up this hill with cleats slung over his shoulder; Buddy leaning against a headstone, talking low to God about some hurt nobody else knew; Buddy promising them, after Gary’s funeral,

“We're gonna keep takin’ care of each other. That's what Holcombs do. That's what this town does.”

The pastor's voice rose behind them, reading familiar words about dust and resurrection. A breeze picked up, slipping through the grass and rattling the leaves in the oaks. It felt, for a heartbeat, like a hand on their backs.

"Blessed are they which do hunger and thirst after righteousness: for they shall be filled. And blessed are the pure in heart: for they shall see God," Pastor Davis almost said in a whisper, tears filling his eyes and his voice trembling over the meadow with his benediction.

When the casket began to lower, Donna's quiet sob broke the hush. Patty's arm went around her shoulders without thinking, both of them watching as the polished wood sank out of sight. Eliza held herself still, only the tremor in her chin betraying the storm inside, her gaze fixed on the space where her boy would rest between stones and saints.

When it was done, the men stepped back from the grave, their hands empty, their fingers trembling with the absence of the weight. The Meadow of Stones stretched around them, bright and merciless and somehow holy.

Danny cleared his throat. "I, uh..." he rubbed the back of his neck, "I keep hearing his voice, you know? 'Plant your feet, boys. Don't let the world knock you sideways.'"

Jared nodded, his eyes rimmed red. "He would say we still got work to do."

"He'd tell us to look out for Eliza," Mark added, "and check on Patty. Make sure Donna doesn't feel alone in all of this." He let out a breath. "He'd expect us to carry on."

They circled up without planning to, shoulders almost touching; their heads bowed. No one called the play. No one led. They just stood there in the Meadow of Stones, the smell of red clay and funeral flowers mixing in the air, and let their grief knit itself into something like resolve.

"We're his boys," Danny said at last, his voice low.

"Still are," Jared replied.

"Then we'll keep doing what he did for us," Mark said, "showing up. Carrying the load. Loving this town out loud."

Late that afternoon, when most of the cars had rolled down the mountain road and the news vans were only dust on the horizon, a pickup eased to a stop at the edge of the meadow. Radford stepped out slowly. His shirt was pressed, his jaw freshly shaved, and for the first time in years, there was no sour trace of alcohol on his breath.

In his hands, he carried a small stone he had chiseled in town. The letters were simple, uneven, like the man who held it:

Little David.

He walked between the rows until he reached the center of the shining field. With a shaky exhale, Radford knelt and set the stone down among the others Buddy had planted. He whispered, his voice breaking,

"Spud, Papa will see you soon."

The wind moved through the grass, catching his gray hair as he stood. For a long moment, he just stayed there, his hat in his hands, sober and still. Then he turned back toward the truck, leaving the stone where it belonged - right in the middle of the meadow of little ones Buddy had carried home. Panther Creek glimmered below, shining like a choir singing to Heaven, telling the song of a quiet life lived in devotion to the God who had made him.

Chapter 31 – Moonlight in the Meadow

Donna slipped out of the back door on bare feet, easing the screen shut so it wouldn't slam and wake Eliza. The only light inside came from the lamp by the rocker, warm and golden over the older woman's bowed head and folded hands. Eliza had drifted off mid-prayer, the Bible still open in her lap, rocker moving just enough to creak a soft rhythm.

"Just a minute, Mrs. Eliza," Donna whispered toward the dimly lit room, "I'll be right back."

The night air met her cool and clean. Crickets chirped in the grass. Far off, Panther Creek's constant roar threaded through the dark like a familiar hymn. A full moon hung over the ridge, bright enough to lay a silver path across the yard.

She pulled Gary's old flannel tight around her shoulders and followed the narrow trail she had walked earlier with

Radford, only this time alone. Laurel leaves brushed her arms, and dew kissed her ankles. Each step down the slope felt like she was walking out of one life and into another. The trees opened and the meadow spread before her, hushed and waiting.

In daylight, it had been green and soft, wildflowers nodding at the edges. Under the full moon, it was something else entirely. The grass shimmered silver. And mist from the creek, hovered at the far end, glowing faintly like a veil. And the stones - those small, white river stones that he had carried in his big hands - caught the moonlight one by one and threw it back, a scatter of pale stars resting on the earth.

Donna stopped at the edge, and her breath caught in her throat.

"Tony," she whispered, the name finally steady on her tongue.

She looked at the stones as the names glimmered as she passed them - Hope, Little Joe, Grace, Baby Girl. A few with only an initial.

When she reached the one she'd traced before, the stone carved with four simple letters, she sank to her knees. Dew began to dampen the hem of her jeans. The ground was cool, solid under her palms.

"Hey, baby," she breathed, "it's Mama."

For a long moment, she just stayed there, her fingertips resting on the stone as she listened to the creek and the wind and her own uneven breathing. The anchor had lived in her chest for years, swelled hard, and then finally cracked. Tears slipped freely and warm on her cold cheeks and fell onto Tony's stone, then flowing into the grass around it.

“I am so sorry,” she said. “I should have fought for you. I should have said no. I let them talk louder than God, louder than my own heart. I went quiet, and I called it no choice, but I now know better. I sinned. I ran. I lied to myself about you and about Him.”

The words didn't come pretty. They tumbled out between sobs and sniffling, more like a child than a polished Atlanta reporter. But they were true.

“I saw him,” she went on. “Your daddy. With his limp and graying, and still trying to stand for what was right. I see what he's done out here - what he did for you and all the others. I watched him bleed on those courthouse steps because he wouldn't keep quiet. And I've been the quiet one all these years.”

She lifted her face toward the moon, and her eyes squeezed shut.

“Jesus,” she whispered, her voice hoarse. “Eliza always said You hear city girls the same as mountain ones. And Gary had told me You died for the scared ones, the stubborn ones, the ones who went along when they should have said no. That's me. I believe You now. I believe You went all the way to the cross for me and for Tony and for Buddy and for every tiny life this world threw away. Please... forgive me. All the way. Don't just forgive what they did. Forgive what I didn't do. Please take this weight."

The wind shifted, drifting down off the ridge, like cool fingers brushing her damp hair back from her face. Leaves whispered overhead. Creek water sang its endless song against the rocks.

"And if...if it is not too much to ask," she added, the words trembling out of her mouth, "tell my boy I'm sorry. Tell him his mama finally said his name out loud under the same moon that shines on him now. Tell him I'll see him when You say so."

She fell quiet, then, spent. For the first time in years, she didn't rush to fill the silence with excuses, plans, or noise. She just knelt there in the wet grass, her hands on the stone, her heart laid bare in a field of little graves.

After a while - she could not have said how long - the tight band around her chest began to loosen. The shame that had always flared hot and choking whenever she thought of the clinic did not flare this time. It lay there, real and wrong, but it was as if something larger had settled over it. Not denial. Not forgetting. Something like... a covering.

"You really did it, didn't you?" she whispered. "You really took this, too."

A picture rose in her mind and unbidding - Buddy standing here, alone in the half-light, shovel in his hands, with tears on his face, whispering scripture over each small bundle. Gary's weathered Bible was open on a stump. Eliza's faithful hands folded in prayer, back up at the house. Tony cradled first in the Carpenter's arms, then in this Earth, never unwanted for a second in his eternal life.

She realized she could think of it - eternal life for him, for her - without flinching.

“I forgive you, Mama and Daddy,” she added softly, surprising even herself. “You were wrong. But you were afraid, too. May the Lord forgive you. I am done carrying all of us.”

The words left her lips, and some last knot loosened. The air seemed clearer, the stars seemed sharper, the stones less like accusations and more like witnesses.

She stayed there until her knees ached and her teeth had chattered once or twice in the mountain chill. When she finally stood, wiping her face with the sleeve of Gary’s flannel, the heaviness in her chest felt different. Not gone-but changed. It was no longer a secret weight pressing down. It was a scar, tender and honest, laid in Someone else's hands.

She laid her palm flat on Tony's stone one more time.

The moonlight caught the wet tracks on the stone, making them shine.

Donna turned and walked back up the path, the dew chilling on her ankles, the creek song at her back. At the top of the rise, she glanced over her shoulder. The meadow lay bathed in silver, the stones glowing soft as lanterns.

In her mind's eye, she could almost see them - the outlines of two men and a boy standing just beyond the mist. Gary with his Bible, Buddy without his cane, Tony between them, whole and laughing. The thought did not hurt. It brought comfort to her.

The lamp inside still burned as Eliza was awake in her rocker, moving slowly, and her lips moving over some half-remembered hymn when Donna finally made it back to the porch.

Donna had a soft hum in her throat as she slipped through the door; her heart was oddly light for how red her eyes were.

"You get some air?" Eliza asked, upon hearing her return and the screen door's soft shutting.

"Yes, ma'am," Donna said, her voice rough but sure. "I think I finally did."

For the first time since she was seventeen, the word finally felt like peace, not defeat.

Chapter 32 –

We Tried

Donna rinsed the last plate and set it in the drainer, watching the evening light slant long and soft across the Holcomb pasture. The familiar creak of Eliza's rocker drifted in from the front room, slow and steady as a heartbeat.

Patty bumped her hip against Donna's, handing over a towel.

“If we leave so much as one fork in that sink, Mrs. Eliza will march in here and show us just how it's done,” she said with a mischievous grin.

“That's why we're not leaving even one fork,” Donna answered, a small smile tugging at her mouth. “Buddy taught me that early on,” Donna added, thinking out loud.

They both went quiet at his name. It had been years now, long enough for the sharp edges of grief to wear down, but his absence still lived in the house like a shadow in every doorway - felt in his empty chair, the quiet barn, and the way Eliza sometimes turned her head as if listening for boots that would never cross that threshold again.

From the front room came Eliza's thin humming, an old hymn Donna had heard her sing since she was a teen. The rocker creaked in rhythm, each pass a soft reminder that time kept moving on even when hearts did not really feel ready.

“Late eighties and still won't let us do her dishes without supervision,” Patty murmured, glancing toward the doorway, “she'll outlast us all.”

“She would argue with the Lord himself if he showed up early,” Donna said fondly, “tell him she's got beans on the stove and folks to pray over.”

They finished in an easy silence, the water running, and the crickets starting up outside. The house was soaking in the sounds it had known for years. When the sink was finally proven to be empty, Patty snapped off the kitchen light and jerked her chin toward the back door.

“Come on,” she said. “My feet are filing a complaint. Let's sit a spell.”

They stepped out onto the back stoop, where the view opened wide to the meadow. The grass moved in gentle waves under a sky just beginning to trade blue for reds and golds. The air smelled of cut hay, damp earth, and the faintest thread of wood smoke drifting from some neighbor’s up the road.

Patty lowered herself onto the top step with a soft sigh, stretching out her legs. Donna took the one below Patty, her elbows bracing on her knees, and her hands clasped. For a while, they simply watched a pair of turkeys picking their way along the far fence line.

"You ever think about how many times we've walked this path?" Patty asked at last. "To the creek and to the town, both of us thinkin' we were the only girls God ever had to straighten out."

Donna's mouth tipped.

"We were late to each other," she said, "It is hard to believe we did not even meet till we were teenagers. Sometimes I wonder how much trouble we could have saved if we had found each other sooner."

"Or how much more we would have gotten into," Patty said dryly. "Don't give us too much credit."

Donna huffed a soft laugh.

"Fair."

The sounds of the evening folded around them - the low growl of a tractor on a distant slope, the whisper of the creek, and the cicadas tuning their rough choir. Behind them, Eliza's rocker kept its faithful rhythm. Every so often, her humming faltered, then caught again, as if she were drifting at the edge of sleep and a prayer both.

Patty cut Donna a sidelong look.

"You talk differently since that night down in the meadow," she said, "like somebody finally turned the volume down on the world in your head."

"Maybe I finally let Him," Donna replied quietly, "or maybe I just ran out of ways to hold Him off."

After a stretch of shared silence, Patty shifted.

"Can I ask you something?" she said. "And you promise not to shut down or circle me with one of your fancy Atlanta answers?"

Donna's shoulders tensed a notch.

"That depends," she responded, looking a little nervous. "Is this about Steve?"

"Not exactly," Patty replied. "It's about... what didn't happen before he left."

Donna drew a slow breath.

"Alright, ask."

Patty twists the hem of her T-shirt between her fingers.

"Why didn't you and Steve ever have kids?" she asked, the words soft, but plain. "You do not have to tell me if you don't want to. I just always wondered. You had been married a long time. You are so good with babies and teenagers. Was it by choice? Or was it... something else?"

Donna went very still.

"That's a big question for a little porch," she said at last.

"I can take it around to the truck bed if the porch is offended," Patty tried, giving a crooked smile. "I just - Don, I love you. And it feels like there is this room in your heart you keep the door shut on. I only see the glimpse of light under it."

Donna stared out over the meadow, her jaw working. The easy answers lined up, the ones she had used for years:

We were busy. It was not the right time. Things just did not work out.

She had worn those phrases thin in the Buckhead dining rooms and around the station.

But this was Patty, and this was Buddy and Eliza's back porch stoop. And out there, between that tree line lay the field where she had knelt under a full moon, said her son's name to the night air, and believed, finally believed, he had heard her in Heaven.

"I did want kids," she said, surprising herself with how quickly the truth came. "More than I let myself say out loud. More than was wise, considering who I married."

Patty's face softened. "So it wasn't that you didn't want them."

"No." Donna shook her head. "Never that."

She wet her lips, and her fingers tightened together.

"When Steve and I first married, we both agreed we would 'wait a while'. That was the phrase we used. He wanted a partnership. I told myself I wanted to get established, be the kind of wife my mom could brag on. The house, the parties, the charity boards. Babies did not fit that picture for them. Not yet."

"And for you?" Patty's voice was barely more than a whisper.

"For me, they always did," Donna admitted.

"Even back when we were teenagers out at the lake, sneaking out to talk about boys and big dreams, I used to picture a little one on my hip. I would walk past the children's section at Rich's and have to pretend I was just browsing for somebody else's shower. I would hold my breath around pregnant women, like if I breathed too deeply, I would fall apart right there in the produce aisle."

Patty's hand found the space between Donna's shoulders and patted her gently.

"After a few years," Donna went on, "when the house was too quiet, and the parties all blurred together, I just... stopped taking my pills. I did not tell Steve. I thought, if it happens, it happens. If not, I will know where I stand with God without having to say anything to anybody."

"Did Steve ever ask?" Patty said gently.

"He noticed I was moody."

A humorless smile tugged at her mouth.

"Blamed hormones, bought me another bracelet. That was Steve's way - throw something shiny at whatever he did not understand and hope it distracted both of us."

The turkeys slipped out of sight beyond the trees as a whip-poor-will called somewhere near the creek.

“Years went by,” Donna said, “nothing. I counted the days in my head, pretending I wasn't doing math every time I was late. Finally, one of the other pilot’s wives cornered me at a fundraiser and said, ‘Don't you think you are leaving it a bit late, dear? Biology is not as kind as you think.’”

Her jaw tightened. “I smiled and laughed it off. Then I went home and made an appointment the next morning.”

“You went alone,” Patty said. It was not a question.

“Of course I did,” Donna's voice sharpened, then softened.

“Steve had a tee time and a Captain's meeting later that day, and I still had not admitted, not even to myself, just how badly I wanted a child. If something were wrong, I figured I would fix it quietly and present him with a done deal. You can hear how much the city got into me, can't you? Always angling, always planning.”

“What did the doctor say?” Patty asked.

Donna's eyes were fixed on the rolling grass, but she was looking miles away.

“She was young, professional. She asked about my history - my cycles, surgery history, and any procedures. When I told her about... about what happened in Atlanta when I was seventeen, she got this look. Like a puzzle piece had clicked into place, and she wished it had not.”

Patty's hand stilled on her back.

"She did an exam. Sent me for tests." Donna's voice thinned and quieted.

"When I went back, she talked about adhesions. Scar tissue. Reduce uterine cavity. Like she was reading off a chart that belonged to somebody else. Then she used a name - Asherman's Syndrome. She said it slowly – it was as if she thought that if she pronounced it carefully, it would hurt less."

Donna swallowed, then continued:

"Scar tissue from that clinic. From that 'procedure' my parents insisted on when I was just a scared seventeen-year-old girl. The one they promised would be over in an afternoon; that it was not really a baby. That I would be just fine. Lies. All lies. It has never been 'over' - for me."

Patty's fingers pressed in. A small anchor between bone and muscle.

"Oh, Don!"

"She told me there were surgeries available, sometimes," Donna continued, "that they could go in and try to cut the adhesions away. But sometimes women conceived after, sometimes they did not. Sometimes they miscarried over and over." Her throat worked. "Then she looked me in the eye and said, 'You need to be prepared for the possibility that carrying a pregnancy to term may be exceedingly difficult for you. It may not be possible at all.'"

The porch blurred, Donna blinked hard, but the tears broke free anyway, tracking down her cheeks.

"I sat there on that noisy paper and nodded like we were talking about changing shampoo," she said. "I thanked her, paid my copay. I walked to my car and gripped the steering wheel so tight my hands hurt. I screamed till my voice gave out. Then I wiped my face, touched up my lipstick in the rearview mirror, and went home to make chicken piccata. Because Steve had some of his friends coming for dinner."

Patty's own eyes were glistening with tears waiting to flow for her dear friend.

"You didn't tell him," she said softly.

"How could I?" Donna turned her head, the tears simply flowing downward.

"He never once said he wanted children. He liked our life loud, glossy, and unencumbered. If I had told him the truth, then I would have had to admit I wanted something he did not seem to want. I would have to say Tony's name. I would have to tie that clinic in Atlanta to every empty room in that Buckhead house."

She faced the meadow again.

"So I buried it. I told myself I had forfeited the right to cry about it. I had stood outside that clinic and gone along with it when my parents said it was the only way. I let other people's fears speak louder than the little voice inside me that whispered 'no'. I decided this was just the bill coming due."

Patty slid down a step, so their shoulders touched.

"And all that time," she said quietly, "you were bleeding on the inside where nobody could see."

Donna let out a shuddering breath.

"I joined more committees. Booked more trips. Let Steve drag me from one shiny thing to the next. If I could not rock a baby at 2:00 a.m. in the morning, then I would dance in some hotel ballroom at 2:00 a.m. in the morning. If I could not pack lunches, then I would pack suitcases. Anything to drown out the sound of what was not there."

Behind them, the rocker's creak paused. Eliza's humming stilled. Donna's spine went taut, but the screen door did not open. After a moment, the soft scrape and the creak resumed, slower now, as if the old woman had only shifted and settled again with a sigh.

"I thought keeping quiet was a way to..." Donna broke off, searching... "to pay for it, I guess. Like if I carried the hurt alone and never asked anyone to look at it with me, maybe I would even the scales somehow. But all it did was wall me off from the folks who might have loved me through it."

Patty laced her fingers through Donna's.

"You are not walled off now," she said. "You're on the Holcomb back steps with a girl and a family who has loved you ever since Buddy loved you, and who wishes she could sit beside that scared version of you and tell you the truth."

A tear ran down Donna's cheek.

They sat like that while the light faded and the pasture softened into the colors of the evening sky.

"You know what I realized down there in the meadow?" Donna said at length, her voice still low.

"All these years, I thought the worst part was that I could not have any more children. That I had lost not just Tony, but every baby after him. But standing down there, saying his name out loud and finally believing where he is... The worst part was believing that God was done with me, that He had stamped me used up and He had moved on!"

Patty turned, studying her face.

"And now?" she asked.

"Now," Donna drew in a shaky breath, "now I know He took the sin. Really took it. The 'blood-on-my-hands' part. I felt it lifted that night. But the scars?"

She laid a hand lightly on her own stomach. "These he seems content to leave, not as punishment. But as... reminders. As markers of where He found me."

Patty's eyes filled again.

"Tony wasn't the only baby you lost that day in Atlanta," she said softly. "You lost all the 'maybe some days' too. Every stocking you might have hung, every science fair project, every graduation picture. That is real. It's right that it hurts."

Donna's chin trembled.

"But God didn't lose a thing," Patty went on, "not Tony. Not your maybes. And certainly not you."

She squeezed her hand.

"He saw that seventeen-year-old girl in a paper gown. He saw the woman on that exam table. He sees the one on this porch, talkin' as she trusts Him now more than she used to trust herself."

From the front of the house, Eliza's voice rose - thin with age, but with joy, wrapping itself around a line they both knew well:

"Jesus Paid It All."

Donna closed her eyes, letting the words wash over the raw places.

"I used to think if Mrs. Eliza ever knew all of it," she whispered, "it would break her heart clean in two."

"It might," Patty said honestly, "but hearts like hers have been broken and mended by the Lord so many times, they are softer, yet stronger at the breaks, not weaker. She can hold more than you think, Don."

"I know." Donna opened her eyes, watching the first pale sliver of the moon peak over the ridge.

"Down there in the meadow, I promised I would stop lying to God. I guess eventually I have got to stop lying by omission to the people who love me too."

They fell quiet.

The moon eased higher, laying a faint silver path across the field. Somewhere out there, Donna knew, the little white stones were catching its light, standing their quiet watch over all the stories buried there and the grace that covered them.

"We tried," she said softly, almost to herself. "Steve and I, we really did. Even if he never knew how hard."

Patty squeezed her hand.

"The Lord knows," she said, "and He's not done with what you've lost."

Donna let out a breath that felt, for the first time, less like punishment and more like release.

"Thank you," she said finally, her voice rough.

"For what?" Patty asked.

"For asking," Donna answered, "and for not looking away when I finally answered."

Chapter 33 -

Eliza's Last Knowing

The winter light lay thin across Eliza Holcomb's quilt, a pale ribbon stretched over faded calico and trembling hands. The room smelled of vapor rub and woodsmoke and a faint hint of lemon from the furniture polish on the dresser. Outside, Panther Creek hummed its same, relaxing song, as if the years had been nothing but a turn of the page.

Patty sat in the chair by the window, knitting forgotten in her lap. Donna stood at the foot of the bed, her fingers resting on the bed rail, watching each rise and fall of Eliza's chest the way a child watches a porch light on a stormy night.

"Pattygirl," she called out suddenly, though weak, there was a hint of mischief reflecting in her dimming eyes, "you got any fellas as a future husband in mind yet?"

Patty looked at Donna in disbelief.

"Mrs. Eliza..." she began, as tears began to well in her eyes, "I'm just gettin' me ready for one, cause you never know."

She softly replayed the words to her like so many times before.

"Truly, Mrs. Eliza, Big Jim will be by soon as he's taking me to Clayton for supper later," she reminded her, as she knew she was already aware of their late-in-life romance.

After what seemed like a very long silence, "Eliza," Patty whispered, "you need anything, honey? Water? Another pillow?"

Eliza's eyes fluttered open, cloudy, but still clear enough to find them both.

"What I need," she murmured, her voice thin, yet determined, "is the truth."

Patty straightened in her chair as Donna's breath caught.

"Eliza..." Patty began.

"Hush now," Eliza said, a hint of her old strength there that had once called the boys in for supper from the fields.

"I am ninety-three years old now. I have buried my husband and my boy. I have outlived half of this county. I can feel the good Lord loosening my fingers from this old world."

She drew a shallow breath.

"I know my Buddy didn't die in no car wreck," she went on, "I let y'all tell me that cause my heart wasn't ready for the truth yet. It is ready now. I do not intend to step into glory on a half-truth."

Tears spilled suddenly and hot down Patty's cheeks. Donna's knuckles whitened on the bedrail.

"Eliza," Donna whispered, "we were only trying to protect you."

"I know you were," Eliza answered gently, "and I forgive you both for that. You were only girls compared to me, carrying more sorrow than most folks carry in a lifetime. But I need to know how my boy really left this Earth. And I need to hear what he did with the years the Lord gave him."

Patty's gaze slid to the small handmade cabinet next to her, and she took out some worn notebooks - Buddy's journals, edges worn by so much handling.

"Here are Buddy's own words, Eliza."

"Go on, Pattygirl, I need to hear some of what he wrote when nobody was lookin', she said, "before I go see him again."

Patty wiped her nose with the back of her hand, reminding Eliza of her when she was just a child back at Grace Fellowship. Then she reached for a tissue.

"Do you want to hear it all?" she asked, her voice a little shaky. "It is... hard, Eliza. The courthouse, the gun..."

Eliza's mouth curved into the ghost of a smile.

"Child, I have lived through hard times," she said, "start where it went wrong. Then tell me where God made it right."

Patty drew a breath.

"It was at the courthouse," she began, "they had found the meadow. Reporters were everywhere. They brought Buddy in for questioning, and when they took him out of the car..."

Her voice faltered. She looked at Donna.

Donna stepped closer, one hand reaching for Eliza's, the other brushing the worn cover of the nearest journal.

"A grandfather from down there, his name Theodore McCall, thought Buddy had something to do with his granddaughter's disappearance," Donna began softly, "he had been listening to the news. To talk radio. To me. To all the wrong voices." Her eyes began to fill. "He came out of the crowd with a gun. He shot Buddy, right there on the steps. I was standing ten feet away."

Eliza's fingers tightened on hers.

"Did he suffer long?" she asked slowly.

"No," Donna answered weakly, "not long. He spoke about Tony. About the little ones. About the Lord. He... he died the way he lived, Eliza. Thinking about other people's children and God's mercy."

A tear slipped from the corner of Eliza's eye into the wrinkles at her temple.

"I felt that," she whispered, "the day it happened; there was a pain in my chest that was not my own. I told the Lord,

'You've taken my boy,' and then I let you girls pour honey over the truth 'cause I was too weary."

She turned her head toward the journals.

"Now," she said, "you read me some of my boy's side of the story."

Patty reached for the top notebook - its cardboard cover worn and soft where Buddy's thumb had rested.

Journal 1992, the ink still dark

She opened near the beginning and read aloud, her voice unsteady, but clear:

"January 3rd

Route #4 - Southside clinic. Cold morning. Frost on the van windshield. Prayed over every car as it pulled in. A young girl in a red coat sat in the passenger seat a long time before she got out. Could see her daddy's knuckles white on the steering wheel. Asked the Lord to give him courage to turn that car around. And he did. They left before the doors opened. Thank you, Jesus."

Eliza's eyes drifted shut, but her lips moved, shaping the words *Thank You* with him.

Patty turned a page.

"February 2nd

rain. Parked the van and sat awhile. Didn't want to crank it yet. Watched folks go in huddled under umbrellas, heads down. All colors. All ages. Sin and sorrow don't care about skin color. Prayed over each one by what I could see - blue dress, green jacket, tired eyes. Felt helpless and somehow useful at the same time. Told the Lord I would rather talk to Him about men than talk to men about God if my talk just makes more noise. Asked Him to send gentler voices than mine when He needs words spoken out loud."

The words hung quietly in the little room.

"He was his daddy's son," Eliza whispered proudly. "Gary always did say you can tell a man by what he does with pain that don't belong to him."

Donna reached for the next journal, the one whose pages had followed her into her dreams.

"This one's from '80," she said. "Listen, Eliza."

She found the page and began.

"September 21st

Swung past the lake house road today on my way back north. Couldn't help it. Thought about Donna. Wondered if she still swims with her hair loose like she used to. Wondered if she ever stands at the falls and remembers. Tried not to let my heart go there, but it did anyway. Told the Lord again I forgave her and her folks. I meant it. Still hurts like a bone that healed crooked. Asked Him to bless her wherever she is. If she's got other children now, pray to give her the courage we were both too scared to grab hold of back then. I still love her. Don't know what to do with that except lay it down at His feet."

Her voice cracked. Her tears fell freely.

For a long moment, Eliza was very still. Then understanding moved across her face like sunrise over the ridge.

"You and my boy..." she breathed, "... a baby...?

Donna's shoulders shook.

"Yes," she whispered. "I was young and scared. My mama pushed hard. I let them take our child. Buddy found out too late. He is the one who... who brought our little one home."

"Brought your little one... home? I don't... understand," Eliza's eyes were lost in confusion.

Donna was overwhelmed with emotion, but she tried her best to regain her composure as she began to tell her about Tony and all that had happened in Buddy's life as a result of his loss.

"Our baby boy. Buddy named him Tony. I followed my parents... and I allowed them to rob me... us... of him. I am so terribly sorry. We... I... was so very wrong. I should have fought for him..." she had to stop as fresh tears and grief overtook her.

"After Buddy brought Tony here and gave him a proper burial in the meadow, he continued to go back to the city. And every time he was able, he would bring another nameless child back home and give them rest. You might not have been able to see, but the meadow is full. It has been dubbed, 'The Meadow of Stones'." She continued with more details of how he took care of each one. "Buddy spent the remainder of his life giving respect and love to so many that were not allowed that in this life otherwise..." Donna stopped there, feeling spent.

Fresh tears spilled down Eliza's face, but there was no accusation in them - only grief and something like wonder.

"You say there are many resting in the meadow?... and... so... the first one," she said softly, "was my grandbaby."

Donna nodded, unable to speak.

Eliza's gaze turned inward, toward a meadow only she could see now.

"And all those others he carried, all those little ones he named and wrapped in the swaddling clothes and laid in this old ground here," she went on, voice thinning but with amazement, "they are mine too, in a way. If my boy loved them like that and commended them back to God, I reckon this heart can claim them as grandchildren just as sure as if they had sat on my lap for Sunday supper!"

A tremendous smile touched her face.

"I have got a whole brood waiting on me then, she whispered, "Gary at the gate, Buddy by his side, and a hillside of grandbabies - ours and the ones nobody else wanted - dancing and laughing where no one can ever throw them away again!"

Donna bowed her head, sobbing.

"I'm so sorry," she choked, "for what we did. For what I let happen."

Eliza squeezed her hand, faint but firmly.

"The Lord has forgiven you," she spoke to her kindly, "and I know my boy forgave you. And now you hear me plain, Donna Hargrove - you gave me a grandchild I will meet in glory. I will not spend eternity frowning at you over that. I will be too busy thanking Jesus that He can take even our worst choices and, somehow, set some part of it right."

She turned her face toward Patty.

"And you, Pattygirl. You gave him an ear and a shoulder. You did not know all of it, but you stood near and faithful. Those babies he buried, they are ours to love now, every one of them."

Patty could only nod through her tears.

Eliza's gaze went back to the window, to the bare limbs scratching the winter sky.

"So my boy spent his days praying over scared girls and burying babies nobody wanted," she said softly. "He wrote their stories down, carved their names, and handed them back to God, one by one. And all this time, I thought I had only one child. Turns out the Lord had a whole flock for me, scattered between here and Heaven."

She let out a small, contented sigh.

"That's enough for this mama's heart," she barely whispered. "I can go now."

"No," Donna choked. "Not yet, Eliza..."

Eliza squeezed their hands, one more time, faint as a leaf's flutter.

"Hush," she said tenderly, "you will see me again. Y'all got work to do, both of you. Pattygirl, you keep tending these hills and these mamas. Donna..." Her eyes found Donna with surprising strength.

"You've spent so many years talking loud for the wrong things. Now you go and talk gentle for the right ones. Let the Lord use that tongue for mercy instead of judgment. That'd please my boy. That would please his mama, too."

Tears streamed down their faces. They nodded, unable to answer.

Eliza drew one last, careful breath.

"Tell Pastor Davis to put it simply on my stone," she murmured. "Eliza Holcomb. Wife, Mama. Loved the Lord. That is enough. Folks can read the rest in Gary's sermons and Buddy's journals."

Her fingers relaxed in theirs. The rise and fall of her chest stilled.

Outside, the creek kept singing. Somewhere, wind moved through pines with a sound like pages turning.

Two women wept, and a third went home, and Heaven leaned down to gather up one more witness - the mama who had prayed her boy into the world and now knew, beyond any headline or half-truth, that he had walked his road well.

The morning of Eliza Holcomb's burial broke clear and cold, the kind of blue-glass sky that made every branch and stone stand out sharp.

Grace Fellowship overflowed again, just as it had for Buddy, though the crowd was smaller now - more locals than cameras, more familiar faces than strangers. The world's curiosity had moved on. The ones who came today came because they knew Eliza: her cornbread, her quiet prayers, her soft "child" when she laid a hand on a shaking arm.

Pastor Davis stood behind the simple pulpit with his Bible open, his eyes damp.

"She asked for it plain," he said, voice carrying over the creak of pews and the sniffles.

"*Eliza Holcomb. Wife. Mama. Loved the Lord.* I have known preachers who would need three pages to say what those few words say."

He spoke of a woman who had held a community together with casseroles and hymn-soft hands, who had prayed heaven down over a husband's sermons and had sat at the bedside of half the town. He did not mention headlines or scandals. He did not need to. Everyone in that room knew the story under the story: a family that had stood in the gap when the world was not watching.

When the hymn faded and the last "amen" was whispered, they followed the casket out into the crisp air and down the familiar road to the Holcomb farm.

The procession went round past the farmhouse, past the old shed, and down toward the meadow behind the house- 'The Potter's Field' Gary once named, which the world now whispered about like a legend. No one stepped on the stones. Even the children, fidgeting in their Sunday shoes, seemed to sense this ground was different.

The hillside shimmered under the winter sun - white and gray markers catching the light, stretching out like a sea of small, silent witnesses. The creek glimmered below, its voice low and reverent.

At the simple granite marker where Gary Holcomb's name had been carved decades ago, and Buddy's name more recently, a new space waited.

Just to the right, a fresh rectangle of earth had been opened, red clay dark against the frosted grass.

Four people gathered closest: Pastor Davis, Patty Hall, Donna Chambers, and the funeral director, standing discreetly at the back with his hat in hand. Behind them, a ring of church folks, neighbors, and a few faces from town spread out along the slope, careful of their steps.

The casket came to rest above the waiting ground.

Pastor Davis cleared his throat, his voice thick.

"Some of y'all were here when we laid Gary down," he said. "Some of you stood here not long ago when we laid Buddy beside him. Today, we place Eliza in the same earth - next to her husband, next to her boy, next to the grandbaby she never rocked but loved just the same. We know what scripture says is true - believe it - she ain't lying here alone."

He gestured slightly to the shimmering stones all around.

"She is surrounded by the very ones she claimed as grandchildren in her last days - the babies Buddy carried from the world's trash to God's treasure. She told the girls, not three days ago, that she thought the Lord had given her only one child. 'Turns out He gave me a meadow full, she said'."

A ripple of emotion moved through the gathered crowd.

Donna's eyes burned as she looked from Gary's stone to Buddy's, then to the small marker with Tony's name, and finally to the newly carved one soon to be eased into place:

Eliza Holcomb

Wife. Mama. Loved the Lord.

Nothing more. Nothing less.

It settled against the earth with a solid, gentle thud.

Patty reached for Donna's hand, fingers intertwining.

"Look," she whispered.

From where they stood, they could see the line of stones as if they were chapters in a book. Gary's name, the pastor who first saw holiness in a rough meadow by the creek. Buddy's name, the son who turned that clearing into a field of witness, Tony's small stone, the first grandchild, redeemed from a dumpster and laid in the river-blessed ground. And now Eliza's - set among them like a final, faithful period at the end of a long, obedient sentence.

Beyond them, the countless little markers shimmered - names and dates Buddy had carved with shaking hands and an obedient heart. Danny, Grace, Michael. Others known only to God Above. The children of a broken land gathered, named, and remembered.

Pastor Davis bowed his head.

"Blessed are they which do hunger and thirst for righteousness: for they shall be filled," he said softly. "Blessed are the pure in heart: for they shall see God."

He let the words hang there, then added, "Gary hungered. Buddy hungered. Eliza hungered. These three saints did not seek after the temporal treasures on Earth, but they laid up eternal treasures in Heaven. They were not perfect. No one is. But they pointed their lives in the right direction - and they left us a witness in stone and in ink to show us how to do the same."

The funeral director gave a small nod. Ropes creaked. The casket descended slowly, gently, into the earth between the stones of husband and son, on a line with Tony and all the others.

Donna felt her knees weaken. For a moment, she thought she might fall, but Patty's arm slipped around her waist, giving her strength.

"This is right," Patty whispered, her voice raw but certain. "She wanted to be here. With her men. With her babies."

Donna could only nod as tears blurred the hillside into a palette of white, green, and sky.

In her mind's eye, she saw it the way Eliza had described it on that last night: Gary at the gate of Heaven, Buddy by his side, and a hillside full of children running whole and laughing; no scars, no secrets, no shame. Somewhere among them, a little one with a name Buddy had chosen and God had sealed - a grandchild Eliza had claimed at last.

As the first shovelful of earth hit the casket lid with a soft thump, Donna closed her eyes and whispered a promise only God and the meadow could hear.

"I'll tell it right," she vowed. "Your story, Buddy. Eliza's. The truth about these stones. I will not waste what you wrote and what you lived."

Wind moved across the field, rattling dry grass, brushing over the carved names, lifting the corners of scarves and bulletins. It felt, for an instant, like a benediction.

When the grave was filled and the mound smooth, Pastor Davis invited those who wished to come closer to do so.

One by one, people stepped forward, laying a hand on the new stone, some speaking a word of thanks, some only standing there in silence.

Patty bowed her head as she approached and then laid a small bundle of fresh flowers on the grave.

"For you and your grandbabies," she murmured.

Donna knelt beside her, her hands reaching out as her gaze roamed over all four stones, spanning names, dates, and generations.

"Thank you," she finally breathed, to Gary, to Buddy, to Eliza, and to the God who had somehow woven their broken lives into a tapestry of grace.

As they walked back up the hill, leaving the meadow bathed in winter light, the stones stood still and shining behind them - a family gathered in earth, a congregation of the smallest saints around them, all of it quietly declaring what the world had almost missed:

One life, offered in quiet devotion, can make even broken ground holy. And one faithful family, laid side by side, can turn a hidden field into a testimony that will outlive all.

Epilogue

It has been nine years since Eliza sat in front of the fireplace at the Holcomb home. She now lies in the meadow between her two men - Gary and Buddy - and the little ones she now knows by name. The God that formed and forged this family of believers now gathers with the 10,204 who are eternally linked with him in the Meadow of Stones.

Well done, good and faithful servants, is the welcome they found.

Donna, long departed from the newsroom lights and worldly fame, runs a crisis clinic at 101 Peach Avenue, where frightened souls find help and sometimes, their first glimpse of heaven's hope. Now she helps build families here on Earth, one mother, one child, one choice for life at a time.

Big Jim and Patty live on the old Holcomb farm with their four adopted children from Donna's clinic, where they tend to the Meadow of Stones. She greets pro-life and church volunteers, and sometimes lone women who sit for hours among the markers, tracing names, and dates until they find Buddy's calling for themselves - a holy invitation to mercy and forgiveness they had sought after.

The End.

www.ingramcontent.com/pod-product-compliance
Lightning Source LLC
LaVergne TN
LVHW090549110826
845146LV00001B/73

* 9 7 9 8 9 9 5 0 9 7 8 1 5 *